BURNING UP

SUSAN ANDERSEN

THORNDIKE
CHIVERS

This Large Print edition is published by Thorndike Press, Waterville, Maine, USA and by AudioGO Ltd, Bath, England.
Thorndike Press, a part of Gale, Cengage Learning.
The text of this Large Print edition is unabridged.
Other aspects of the book may vary from the original edition.
Set in 16 pt. Plantin.

LIBRARY OF CONGRESS CATALOGING-IN-PUBLICATION DATA

Andersen, Susan, 1950–
  Burning up / by Susan Andersen.
    p. cm. — (Thorndike Press large print romance)
  ISBN-13: 978-1-4104-3079-3
  ISBN-10: 1-4104-3079-0
  1. Large type books. I. Title.
PS3551.N34555B87 2010
813'.54—dc22   2010029270

BRITISH LIBRARY CATALOGUING-IN-PUBLICATION DATA AVAILABLE
Published in 2010 in the U.S. by arrangement with Harlequin Books S.A.
Published in 2011 in the U.K. by arrangement with Harlequin Enterprises II B.V.

U.K. Hardcover: 978 1 408 49305 2 (Chivers Large Print)
U.K. Softcover: 978 1 408 49306 9 (Camden Large Print)

Printed and bound in Great Britain by the MPG Books Group
1 2 3 4 5 6 7 14 13 12 11 10

Dear Reader,

The past year has been kind of taxing, so when I started this book I only had one criteria: to have fun. To that end my imagination presented me with MTV queen Macy O'James — a one-time small-town girl with a big, bad reputation and a penchant for in-your-face clothing. The minute the ink on her high school diploma dried, she kicked the dust of farming community Sugarville, Washington, from her boots. But now she's back, and if the citizens of S'ville don't like it — and she fully expects many of them to be vocal in their displeasure — well, she's prepared to live with that.

What she's not prepared for is her unwelcome response to Sugarville's new fire chief, Gabriel Donovan.

Gabe left a career as a big-city arson investigator to simplify and de-stress his life. But things aren't turning out according to plan. This placid little town is suddenly plagued by a raft of fires. Those, he knows how to handle. The infamous woman he heard reams about even before she came home is another story. He was prepared to discount the gossip, but up close and personal, Macy threatens the even-keeled existence he's carved for himself. She's trouble, and that's

5

the last thing he's looking for. After a hard-scrabble childhood and a wild adolescence, there is no way Gabe's falling for a too-hot-to-handle firecracker like Macy O'James.

Still, that up-close-and-personal thing is pretty hard to resist.

I had a ball writing Macy and Gabe's story. I hope, hope, hope you have even more fun reading it.

Susan

But wait! There's more! (Yeah, I know, I've gotta cut back on watching infomercials.) As an extra added treat, be sure to check out Auntie Lenore's recipes in the back of the book.

This is dedicated, with love,
to
Joey Zderic Gaviglio

For
Long walks, lotsa laughs and non-stop
conversations.

I'm so tickled we reconnected after all
these years.
Thanks for all the shared goodies and
recipes — not to
mention turning me on to some great
walking shoes and
sandals.

I always look forward to Wednesdays.
— Susie

ACKNOWLEDGMENTS

I also owe a huge thank-you to the firefighters who took time to help me with the technical aspects of this book. My gratitude to King County Fire Marshall Gary Owens, Assistant Fire Chief Robert Young of Mountain View Fire and Rescue, and Doug Napoli of the Tualatin Valley, Oregon, fire district. You guys rock; any and all mistakes I may have made in the use of the information you gave me are mine alone.

CHAPTER ONE

Gabriel Donovan knew Macy O'James was trouble the minute she rolled into town.

Hell, he knew it before she even hit the city limits. He and Johnny Angelini were sitting in Johnny's police cruiser out near the county line, shooting the bull and discussing ways to improve workplace efficiency, when he had his first Macy O'James sighting.

Not that he knew it was her at that moment. Despite old Sheriff Baxter's objection to what he considered the newfangled notion of interdepartmental information sharing between Johnny, Sugarville's sole deputy, and Gabe, the town's fire chief, the two men liked putting their heads together every now and then to talk out problems they felt had cross-over potential. And that particular hot July afternoon, Gabe had just finished recounting why he thought Johnny should check out a ramshackle trailer out

11

near Leavenston that he suspected might be a meth lab, when a candy-apple-red, drop-top Corvette roared by, trailing screaming rock and roll in its wake.

The two men exchanged a look. "Not going that much above the limit," Gabe commented laconically.

"True." Johnny nodded. "Ten over hardly seems worth the time to write up a ticket."

"That was my thought."

"Still," Johnny said. "Hot car, hotter driver, man. *Blonde.* Could be my future bride."

"There is that," he agreed, although how his friend could state the driver's hair color, much less her hotness factor, from the one quick glimpse they'd gotten as she'd blown past was beyond him. He didn't, however, doubt it was true. Johnny had eyes like a raptor when it came to the female portion of the human race.

The deputy scratched a thumbnail across his jaw. "And it *is* a hot day. Be a real mess if Myerson chose now to let his cows cross the road."

"Little car, big cattle," he granted.

"My civic duty to do my job. It's not like they pay me the big bucks for sitting under the trees. So." He raised an eyebrow. "You in?"

Gabe considered. Common sense dictated he get out of the cruiser, get back in his rig and go about his business. He had no real reason or even desire to check out Johnny's "future bride." Beyond the fact he was currently dating a nice woman, he was nowhere close to being the hound with the babes that Johnny was.

Not anymore.

On the other hand, it was pretty much the male code not to let your friends have too much fun if there was any chance you could throw a wrench in their good times. "S'pose I better," he said dryly. "When she files the sexual harassment suit, she's gonna need a witness."

Grinning, the deputy started up the Ford Ranger. He eased the cruiser out from beneath a stand of Douglas firs and alders that had done a decent job of shielding their cars from passing traffic, bumped over the uneven turf and onto the highway, then hit the siren at the same time he punched the gas.

They caught up with the Corvette moments later and watched as it first slowed, then pulled to the side of the road. The blaring music cut off midnote.

Two suitcases sticking up from behind the car seats blocked the driver from view. But her door opened in the sudden silence and a long, bare leg appeared, a blue peep-toed, platform-soled, Cuban-heel-shod foot stretching for the ground.

"You can wait here," Johnny said, reaching for the door handle. "This is clearly a job for a trained professional."

Gabe snorted. "Not a chance. What kind of bud would I be if I didn't have your back?" Climbing from the cruiser, he looked at Johnny over its top. "For all we know, the woman's armed and dangerous."

"Yeah, I'm worried about that. Might have to pat her down for weapons."

That would be the day. Johnny loved flirting up females, but he also had an appreciation and bedrock respect for them. Besides, he wasn't the type to abuse his authority any more than Gabe was.

By the time he'd cleared the hood, the woman had eased out of the low-slung car and risen to stand hipshot on the highway beside it. She relaxed her rump back against the driver-side door as she watched them approach, the heels of her hands braced on either side of her hips.

"Holy shit," he muttered, because she looked for all the world like one of those World War II pinup girls, dressed as she was in a white sailor shirt trimmed in blue, those

14

retro shoes and even more retro little blue tap pants that showcased yard-long legs.

Hell, she was even wearing a white sailor cap, its wide turned-up brim tilted rakishly off-kilter atop a froth of curls that clung in wisps to its brim and her cheekbones.

And sure enough, she was a blonde. Shooting his friend a sideways glance, he shook his head. "I don't know how you do it, man."

"It's a gift," Johnny said over his shoulder as Gabe stopped and leaned against the cruiser's hood. Continuing to the Corvette, the deputy raised his voice to address its driver, saying easily, "Hey, sailor. New in town?"

"No newer than you, Angelini," the woman replied in a low, husky voice that ruffled Gabe's nerve endings. "Considering you and I moved here around the same time." Her shoulder hitched lazily. " 'Course, I've moved on, while you . . . well, here you still are." Her gaze cut to Gabe and she gave him a leisurely up-and-down examination that, to his disgust, elicited a down-and-dirty level of sexual awareness he thought he'd left in the dust long ago. "I'd say the honor of new in town probably goes to your friend there."

Johnny came to attention. "Macy?" he said

incredulously. "Macy O'James?"

Hearing the name, Gabe's own interest was piqued, and he gave the woman a closer inspection. They'd never met, but he'd sure as hell heard of her. Macy O'James, Sugarville's own wild child, heartbreaker — and ultimate pariah. From his first day in this little eastern Washington prairie town, he'd been inundated with tales of Macy, a girl whose morals were no better than they should be and who had left a trail of wreckage in her wake when she'd blown town for L.A., where she'd starred in a series of music videos. *Steamy* videos, it was always amended. Depending on who was relating a story to Gabe, she was Sugarville's version of Pamela Anderson/Carmen Electra/Paris Hilton. Except — and this was always grudgingly admitted — Macy mostly kept her clothes on.

All of which he had supposed was marginally titillating. It was a helluva lot more so now. Because, looking at her lounging provocatively against her red convertible, the sun shining on the creamy expanse of those long legs and limning the curves of pink lips that were currently crooked in a sardonic smile, it was easy to understand the town's preoccupation with her exploits. Once upon a time, he, too, had allowed girls like her — sexual girls with magnetism to spare, too pretty and knowing for their own good — to consume too many of his waking hours.

Well, hey, that was then. This was now. No skin off his ass what she did. He believed in live and let live, in allowing people to be who and what they were. While he had a self-acknowledged issue or two with good-time girls, having been, loosely speaking, raised by one, he'd do his best to accord O'James the same courtesy he'd show anyone else.

Settling more firmly against the hood, he crossed his arms over his chest, watching as she gave his friend a sultry smile.

"Hello, Johnny," she murmured to the deputy. "Long time no see." She raised a slender brow. "You planning on writing me a ticket for going a few miles over the speed limit?"

Her tone was negligent, but even as Johnny appeared to consider the question, the hint of dare-ya attitude beneath her casualness rubbed at Gabe's edges, abrading the Zen calm he prided himself on. The realization was surprising, and more than a little annoying. Yet even so, he couldn't stop himself from watching her.

As if sensing it, she turned to him and

17

slowly slid her sunglasses down her slender nose. Her eyes were big and green. Or possibly hazel; it was hard to tell for sure with the sun hitting her from that angle.

Whatever the color, they were set for stun when she trained them on him. And it bugged the bejesus out of him that if he were any other man, he'd find the ploy's effectiveness factor off the charts.

"Well, you're certainly taking in the scenery," she said. "Here. Let me give you the nickel tour." And, her elbows bent close to her waist and slender-fingered hands held palms up in the air, she spread her arms and slowly pivoted to display first the view from the left, then the back, then the right.

And they all looked good.

Turning face-front once again, she gazed at him from up under her lashes. "Like the view, sugar?"

He shrugged. "Not bad."

One corner of her mouth curved up. "To say the least."

But inside Macy wasn't smiling. That was the trouble with this burg — you couldn't live down your reputation no matter how long you'd been away or what you had accomplished in your absence.

But she'd had years of practice slapping on an insouciant expression and she did so now as she considered Johnny's sidekick.

My God, he was huge. The guy was six-six if he was an inch and must weigh in at about two-thirty.

Nary an ounce of which was fat. Unexpected heat scalded her veins, and her heartbeat performed a quick pitty-pat. In a knee-jerk attempt to negate the awareness she felt, she consciously bumped up the wattage on her bimbo meter. Slicking her tongue over her bottom lip was inadvertent. But the aren't-you-just-so-big-and-strong look she gave him was definitely deliberate. "And you are . . . ?"

"This is Gabe Donovan, Macy," Johnny said. "Sugarville's fire chief. Gabe, this is Macy O'James."

"Sugarville's celebrity tramp," she murmured.

Johnny, bless him, winced. While he'd always been hot for anything in skirts back in high school, he'd still been a fairly decent guy.

Fire Chief Donovan, on the other hand, merely gave her a clipped nod as if he wasn't the least bit surprised. And for some reason that stung. For a nanosecond when she had met the guy's intense gray eyes, looked at his big, hard body, she'd felt . . . something. Something that made losing it in almost the next heartbeat a crying shame. It was clear, however, that whatever-it-had-been had zero chance of going anywhere now that he knew who she was.

But that felt a bit too boo-hoo, I'm-just-a-poor-misunderstood-waif for a woman who had learned young that life was messy, life was unfair, but you sucked it up and dealt with it. Her shoulders squared. *Well, guess what, pal? I'm not wild about you, either.*

And she wasn't, whether the guy was a big hot number with pretty, cool eyes or no. Not when he'd taken one look at her and embraced the role assigned her by the good people of Sugarville without even bothering to find out if there was any validity to it.

Not when he made her feel like that girl the town loved to hate.

As if, she reminded herself, *I give a great big rip.* She was what she was. She had no regrets.

None.

But she did know she'd had enough of this. Tilting her chin up, she looked at Johnny. "So," she said. "What's it gonna be? Yes or no on the ticket?"

"I'll give you a pass this time."

"That's my preferred option," she agreed, opening the car door and sliding inside. She started up the car with a roar and slid it into first gear. "See you around, boys."

And without sparing either man another glance, she eased her Corvette off the shoulder and headed down the road toward home.

CHAPTER TWO

"Love the getup," Macy's cousin Janna commented dryly. "But I can't believe you wore it all the way from wherever you spent last night."

Macy paused, glancing from the closet where she was unpacking to her cousin, who sat in a chintz chair in the study of their family's boardinghouse. Her leg was encased in plaster from knee to crotch, a pair of crutches propped within easy reach.

"Medford," she replied, naming the Oregon town six hours away. "And please. Of course I didn't wear it the entire way. Do I look crazy to you?"

"That's probably not the question you wanna ask when you're wearing the wet-dream version of a sailor suit."

Macy grinned. "Let me rephrase it then. Have you ever known me to be a martyr? No, you haven't," she hastily asserted when she saw her cousin open her mouth and just

22

knew it was to bring up That Night.

But she wasn't going there — it had all happened too long ago to rehash at this late date. "I changed in Wenatchee, baby. Hey, I could hardly arrive in town looking halfway normal and deprive the good folks of Sugarville of yet another chance to be scandalized."

Janna rolled her eyes. "Yeah, heaven forbid people should have nothing to talk about."

"Damn straight. Life as we know it would cease to exist." She reached for a hanger in the closet. Whipping it beneath the skinny straps of a gauzy summer dress, she shook out the garment with a snap, then hung it on the rod above the tangle of shoes she'd already dumped onto the closet floor. "They gave me the name. The least I can do is have a little fun playing the game."

"Right. Because you're so tough."

"Yes." Looking up, she caught Janna's who-are-you-trying-to-kid expression. "Don't give me that look — I am. You, on the other hand —" her voice softened with concern as she took in the other woman's pale face "— look like a harsh word could knock you on your butt, let alone the proverbial puff of wind."

"I'm okay." Belying her assertion, Janna shifted uncomfortably. "It's just hard to find a position that doesn't hurt. The doctor told me to try to keep my leg elevated as much as possible, but —"

Contrition hit Macy like a freight train. "Oh, crap, Janna, why didn't you say something?" She shifted the suitcase that she'd crammed with clothes two nights before in L.A. onto the floor and shoved the ottoman it had been sitting on toward her cousin. Easing it into position, she winced in sympathy when pain clouded Janna's expression during the moment it took to lift her cast-encased leg onto it.

Dammit, Janna was the closest thing she had to a sister, and seeing her hurt made Macy want to wrap her in yards of warm chenille and ply her with cup after cup of hot tea. This, despite the fact that it must be ninety degrees outside.

Janna sighed. "I hate being an invalid, so I tend to overdo. Which is why Mom wants you here — when *you* ride herd on me I don't get all defensive." Spearing her fingers through her normally shiny but currently dull ear-length chestnut bob, she flashed a tired smile. "Thanks for dropping everything and coming so fast."

"Are you kidding me?" She sank to her haunches in front of the other woman and, picking up Janna's hand, held it gently between her own. "Where else would I be — you're family. Do you have any idea how much I loved this town before all the crap began? And it was all because of you and Uncle Bud and Auntie Lenore. Not to take anything away from Mom or anything, but living with you guys? That was the first time in my life I felt as if I had a real home."

"I thought it was so cool when you got to come here."

Embarrassed by the sentimental tears that rose in her eyes, Macy looked around the room. Even with all the regular furniture moved out, there wasn't much space to spare with the addition of two beds and two dressers. "Are you sure you want me to bunk in here with you?" she asked. "I can easily make do with the Closet."

"It's not available," Janna said. "We had to do some switching around in February to accommodate a new boarder, and we moved Tyler in there. Wait until you meet —"

"Tyler got shoved out of his room and ended up in the *Closet?*" she interrupted indignantly. "Janna, that's just wrong!"

Her cousin laughed. "Not in Ty's eyes, it isn't. He actually loves it. He likes pretending it's a nuclear-class submarine and he's the master spy. It doesn't hurt that his best

25

friend, Charlie, thinks it's beyond cool, either." Her mouth crooked in a wry smile.

"Only a nine-year-old," Macy said, shaking her head at the notion of anyone thinking that sweatbox of a six-by-ten-foot room was "beyond cool." "Then how about our old room?" They'd shared an upstairs room for several years as teens. "Auntie Lenore said they're keeping it open for when you can navigate the stairs again, and I'd be out of your way but still close enough to help."

"Uh, the thing is, I can't use these crutches and carry anything bigger than a pair of undies at the same time. So I need help with the fetching and toting. I'm sorry, Macy, I know it's cramped in here and not what you're used to —"

"No, no, no, no, no!" She shook her head in vigorous denial. "I didn't mean it that way at all!" The action made her realize she still had on the sailor hat and she reached up to lift it off. Tossing it onto the bed Janna had assigned for her use, she tugged free the blond wig she'd worn beneath it. "I was afraid I'd be crowding *you,* not the other way around!"

"Then we're talking apples and oranges and don't have a problem. Here. Fork that over." Janna crooked "gimme" fingers at the wig. "I always wondered what I'd look like as a blonde."

Macy tossed it to her, then ran her fingers through her own super-straight hair, which was more caramel colored than the do-me-daddy platinum of her wig. She rubbed her scalp to lift the roots and sighed as a breeze ruffled through the white curtains, combing cool fingers through the freed strands and setting them to dancing against her collarbones. Toeing off her Cuban heels, she kicked them aside, then breathed a long, attenuated "Ahhh," and wiggled her toes. "Lovely."

"I'm glad one of us is," Janna murmured, making a face as she tugged at the wig and a pale blond strand flopped over her eye.

"It's hard being adept in the beauty department without a mirror." Macy crossed to her cousin and shifted the hairpiece into proper position, then finessed the curls into a sassy style. Standing back, she surveyed her handiwork.

"You need a little makeup." Grabbing her purse, she upended it over her bed and picked her cosmetic case out of the resulting jumble. Handing a tube of lipstick to Janna with instructions to dab some on, she applied a pale rose blusher to her cousin's poreless cheeks, then mixed brown eye shadow into a daub of Vaseline she'd

27

smeared on the back of her hand. She applied the concoction over Janna's eyelids with a deftness gained through years spent taking mental notes while makeup artists got her camera-ready for this, that or the other video shoot. After smoothing the gleaming eye shadow to just above the crease in Jenna's eyelid to give her cousin a thirties silent-movie-star look, she finished it off with a coat of mascara, then leaned back to inspect her work.

"*Now* you look like the coz I remember." Twisting around, she reached behind her for the hand mirror atop Janna's dresser and turned back to extend it to her. "Here. Check it out."

Janna stared at her reflection for several silent seconds. Then, the hand holding the mirror dropping to her lap, she looked up, a slow well of tears pooling in her eyes.

Remorse slammed through Macy. "Oh, my God, Janny, I'm sorry! I'll take it off!" She snatched several tissues from the box on the dresser where she'd gotten the mirror. "Don't cry, it'll only take me a second to remove it!"

"No! Don't you dare." A choked sound rose from Janna's throat and she dashed the sides of her hands beneath her eyes. Then she let out a watery laugh. "Well, don't I feel like an idiot. It's just . . . I look like a woman again. For the first time since that car hit me and took off — no, since even before that, when Sean walked out — I look like an honest-to-gawd woman instead of somebody's patient or a woman whose husband dumped her for a twenty-year-old or, I don't know, whatever it is I've been these past six months. Jeez," she said. "Can you say *overreaction?*" Bringing the mirror up to study her reflection again, she turned her head this way and that to take in the full effect.

And smiled. "I make a pretty hot blonde, if I do say so myself."

"Yes, you do. And it's my fervent hope that the bastard who put you in the hospital *and* that little prick Sean contract a raging case of the —"

Janna brought her hands together in a single loud clap. And wiggled her eyebrows.

Macy laughed. "Precisely."

Her cousin sighed. "What is it about men, anyway? You can't live with 'em and the law frowns on neutering them. It's not exactly a win-win situation."

For no good reason, an image of Gabe Donovan popped into her mind. With his big body and near-black hair. Those gray eyes. His strong nose, strong chin, strong . . .

29

well, everything — or at least that was how it had appeared to her.

Damn. She hadn't even realized she'd been paying such close attention, but here she was with warm blood rushing to places it had no business going and her heart beating much too rapidly. And all because of an unbidden mental slide show featuring a man she'd met for all of maybe two minutes.

Well, get a grip, girl! She slammed a lid on the images. She had zero time for this.

As if on cue, the door banged open, bouncing off the wall with a crash and creating a welcome diversion. "Mom, can Charlie stay for dinner — hey!" Macy's nephew, Tyler, spotted her and his entire face lit up. "You're here!"

"Hey, pard!" She closed the distance between them, but rocked to a halt in front of Tyler, uncertain how to greet him. What she wanted was to haul him into her arms. But she was afraid that, at nine, he might have reached the age where he'd rather stick needles in his eyes than have a relative hug him in front of his friends.

Or not, she thought with a big smile as Tyler hurled himself at her, wrapping matchstick arms around her waist and squeezing with surprising strength. Then, without relinquishing his hold, he leaned back and grinned up at her. "I'm glad you're here. Mom's been either in the hospital or that rehabib, rehabibl — that nursing place — for*ever* and she still can't get around very good. But she says you're gonna stay with us and take me to my practices and games and stuff 'til she's better. Dintja, Mom?" He turned his head to get Janna's endorsement — and did a double take.

His jaw sagging, he dropped his arms from Macy's waist. "*Mom?* Is that — ? Wow. You look . . . uh, you look really —" He blinked at her.

"Pretty," said the little redheaded boy who had followed Tyler into the room.

"Yeah." Tyler nodded and, once in motion, his head continued to bob like a marionette's in the hands of a mad puppeteer. "Did you use one of them boxes the ladies buy at Sheppard Drugs to change their hair color?"

"No, it's a wig of Aunt Macy's."

"Can you wear it again at my Little League game?"

"Oh, honey, I don't know about tha—"

"Is that my baby girl's car I see parked out back?" a feminine voice bawled from the kitchen. "Macy O'James, you get your tush in here this minute and give your Auntie a hug!"

Laughing, Macy left Tyler and Janna to their discussion, whirled on her bare heel and raced from the room. Long-legged strides carried her down the hallway and into the kitchen, where she embraced the woman who had just dumped an armload of grocery bags onto the counter.

Warm, plump arms wrapped around her in return and when she bent her head to bring them to a more equitable level, Macy was enveloped in Lenore's signature scent: a combination of comfort food and sugar cookies. This, *this,* was the reason she braved the condemnation of this town. Because of Aunt Lenore and Uncle Bud and Janna and Ty, this was home. *They* were her home.

"Let me look at you." Stepping back, Lenore held Macy at arm's length. A wry smile tipped up the corner of her lips. "You get separated from the cast of *42nd Street?*"

She laughed. "You should have seen the full effect before I took off my wig, shoes and sailor cap."

"That's my Macy." Her aunt reached out an age-spotted hand and brushed Macy's bangs out of her eyes. "It's good to have you home, girl."

"I'm sorry I don't get back here more often, Auntie Lenore. It's just —"

"Difficult. I know. I still want to skin that Mayfield boy alive every time I clap eyes on him. If it wasn't for him and his lies —"

"I brought along some wickedly hot outfits." Macy grinned, but avoided Lenore's eagle-eyed gaze so her aunt wouldn't see the lack of humor in her own. "I plan on giving him and all his sycophants an eat-your-heart-out eyeful while I'm here."

"I don't suppose you could just let it go."

Her stomach clenched at the thought of disappointing her aunt any more than she already had over the years, but she looked Lenore in the eye. "No. I won't go looking for trouble, but I won't step away from it, either." Then honesty compelled her to amend her statement. "Okay, I suppose I do look for it, in a way, with the clothes I choose to wear to town."

She rubbed her temples, looking at her aunt from beneath the bridge formed by her thumb and fingers. "I know you probably think I lie awake nights plotting ways to make people squirm, but I truly don't. I rarely even think about this stuff when I'm away from here. But the minute I cross the county line, something happens to me. And I'm sorry, Auntie, I know it would make things so much easier on the family if I could just be less problematic, but —"

"You can stop right there, Macy Joleen — no one here wants or expects you to be anything but exactly what you are. I do believe, however, that *you* would be a lot happier if you could walk away from it." Lenore patted Macy's cheek. "But you're gonna do what you gotta do until you no longer gotta do it."

Stepping back, she added briskly, "But not today. Today, you're all mine. Stick around while I put the groceries away and get the pork chops going. Have you seen your Uncle Bud yet?"

"No. Janna said he went in to pick something up at the Feed and Seed." She cocked her eyebrows at her aunt. "You two ever considered carpooling?"

"Aren't you the smart-mouthed little missy!"

"A smart-mouth, maybe, but hardly little. I'm way bigger than you are, Madam Short Stuff." Stepping close, she wrapped an arm around her aunt to showcase the disparity between her five-eight and Lenore's five-four, then had to hide a frown when she realized her aunt had lost weight since she'd seen her at the hospital in Spokane just five weeks ago after Janna's encounter with a hit-and-run driver. The new frailness suggested an even greater discrepancy between

34

their heights now — and she was barefoot while her aunt wore her usual sturdy clogs.

Lenore was almost seventeen years older than Macy's mother. But she'd had Janna just a month before Macy was born. She and Uncle Bud had always been closer to grandparent age than that of a parent, but Macy had never invested much thought in the difference between them and her classmates' folks when she was a kid. Her aunt and uncle had provided her a stable place to escape her mother's perpetual wanderlust and had been, in her estimation, simply the best parents any kid could hope to have.

She rubbed her aunt's upper arm. "What can I do to help?"

"Just what you came here for, sweetheart. Help Janna all she'll let you and take the burden of worry off her by looking out for Ty."

"I meant right now, for you," she said with a laugh. "But I'm definitely here for Janna. How is she doing, Auntie? She looks so pale."

"She's improving. You already know what a rough go she had of it at first, and she certainly didn't love rehab in that interim nursing home after they sprung her from the hospital. But she's home now and improving a little every day. The doctor expects her recovery to pick up its pace once she starts physical therapy."

"Good. I was so excited to see you when you got home that I kind of raced off and left her. Let me just run down the hall to see if she has everything she needs, then I'll come back and peel potatoes or do whatever other KP you need. You want me to set the table in the dining room first?"

"No, that's Ty's job, but I think I just heard him thunder up the stairs. Dinner's not until six, as usual, but if you wouldn't mind going up and asking him to come down and do it now I'd appreciate it. And tell Charlie if he's eating here he can lend a hand, as well." She shook her head. "Those two," she said gruffly. "I swear they're permanently joined at the hip." But Macy saw the smile that curved her lips as her aunt turned away.

She went up and passed on the message to Ty and his friend, smiling when the boys complained loudly, yet immediately clattered down the stairs to do as they were bid. Sauntering behind them, she paused for a second outside her and Janna's old room. Then she turned the knob and let herself in.

The two twin beds they'd slept in had been replaced by a queen with a sleigh headboard she remembered from Old Mrs. Matheson's room. But the illusion curtains the breeze blew into the room were the same, as was were the dotted swiss tiebacks that framed them. And it smelled the same in here — a combination of floor wax, fresh linens and a hint of the cheap girlish cologne they'd applied so lavishly it must be imbedded in the very walls. There was a world of memories associated with this room, both of the good and the bad variety.

Mostly, though, they were good.

Her cousin was asleep sitting up in the chair when she let herself into the converted study several minutes later, and Macy debated waking her to get her into bed where she'd be more comfortable. Deciding the pain of the move probably wouldn't be worth what Janna would gain in exchange, she left her where she was. Gently, however, she straightened Janna's head and propped a pillow alongside it to keep her cousin from getting a nasty crick in her neck on top of everything else. Then she grabbed an ancient pair of jeans out of the suitcase she'd yet to finish unpacking and exchanged her tap pants for them before going back to lend a hand to Aunt Lenore.

Her uncle got home a short while later, and they sat at the worktable catching up as she shucked peas into a bowl. At a quarter to six, she went back to the study and found Janna leaning on one crutch, peering into the mirror as she tried to fluff up the wig where it had flattened on one side. Fixing it for her, she then handed her cousin the lipstick to refresh her makeup and ushered her in baby steps down the hall.

Voices could be heard coming from the dining room, along with the sound of chairs scraping back from the table as her relatives' boarders gathered for dinner. Macy smiled to herself at the discovery that she was still every bit as curious and fascinated to see what the dynamics would be of the current group Lenore and Bud had taken in as she'd been as a kid.

But when she reached the doorway she stopped in her tracks, causing Janna to bump her crutch's rubber tip against her heel. *"Seriously?"* she demanded incredulously.

Because there, seated midtable, his big shoulders taking up a small person's worth of space on either side of him, a slight smile on his face as he placed a napkin on his lap and listened to a young man she didn't recognize, sat the very last man she expected to see.

Freaking Fire Chief Gabriel Donovan.

CHAPTER THREE

Gabe heard Macy's voice and for a second everything stilled.

Then the planet recommenced its rotation, platters clattered onto the table as Lenore transferred them from the cart and he got his game face on before turning away from Mike Schwab, one of the three boarders studying farming methods at AAE, the experimental agricultural project outside of town. Because what the hell? Women didn't stop his world. Not to mention it didn't say a helluva lot for his deductive abilities to be caught flat-footed at finding O'James here. He knew she was the Watsons' niece; this was the only logical place for her *to* be.

But, observant wonder boy that he was, he looked across the table and didn't even recognize her at first. His gaze went straight to that sassy blond hair, only to realize it didn't jibe with the face of the wearer. Janna's full-leg cast probably should have been his first clue, and he looked away from her to the woman holding Janna's crutches while she eased onto a chair.

Heat promptly streaked down his spine.

He ignored it by focusing on the reasons he hadn't copped to Macy being Macy right away, because, face it, she wasn't exactly a woman who was easy to ignore. Yet except for the sailor shirt she still wore, nothing about her looked the way it had out on the road.

Her hair was a different shade of blond — actually more the amber-brown of good ale — and its long style and blunt-cut bangs emphasized her cheekbones while the short platinum wig had been all about her eyes. Which, he saw in the early-evening sunshine pouring through the windows, were hazel, not green. Well, part of her irises were a clear green, but they were ringed in a darker shade and striated with amber near the pupils. As for her clothing, she'd ditched the shorts for worn, snug jeans and was currently barefoot. She looked more farmer's daughter than forties pinup. Same woman, different fantasy.

Maybe that was why she did so well on all those music videos — she was a chameleon, able to change her look at will without losing her ability to remain the average guy's dream girl.

"Hey there, Mr. Grandview," the dream girl said in her throaty voice, looking at the old man two seats down from him as if he were God's gift. "It's so nice to see you again. You still breaking hearts right and left?"

For God's sake, Gabe thought in disgust, the man was eighty-five if he was a day. Apparently O'James's sole requirement for flirting was a pulse.

Not that Grandview appeared to object. "Yes, ma'am." He agreed with a chuckle. "Come senior afternoons down at the grange hall, I got wimmen buzzing around me like bees on mint."

She flashed him a smile of admiration. "You always were a devil with the ladies."

Lenore handed a big bowl of peas to Dawson on her left and took her seat. "Let's get my food passed around before it gets cold, people. Everyone, this is my niece, Macy O'James. Macy, this here is Brian Dawson," she said of the man with the bowl. "He and Mike Schwab and Jim Holstrom —" she indicated the men as she introduced them "— are studying farming methods at the Experimental. The lovebirds there," she continued, nodding to a young couple whispering and exchanging surreptitious

41

touches at the far end of the table, "are Justin and Tiffany McMann."

"Newlyweds?" Macy asked them, accepting the platter of pork chops from Tyler and spearing one onto her plate. She turned to her cousin. "You want to split one of these?"

"Sure," Janna agreed, taking the platter and passing it on. "Just don't expect me to relinquish my share of the potatoes."

Macy turned back to the couple. "Sorry. I didn't mean to ask a question, then not listen to the answer." But tumbling to what the rest of them already knew — that the just-wed teens paid attention to no one but each other — her lips crooked in a wry smile. "O-kay. Who says talking's required to get a straight answer?"

Lenore snorted. Pointing to Gabe as he speared two pork chops onto his plate, she said, "The big boy across from you is Gabriel Donovan. Our new fire chief."

He half expected Macy to pretend this was the first time they'd seen each other. But she merely gave him a brief nod before turning her attention on her aunt. "We actually met out on the highway," she said. "Johnny Angelini pulled me over for driving ten above the limit and Fire Chief Donovan was with him. I didn't know he was living here, though."

"I'm in the process of building a house," he said with the aloof courtesy that was his default manner with anyone he didn't know, then shot Lenore a smile. "I'm not sure how I'm going to tear myself away from your cooking, though, when the place is finished." Turning his attention back to Macy, he invited perfunctorily, "Call me Gabe."

When Brian, Mike and Jim tripped all over themselves inviting her to call them by their first names as well, he shook his head. Not that he had a problem with them seconding his invitation. But Jesus. You'd think three grown men would have more pride than to tumble all over themselves like a litter of eager puppies.

He transferred his attention to Janna, absorbing the change in her appearance. "You sure look nice tonight."

Color touched her cheeks. "Thank you. Macy dolled me up."

"Mom looks really pretty, doesn't she?" Tyler piped up. "And she didn't even hafta dye her hair from one of those boxes."

"Yeah," Charlie agreed around a mouthful of sweet potato fries. "That's a wig of Ty's Aunt Macy's."

Resisting an unusual urge to check out Aunt Macy sans her wig in more microscopic detail than he'd already done, he kept his focus determinedly on Janna. "It looks good on you."

"Doesn't it?" Lenore agreed. "And it's sure nice to see some color in her cheeks."

"Johnny slap you with a ticket, sweetheart?" Bud asked Macy in a low voice, promptly diverting Gabe's attention. He looked across the table at her, wondering if she'd invest the story of being pulled over with the same hint of attitude he'd sensed when it had been happening.

But she merely shrugged. "Nah. Johnny's always been a pretty decent guy. He just gave me a warning."

Charlie leaned forward to look around Janna's boy at Macy. "My sister says you're, like, a movie star, or something."

Tyler rolled his eyes. "I've tol' him and tol' him you ain't."

"You've told him she's not," his mother corrected.

"I know! But his sister Amy keeps insistin' she is."

Macy gave the boys a crooked smile. "Tyler's right, Charlie. I've made a name for myself in the music-video industry, but movie star–wise I'm not even a little fish in a big pond. I'm more like a minnow in the ocean." She indicated the basket next to his elbow. "Pass me those rolls, will you?"

The basket was handed to her, and holding it in both hands, she brought it up to her nose and inhaled deeply, her lips quirking up and her eyes sliding closed in appreciation.

But her eyelids promptly reopened and she gazed straight at Gabe, catching him watching her. He felt that look like fingers running down his chest. Then her tongue commenced a slow glide across her full bottom lip and his balls tightened.

Damn. He didn't understand why those eyes and that voice and, hell, every goddamn thing about her kept having such an impact on him. Women didn't usually get under his skin. He didn't allow it.

Yet here he sat, waiting to see how outrageous she'd be in the company of her aunt and uncle.

"You're right to worry about who'll do the cooking when you move into your new house," she murmured. "Because Auntie Lenore is, hands down, the greatest cook in the world."

And as fast as she'd locked gazes with him, she turned her attention to selecting a roll and passing the basket to Janna.

Leaving him irritated as hell that he felt . . . let down.

And itching for something he couldn't

even name.

Macy had just gotten Janna settled in the overstuffed chair in their room when her cousin swore and started levering herself out of it again.

"Whoa!" Macy put a hand on her shoulder. "Sit. Stay. What do you need?"

"Me, nothing. But I forgot all about Ty's uniform for tomorrow's Little League game. Dammit, I meant to check earlier to make sure it was clean and not moldering under his bed since the last game." She planted her hands on the arms of the chair as if preparing to push herself back onto her feet.

"Plant your butt," Macy ordered. When Janna narrowed her eyes at her, she snapped, "Don't give me that look. This is exactly the kind of thing you wanted me here for. So take a deep breath. I'll run up and see if he has it. And if it is under the bed, I'll make him fish it out and we'll bring it down and run a load of laundry. You know that's no biggie. There's always something needs washing in this house."

"Okay." Blowing out a breath, her cousin sagged against the cushions. "Thank you." She scrubbed a hand over her mouth. "God, I hate this. Every little molehill turns into frigging Mount Everest."

"I know. But that's what you've got me for — I'm your designated mountain climber. So prop that leg up. Grab your book. Or I can turn on *Wheel,* if you prefer. You always were better at that game than me. You want anything from the kitchen?"

"God, no. I'm still stuffed from dinner."

She grinned. "Yeah. I wasn't kidding when I told the fire chief your mom puts on one dynamite spread."

But the last thing she wanted to think about was Gabriel Donovan. She hated the fact she was so aware of the man while he was all cool-eyed disinterest when he looked at her.

"All right, then," she said briskly. "I'll go find out the status of Ty's uniform."

She took the stairs two at a time up to the second floor and strode down the hall to the Closet, where she rapped on the door.

"Who is it?" Tyler's muffled voice demanded.

"Emissary from your commanding officer, Seaman Purcell. Open up."

The door whipped open. "I'm not a *seaman,* Aunt Macy — I'm captain of the sub!"

"My mistake, Cap'n. So, you all ready for tomorrow's game? You have your uniform in tiptop shape?"

"Yep. Grandma washed it up for me and

it's in my closet. On a hanger and every-thing."

"Excellent. How 'bout your shoes, mitt, all that sorta thing? They ready, too?"

"Uh-huh." He gave a long-suffering sigh. "Can me and Charlie get back to our game now?"

Over his shoulder she saw Charlie twist around to stare at her and hooked her elbow around Tyler's neck to haul him in for a noogie. "Yes, you may," she said, turning him loose. "As you were —"

He shut the door in her face.

"— men." A huff of laughter escaped her. "Am I racking up the points with the under-twenty crowd tonight, or what?"

She was smiling when she turned around, but yelped in surprise as she smacked into someone. Reaching out a hand to steady herself, she jerked it back when it touched the abdomen of whatshisname, one of the guys studying at the Experimental.

"Steady there." His hands grasped her up-per arms.

"I'm sorry, I didn't see you." She stepped back, breathing easier when the man's hands dropped away. *Jeez, girl, get a grip.* This was a shy young man, not Jack the Ripper. "Um, Brian, right?"

"Yeah. Hey, at dinner, I didn't get a

chance to say how much I enjoy your videos. That Aussie Kiss one, *Burn, Baby, Burn*? Man, you *smoked* in that!"

A corner of her mouth ticked up. "Mr. Dawson, are you punning me?"

"Huh?" Then he chuckled. "Oh. I guess I did make a pun. Not on purpose, though. I just can't believe I'm meeting you and want you to know how hot I thought you were in that video."

Because he didn't leer at her as he said it, she swallowed a sigh. But, God, she was tired of being told how hot she was and so glad to know that her career had recently shifted from being on-camera to working behind the scenes. All the same, because the guy was perfectly sincere and he *hadn't* leered, she slapped on some sass and ramped up the appreciation factor. "Aren't you a doll? I'm so gratified you enjoyed it."

"Oh, man, I really did. I liked all of them, but especially that —" he cut himself off as the bathroom door opened behind her and shampoo-scented steam rolled out into the hallway. "Oh. Hey, Gabe."

Damn.

"I was just telling Macy here how much I enjoyed her in *Burn, Baby, Burn*."

"Isn't he just the *sweetest?*" Bracing herself, she turned around — and nearly

49

swallowed her tongue when she saw Gabe clad in nothing but two towels, one wrapped low around his hips and the other slung around his strong neck. Skin warming, she forced herself to give him a cool once-over from the top of his damp hair, to the large hands grasping the ends of the neck towel, to his long bare feet. "Well, aren't you the picture of big and strong. Do you always walk around half naked, Fire Chief Call-me-Gabe?"

"Difficult to shower with your clothes on."

"And yet so easy to dry off and dress in the bathroom."

"I think we all got used to it being the Boy's Club up here," Brian said edging away. "Well, uh, hey. I better get going. Nice talking to you, Macy."

"You, too, cupcake." She swiveled back to face him. "I'm sure we'll run into each other regularly." Watching as he backed down the hall, she gave him a friendly finger wiggle when he stopped in front of the Green Room.

Ducking his head, he smiled shyly, then entered the room. She drew a deep breath and turned back to Gabe.

Only to find that he'd taken a giant silent step forward while her back was turned and her nose was practically touching the hard curve of his lightly furred chest.

"Hel-lo!" Surrounded by his soap-and-shaving-cream scent, she took a nonchalant step back and looked up at him, taking in the gleam of the freshly shaven skin on his cheeks and jaw. "Sneaky son of a gun, aren't you." Against her will, her gaze was drawn back to the fine cloud of black hair covering his pectorals.

"You just can't help yourself, can you?"

A bead of water slid down his tan neck and rolled over his clavicle, heading for the fan of hair. *I will not lick it, I will not lick it.* She forced her gaze back to his face. "Excuse me?" Her mind replayed his question and she straightened. "Can't help myself from what?"

"Flirting. It's like breathing to you, isn't it? Wet-behind-the-ears boys, old duffers with one foot in the grave — is there no one you won't flirt up?"

"I don't recall flirting with you. Is that what's got your boxers in a twist, sugar — you don't like being left out?" She had a pretty strong hunch this wasn't a man to mess with and felt her heart gallop. But she'd learned young never to back down, and knew she was going to mess with him anyway.

Reversing the backward step she'd taken,

she touched her fingertip to the drop of water now clinging to his chest hair.

She wasn't prepared for the shock such simple contact sent skittering along her nerve endings. Praying its impact didn't show, she raised the now damp finger to her lips.

His hand shot out and captured her wrist before she could lick the smear of water from it. Bringing it to his own lips, he slid her finger into his mouth. Slick, moist heat promptly pulled forth a like condition in every tissue in her body capable of producing it. He wrapped his lips around her finger and sucked hard as he slowly pulled the digit free, and that secret entrance deep between her thighs clenched like the mouth of a drawstring purse.

In the next heartbeat he'd set her loose. "I'm neither a boy nor an old man," he said in a low, even voice. "And you might want to rethink making me any offers, implicit or otherwise, if you're not prepared to follow through on them." He stepped past her, spreading warmth along her entire left side when the bare skin of his arm brushed her.

Her heart threatened to hammer its way out of her chest as she turned to watch him, all wide shoulders, long back and longer legs, stalking down the hallway. *Yes,* she thought hazily, clasping her damp finger with her other hand. *I probably oughtta do that.* Because, holy shit.

Holy, holy shit. It had been a simple little suck on one lousy finger, for pity's sake. He hadn't dropped his towel, pressed her up against the nearest wall and had his wicked way with her.

Yet here she stood, rattled so hard that for perhaps the first time in her life not a single comeback popped to mind.

Because she had a bad feeling she would've really liked it if he had.

CHAPTER FOUR

Gabe gently closed his room door behind him, then ripped the towel from around his neck and flung it at the nearest wall.

It fell far short, drifting harmlessly to the old hardwood floor.

"Hell." Covering the distance to the crumpled terry in a single long stride, he bent and swept it up.

Only to have the towel around his waist come untucked and slide down his legs to take its place. "Son of a fucking *bitch!*"

He swept that one up, as well. Breathing heavily, he stood clutching both linens in white-knuckled fists as he stared blindly at the wall.

Then he gave a sharp shake of his head and got a grip. He sucked in deep, measured inhalations and slowly exhaled them until his breathing was regulated again.

Jesus. What *was* this? He never had to struggle for control, because he never lost it in the first place.

Not since he was sixteen, at any rate. For a couple of years there, he'd been monkey wild. Fighting anything in pants. Screwing anything in skirts.

But that was a long time ago. The man he was now was deliberate. In control. Master of his rare wayward impulse.

So what had he been doing out in the hallway with the music-video princess? What the holy hell had he been thinking?

He snorted. Yeah, right. Like *thought* had been a big part of the equation. He'd simply acted on instinct. Because he'd known in his gut that he couldn't watch her close that soft, pink, smart-ass mouth around her finger. Still, he could have, *should* have just released her hand and walked away.

Tossing his towels aside, he strode for the dresser. *Yeah, well, you didn't, so get over it.* The deed was done. He thought of the series of garbage-can fires around town that he'd been dealing with for the past few weeks. *That* was what he should be concentrating on, tracking down the reason for those, not wasting his time rewriting a here-and-gone run-in with the new resident flirt. Either that or . . .

"Shit!" *Grace.* How the hell had he forgotten his date with Grace, even if only for a few minutes? Guilt crawled down his spine. This was the second time he'd gotten so caught up in Macy's sexual pull that it had blown every single thought of the woman he was actually dating clean out of his mind.

Yanking open the second drawer, he collected a clean pair of jeans, then strode to the closet and ripped a cotton shirt from its hanger.

As he dressed, however, he found that merely thinking of the teacher he was scheduled to take out for a glass of wine smoothed over the minor irritations of his day. Because Grace was aptly named. She was quiet. Restful. *Nice.*

All of which were attributes he appreciated more than he could say considering his early life with his tumultuous party-girl mom, the fury years after she'd abdicated her responsibilities by dumping him on the system, and his time in the Detroit FD, the last six years of which he'd spent as an arson investigator forever juggling too many fires and not enough hours in the day. Taking this county fire-chief job had been the first step in alleviating the overload of stress he'd lived with for too long. Being with Grace, absorbing the tranquility she radiated, felt like the next.

A little peace was something he'd been in

search of for a long time. He'd had enough craziness and tension to last a lifetime. So, hell, yeah. Given even the prospect of a little serenity injected into his life?

He'd be a fool *not* to latch on to Grace.

Macy strode into the kitchen where her aunt was washing up the pans from breakfast. "Hey, Auntie Lenore," she said, grabbing an apple out of the bowl on the counter and polishing it on her shirt. "Janna's settled in our room for a while and Tyler's over at Charlie's. Charlie's mom said she'd get the boys to their game, so I sent along everything I thought he might need." She bit into the apple. Seeing her aunt in her natural milieu gave her a surge of pleasure every bit as strong as her first glimpse had last week.

Lenore turned off the faucet and turned to face her, taking in Macy's severe ponytail, bloodred lipstick and Goth eye makeup. "Let me guess," she said dryly. "You're heading into town."

Macy took another bite as her aunt inventoried her short pin-striped pleated skirt and stretchy black U-neck girl-T. The older woman's gaze lingered for a moment on her black spiked dog collar before moving on to —

"Oh, honey, no. You got a tattoo?"

57

"Nah." She smiled at the pained expression her aunt couldn't hide, then glanced down at the flame-winged skull on her inner forearm. "Though I may be one of the few of my generation who hasn't — at least in L.A. This is just for fun, a press-on/wash-off. And yeah, if it's okay with you, I am gonna run into town. I won't be gone long. I have a check I need to cash. I should have done it earlier in the week but I enjoyed just hanging around and catching up with you guys. Don't worry, though, I'll be back in plenty of time to get Janna ready for Tyler's game. Do you need anything while I'm there?"

"No, sweetheart, thanks. I'm good for a while." Lenore flashed a crooked smile. "I actually remembered my shopping list the other day. It's amazing what a difference that makes."

Macy laughed and slung an arm around her aunt, stooping to press a kiss on her cheek before heading out the back door.

It was only a couple of miles to town, and within minutes she was whipping her Corvette into a parking space a few doors down from Sterling Savings and Trust. But then she simply sat in her car, staring at the gold lettering on the plate glass window of Smokey's Grill.

She'd reached the turnoff to Bud and Lenore's boardinghouse the other day before the highway passed through Sugarville, so this was her first time in town in . . . Wow. More than a couple of years now.

Not that anything had changed. It still looked like a town caught in a time capsule, with its lack of fast-food chains and its two-story-maximum historic brick or stone buildings that comprised the three blocks of Commerce Street. For the same reasons, it was an exceptionally pretty town.

And despite her trying junior and senior years in high school or the fact that she'd barely flipped her tassel to the other side of her mortarboard before blowing town, there had been times she'd missed it dreadfully.

But mostly, she acknowledged, leaving had been the best present she'd ever given herself.

Sitting here patting herself on the back over it wasn't getting her check cashed, however, and impatient with her procrastination, she snatched her purse off the passenger seat and climbed from the car. She sauntered to the bank on the corner, feeling as if prying eyes were watching her every move but knowing she was likely being paranoid.

Air-conditioning pebbled her nearly bare

arms as she stepped into the oak-walled, marble-floored lobby a moment later. Digging her check from her purse, she crossed to the nearest old-fashioned, iron-barred teller's window. "Hello —" smiling at the maybe-twenty brunette manning it, she read the girl's name plate "— Lucy. Can you cash this for me?"

She signed the back of the check and slipped it beneath the iron grill, then pulled her wallet from her bag to root for the identification that, given the size of the check, she was sure to need. But as she withdrew her driver's license she realized the girl hadn't responded and, raising her head, discovered the brunette staring at her.

"Omigawd," the young woman breathed. "I can't believe it. It *is* you. You're That Girl."

Damn. She would've thought the teller was too young to remember her, but apparently her fricking reputation back in high school had filtered down even to the elementary level.

"You're that girl in all the videos — Jack Savage's girlfriend."

Ah. It wasn't her old rep the brunette was talking about but rather her newer claim to fame. Some of the tension went out of her shoulders. "Jack and I are just friends," she said cheerfully. "We're not — and never have been — lovers."

"No kidding? Wait 'til I tell my friends I got the inside scoop straight from the horse's mouth! This is ginormous!"

"I'm happy to help you one-up." She inched the check farther beneath the grill with her fingertips. "Would you mind cashing my check?"

"Oh! Sure." But when the teller looked at it, she frowned. "Oh," she said, glancing back at Macy. "This isn't drawn on us. Do you have an account here?"

"No."

"I'm sorry, Ms. O'James," she said with patent regret, "but this is something I have to have approved. Let me just get our manager, Mrs. Thorensen."

The young woman let herself out of the teller's cage and Macy turned to watch her cross the lobby to a woman in a black suit presiding over an ornate desk in the corner. The manager glanced across the room at her, then rose to her feet and came over.

Extending a hand, she said, "Macy? You probably don't remember me, but I'm —"

"Kelly Sherman," she supplied, recognizing the Sugarville High class treasurer in the slightly plumper, ten-years-older woman standing before her.

The bank manager gave her a surprisingly friendly smile for someone Macy remembered as perpetually desperate back in the day to please Liz Picket.

Liz, who had hated Macy's guts.

"It's Kelly Thorensen now. Why don't you come over to my desk and we'll see what we can do about getting you your money."

When they'd settled themselves across from each other, Kelly looked at her and said, "Are you in town for a while?"

"Yes. You may have heard that my cousin, Janna, was hit by a car a while back. I'm here to lend a hand until she gets back on her feet."

"Yes, I did hear that, and I'm so sorry. The main reason I asked, though, is we can't cash a check of this size for a noncustomer."

And *there* was the knife in the ribs she'd expected upon recognizing the banker. She had to hand it to Kelly, though, the woman managed not to let her satisfaction show. She was clearly worlds more sophisticated than she'd been in high school.

But then the banker grimaced with genuine regret and said, "I truly am sorry, Macy. If you're going to be in town for a while, though, perhaps you'd like to open a savings account with us. We still have to wait for the check to clear, but the balance will of course accrue interest from today's date."

"That sounds fair," she agreed slowly. She'd run into this situation a time or two; she'd simply forgotten about them because most of her employment checks were drawn on the bank where she had her account. She blew out a breath. "I meant to take care of this before I left home, but I forgot in my rush to pack and get on the road."

Kelly opened a form on her computer and started keying in information Macy supplied in answer to the manager's questions. Within minutes, she'd sent it to the printer. Sitting back in her chair, she smiled at Macy. "What a glamorous life you must lead in L.A."

"I don't know about glamorous," Macy replied, because mostly the work she did *was* work. And there was a phoniness prevalent in the industry that often wore thin. "But it's satisfying work." Especially now that she was in the creative end of producing music videos rather than acting in someone else's vision of a song.

"You going to our ten-year reunion next month?"

God, no. "Oh. Wow. Has it been ten years already? A reunion, huh? This is the first I've heard of it."

"Well, you should come. It'll be fun."

Uh-huh. Because I had so many friends in high school. "I'll keep it in mind, but so much depends on how well Janna's leg improves. Did I tell you she's starting physical therapy next week?"

They exchanged a few more pleasantries before she headed back to the car. All things considered, she thought in bemusement as she climbed in, that hadn't gone half badly.

When she said as much to Janna a short while later, after recounting her experience, her cousin gave her a wry smile. "So maybe the good citizens of Sugarville have moved on more than you've given them credit for." Then she teased, "I mean, I know you think it's all about you —"

"You mean it's *not?* What's with that?" But she wasn't up to kidding about this, and rubbing her forehead, she stared at her cousin. "You know, I never gave it much thought, since I was only here for a few days at a time to see you and the rest of the family. But I guess I've sort of been braced for the whole hornet's nest response to my return," she admitted soberly, "and I'm grateful as can be that Kelly was professional and gracious instead. But I doubt it's realistic to expect that everyone will be so nice." She shook her head. "I just wonder how *not* nice they're going to be."

Janna nodded, her expression troubled. "Yeah. That's the million-dollar question."

"Is that Macy O'James?"

"I heard she was back in town."

"She's got some nerve showing her face after all the heartache she's caused!"

"Hey, you know what they say. No-class white trash then, no-class white trash now."

The voices carried clearly in the hot summer air as Macy unfolded a lawn chair under the spreading oak trees next to the bleachers and helped her cousin settle into it. "Well, I guess that answers that big-bucks question," she murmured and made a moue of distaste. "Apparently Kelly was a fluke."

"Oh, I imagine there's more people like Kelly than you think." Janna cautiously propped the heel of her cast on the plastic bucket Macy upended in front of her. "There are always going to be idiots in this town, though. So do as I do, sweetie. Ignore 'em."

"I intend to." Knowing better than to expect an offer from the people on the bleachers nearest Janna to make room so she could sit next to her cousin, she snapped open the blanket she'd brought along for this precise contingency and spread it on the ground on Janna's other side. Careful to keep her knees together in deference to the shortness of her pin-striped skirt, she lowered herself upon it.

And swallowed a snort. Because wouldn't *that* be just what she needed to round out this outing — to flash the young players warming up on the field? As if she didn't have a bad enough name in this town as it was.

It would have been smarter to wear a nice conservative pair of shorts, she knew, but she was glad she hadn't changed her clothes. For a short while, in the wake of her better-than-expected encounter with Kelly, she'd considered it. But in the end, she'd decided that a girl could simply never predict when her armor might come in handy in this town. Outrageous clothing was her armor of choice. And it was coming in handy now.

Then Janna's words sank in, and she scooted closer to her cousin, leaning in to ask in a low voice, "What do you mean, do as you do?"

Janna shrugged. "When Sean and I divorced, I lost most of my social circle," she answered with matter-of-fact equanimity.

Macy stared. "He screwed around on you with a barely legal bimbo and your friends took *his* side?"

"Except for one or two of them, they were never really my friends, anyhow. Sean is a Purcell — I married up in their eyes."

"Are you kidding?" An incredulous laugh escaped her. "Someone actually said that?"

"Nah, it wasn't that blatant. But the cliques in this town continue long after high school." She gave an impatient shake of her head. "No. That makes it sound like it's a Sugarville thing, and it's not. This sort of social maneuvering goes on everywhere. Everyone was friendly while Sean and I were married — and a few of them I've remained friends with. But for the most part, when he dumped me, so did the group we socialized with."

Macy blew out a quiet breath. "I'm sorry, Janny. That must have been rough."

Janna shrugged again. "Shit happens. You know that better than most."

"She's wearing a damn dog collar," a woman on the bleachers said loudly. "I've never seen anything so stupid."

Twisting around, Macy located the speaker and gave her a slow appraisal. "Interesting fashion criticism, sugar, coming from a woman who wears burgundy lip liner with pink lipstick."

Angry color scalded the woman's cheeks. "Bitch."

"Yes. I am. Hence the collar."

She heard a muffled laugh and turned back around. Charlie's mother, Shannon, stood nearby with another woman, but if the snicker she'd heard came from either of them she saw no evidence of it now.

"Hey, ladies." Shannon greeted them with easy cheer, flashing the ready smile Macy had noticed when she'd dropped the boys off at Charlie's house earlier. She was a big woman with a big laugh and the same orangy-red hair as her son's. "Mind if we join you?"

"Please do." She patted the blanket next to her.

"Thanks. You've got a primo spot here." The women settled on the blanket next to her, then Shannon leaned back so Macy could see the quietly pretty brunette on her other side. "Grace, this is Macy O'James. Macy, Grace Burdette."

"Hi, nice to meet you." She reached around Shannon to offer her hand, but froze midshake after the woman accepted it. "Wait. You're *Miss* Burdette? As in the fourth-grade teacher?"

"You've heard of me?"

"I'll say." Belatedly, she released the other woman's hand. And grinned. "My nephew Tyler's going to be in your class this fall and he talks about it as if he won the lottery in the teacher sweepstakes."

Grace's face pinked up. "Isn't that nice? Not to mention flattering." She smiled crookedly. "I mean, it's not like I'm a famous MTV video star."

"No, you're a teacher with serious word-of-mouth buzz going for her. That's much cooler."

Grace smiled in pleasure, then the game started and their attention focused on the Sugarville Sentinels who, as home team, fielded first.

Uncle Bud had given Macy the skinny on this league. Apparently, Little League sanctioned teams played in the spring, which tended to be a busy time in the farming communities. So several towns in the county had banded together to form a youth league of its own. The junior and high schools played teams from all over the state, so they had to adhere to the regular schedule. But the younger kids drew their competition from a smaller pool, which gave the parents more leeway to work around planting and harvesting schedules.

Not that it would have ever occurred to her to question the timing if Uncle Bud hadn't told her about it last night.

Watching Tyler, who was out in right field,

his baseball mitt atop his cap as he alternated gazing up at the sky and kicking tufts of grass, she grinned. She poked Janna. "I'm thinking Ty gets his attention span from the Purcell side of the family."

Janna laughed.

Denser shade than that provided by the leafy trees suddenly blocked her light, and expecting to see rain clouds had blown in, she tipped her head back.

Only it wasn't clouds. Instead, she found herself looking up at Gabe. His dark brows pleated over the strong thrust of his nose, he stared back down at her.

Her heart beat double time. Because as their gazes locked, an electric current seemed to pulse between them.

Then Grace leaned forward and Macy saw her smile up at him. "There you are," the teacher said.

And gave the blanket next to her hip a sit-next-to-me pat.

CHAPTER FIVE

Lounging back on his elbows next to Grace, Gabe watched Macy's animated gestures as she laughed and talked with Janna, Shannon and his date. Jesus. Was there no escaping this woman? It just went to show it didn't pay to get too complacent. Because Macy O'James was *not* a restful female to be around, and more than once since that night in the hall he'd mentally congratulated himself on the wide berth he'd managed to give her. Yes, they had to share the dinner table. But he'd avoided being in any other common room she might occupy.

Which wasn't to say he hadn't heard her laughing and flirting up a storm with the AAE boys. The chick was a freaking magnetar — a powerful force drawing anything that even *approached* her orbit. Hell, she'd even gotten the honeymoon kids to occasionally come up for air and interact with her.

It wasn't as if he'd assumed she wouldn't be here today. She was actually pretty attentive to her cousin's needs — he'd give her that — so he'd figured she might bring Janna to Tyler's game. But he sure as hell hadn't expected to find *Grace* sharing a blanket with her.

As if she could read his thoughts, the brunette schoolteacher turned to him and smiled. "Isn't this fun?"

"Yeah. Great. I sort of expected to spend the time with just you, but either way, it's good to have some time together."

"This is like an unexpected party, though, don't you think? Did I tell you what Macy said about her nephew Tyler having me as his teacher this fall?"

"I don't think the kid is actually her nephew." Okay, he was being a boor, but he couldn't seem to help it. He'd been looking forward to having a relaxing hour or two with Grace and here *Macy* was. Butting in. Getting in the way of his absorbing some of the teacher's serenity. Making his heart rate spike.

"Oh, I know," Grace agreed in her sweet-natured way. "I guess he'd be her second cousin. Still, that's what she calls him. And apparently he calls her Aunt. Anyway —" She launched into a tale of what-Macy-said.

The woman under discussion suddenly shrieked Tyler's name and shot up onto her knees. "C'mon, c'mon, c'mon," she and Janna, who'd leaned forward in her chair, chanted with almost perfect synchronism.

Gabe's gaze flew to the field and homed in on Ty, and he sat up with a jerk. Number eleven on the visiting team had hit a long pop-up and was racing for first base, slinging his bat to the side as he ran. Ty, his eyes narrowed in fierce concentration, had his hands overhead, his mitt cupped toward the descending ball, as he backpedaled . . . danced several steps to the left . . . then corrected by taking a short step back toward center. He was positioned under the ball when it came down, hit the tip of his mitt, balanced for one breathless moment —

Then bobbled over the edge and fell into the space between his raised arms and his body.

"Nooooooo," Janna and Macy groaned.

Tyler slapped his mitt and free hand at his narrow little chest, his stomach, his groin, his thighs, hunching in on himself as he chased the ball rolling down his torso. Then he suddenly straightened.

And held the ball high.

"Oh, my," Grace whispered as Janna, Macy and Shannon screamed their approval along with several parents on the bleachers. Macy executed an impromptu little upper-body dance, then exchanged high fives with her cousin and Shannon. Kneewalking around the big redhead, she held out her hand in low-five position to Grace. "Gimme fiiive."

Grace laughed and slapped palms, then Macy leaned around her to offer the same to him.

He saw the instant she thought better of the idea, but he knew that for once this had nothing to do with that playful, sexually aware teasing she excelled at. This was sheer exuberance over Ty's triumph — and he reached out to slap hands.

Hers was supple and cool, and instead of giving it the quick spank-and-snatch he'd intended, he executed the former but found his fingers developing a life of their own as they slid slowly away, brushing from her palm to her fingertips. The contrast between the hard-edged Goth look she sported today and the softness of her skin made his brows furrow, and when her eyes widened and she curled her fingers in as if to hang on to the same sensation sparking in him, he dropped back onto his elbows. He couldn't figure her out at all.

It was almost a relief when some guy

showed up a short while later and Macy started flirting with him, sliding effortlessly back into a niche Gabe understood.

At least it was for a while. Then the verbal slap and tickle between the two started getting on his nerves. Sitting up again, he leaned around Grace to look at the guy squatting in front of Macy. "I don't think we've met," he said. "I'm Gabe Donovan."

The guy barely spared him a glance. "Adam Westler. My son, Zach, plays on the team."

"No kidding? Huh. I stop by pretty often to catch at least part of the games. I don't remember ever seeing you here before."

The man shrugged. "Guy's gotta work."

But apparently not once word got out that Macy O'James is in town.

Before he could make an issue of it, however — or even figure out why he would want to — Lenore and Bud arrived, carrying folding camp chairs. "Sorry we're late," the older lady said cheerfully. "Bud insisted on weeding the vegetable garden, then didn't want to leave the job half-done."

"In this heat?" Macy demanded, jumping to her feet and taking the chair from her aunt. She unfolded it and set it on the other side of Gabe while Bud set up his own next to it. For a moment, Gabe was as mesmerized as a pubescent boy by the straight shot up her yard-long legs to a glimpse of schoolgirl-white panties that his position on the ground afforded him.

Then, he gave himself a mental head slap and looked away. What was he, twelve?

"Auntie," he heard Macy say with a low-voiced intensity that snapped his gaze to her face. "Didn't you receive the check I sent last month? You were supposed to hire some help with it."

"Oh, we put that away for a rainy day. Along with all the others you've sent." Reaching out, she patted Macy's hand. "Don't fret, sweetheart. Your uncle's been gardening since he was old enough to pick up a hoe. Pulling a few weeds in the heat's not gonna do him in."

"Me big strong man," Bud agreed with a grin.

"I know you are," Macy circled her aunt and stooped to plant a kiss on his bald, sun-spotted head. "The biggest, strongest man it's my privilege to know. I just don't want you overdoing."

"Not gonna happen, baby girl. So, how's the game gone so far?"

"Oh!" Her face alight with enthusiasm, she turned to her cousin. "Janna! Tell your folks about Ty's fly ball."

The Sentinels ended up losing by two points, but Tyler and Charlie were so pumped over Ty's save that the loss didn't seem to faze them. With great drama and exaggerated staggering, they performed a reenactment of the play.

Laughing at their antics, Lenore said, "Well, this is just too much fun to break up. I think everyone should come back to the boardinghouse and have dinner with us. Call your husband, Shannon, and tell him to grab Amy and come on over." She turned to Westler and looked pointedly at the pale band of white Gabe hadn't even noticed encircling the other man's ring finger. "And your wife is welcome, too, of course."

Westler gave her a wry smile. "I'm divorced, ma'am. That's my ex over there with my son, Zach." He indicated a plump, sandy-haired woman stepping off the bottom riser of the bleachers and reaching out to haul a dejected-looking kid into her arms for a hug.

"Then I guess you'll have to come on your own. Or maybe Zach would like to join us."

"He's pretty mad at me over the divorce right now, so I doubt it. But let me go ask."

Watching the interaction between father and son at the far end of the bleachers, Gabe didn't need to hear their exchange to know Westler would be joining them stag. The sullen expression on the kid's face said it all.

He blew out a quiet, irritated breath. Great. That's what they needed around the dinner table tonight, another contender for the always-happenin' Flirt-a-rama.

But Grace was clearly pleased by the prospect of the get-together continuing. So, sucking it up, he rose and extended a hand to pull her to her feet.

"Didn't you date my niece one time in high school?" Bud suddenly asked Adam over Lenore's taco salad and homemade rolls.

Damn, Macy thought at the same time Adam agreed, "I did."

Fork suspended halfway to his mouth, her uncle gave the younger man a level stare and demanded in a low voice, "You one of those fools who took her out because you believed Mayfield's lies?"

Damn, damn, *damn.* Her heart sank as Gabe's head snapped around from his tête-à-tête with Grace on the other side of Bud.

Color bloomed in Adam's cheeks. "Uh —"

"How's he supposed to answer that, Uncle Bud?" she demanded in a voice as quiet as her uncle's had been. Turning to the Experimental boys, she said in a more conversational tone, "I'm not sure if Adam mentioned this, but he works at AAE." She gave the American Agricultural Experiment, which most folks in Sugarville simply called the Experimental, its proper acronym. "Have any of you had a chance to work with him yet?"

Jim Holstrom said that he had, which started the conversational ball rolling when the remaining Experimental grant holders told Adam where they were currently studying within the project. Ignoring the intent gaze that Gabriel was drilling into her temporal lobe, Macy rearranged her salad on her plate.

She *hated* that her aunt and uncle knew about that time in her life. She'd done her best to keep them from learning of it, but somehow they'd found out anyway. They'd never said exactly how.

The whole screwed-up mess had started because she'd forgotten the first rule of self-preservation. Growing up, she'd been dragged from pillar to post by her mother, the queen of Moving On. Macy had been the perpetual new kid in school — all twenty-three of them — and was savvy about not setting herself up for disappointment. She simply avoided getting attached to anyone, because she knew that sooner rather than later, Mom would get that restless look in her eye again and Macy would be shaken awake in the dead of night or greeted at the door when she came in from school by her mother's gratingly cheerful, "Pack your bags, kiddo. We're off on a big adventure." It wasn't until she'd hit high school age and Auntie Lenore talked her mom into letting her stay with them that she'd spent an entire year at one school.

And man, she'd adored it. She'd loved the continuity, the regular-kid home life with her relatives, the having a dresser of her own and half a closet in the room she and Janna shared so her clothes had a permanent spot. She'd really loved putting her suitcase in the attic instead of having to keep it handy because after a couple of months — or sometimes even weeks — it would be time to hit the road again.

It hadn't been utopian, of course. Small schools had the most rigid cliques in the world and were notoriously slow at welcoming outsiders. Still, she'd figured that for once in her life she had time to carve out a spot for herself. And she'd deemed life good.

Then she'd gone and developed a huge crush on Drew Mayfield and everything had turned to shit.

"You gonna just push that around your plate, or are you actually going to eat the damn thing?"

Macy jerked her head up and found Gabe shooting her an irritated look from across the table. "*Excuse* me?"

"I asked if you're going to eat your aunt's salad." His gray-eyed gaze traveled her long, lean body before raising to meet her own. "Or are you one of those Hollywood anorexics?"

"Jesus, Donovan," Adam said at the same time that Grace emitted a shocked, "Gabe!"

"Well, look at her plate. She hasn't eaten more than three bites."

"What are you, the dinner police?" She looked him in the eye, the easy charm she'd worked to make her default mode on temporary hiatus. "Considering you've been at a lot of the meals I've scarfed down this week, for all you know I could simply have something on my mind."

He merely raised a thick, beautifully curved eyebrow at her.

Causing her to expel an impatient breath. "Fine. Here." Holding his gaze, she shoveled a huge bite into her mouth and chewed. Not as adequately as she should have before she swallowed, maybe, but what the hell. "Happy?" But her taste buds tingled with delight at the textures and flavors and the hint of heat in her aunt's secret Thousand Island dressing recipe.

"Ooh. That's good." She forked up a more reasonably sized bite, but turned to Adam before carrying it to her lips. "Could you pass the rolls?" Then she popped it in her mouth and ate two additional bites before the basket made its way down the table.

Licking a dab of the dressing off the corner of her lips, she shot Gabe a grin as she broke open her roll. Then she turned to Adam to do what she did best when she wanted to keep someone at arm's length without appearing unfriendly: flirted. Because Gabriel was right about one thing. Pushing her food around her plate while she brooded was a prodigious waste of time.

She wished Aunt Lenore hadn't invited Adam for dinner, but at least the guy had been one of her few nice dates in high school. Unlike so many other boys in her class, he'd never asked her out expecting her to drop her drawers in the backseat of his car in exchange for a second-run movie at the Majestic and a burger basket at Smokey's — then regaled his buddies with what a hot number she was after she declined to put out.

The legend of her so-called sexual prowess began with Andrew "Drew" Mayfield, the object of her fervent first crush. He'd been golden to her then-impressionable eyes, everything her young heart considered desirable. Reasonably tall, which meant a guy she wouldn't be afraid to wear heels with, and fit, he was an athlete revered for his prowess on the football field, confident in the way only a young man with money, looks and outstanding physical ability can be. But she didn't understand that until later. At the time she took the fact that he rarely laughed for intelligence, and it was the confidence that truly sucked her in, for it had made him stand apart from the usual high school boys.

God, she'd been excited when he'd asked her out. She'd carried a torch for the football star since her first week as a sophomore at Sugarville High, and to have him suddenly focus his attention on her midway through her junior year had thrilled her no end.

The thrill had waned considerably after their date, when he'd driven her to Buzzard Canyon, one of the more popular partying and make-out areas along the wooded draw climbing up from Wenatchee. Not that she'd objected to necking with a guy she'd wanted to kiss for what seemed like forever. But he had quickly pushed for far more than she was willing to give. And for the first time since coming to Sugarville, she'd refused to rein in her time-honored defense against being an outsider — her zero tolerance for taking crap. Instead, she'd fought her way upright and put a halt to the make-out session in no uncertain terms. He'd taken it like a gent, though, and driven her home, so she'd assumed that was the end of it.

Until the following Monday, when sniggers had followed her down the hallways of Sugarville High and she'd discovered her once-idol had told all his friends she was a pushover in the backseat of his car.

And the rush to date her began.

She'd known better than to think anyone would believe her over a guy who was the high school equivalent of royalty. So, except with Janna, she hadn't even tried to set the record straight. What was the point? Once an outsider, always an outsider.

But enough with the trip down memory lane. Impatient with herself, she joined in the conversations swirling around her. It had been a long day, however, and given a choice when dinner ended she would have retired to her room in a heartbeat. But Adam was there. Not feeling like dealing with him, however, she quickly offered to help with the dishes. Hey, a girl could always hope Inconvenient Guy would take off if she just stayed busy long enough.

Her aunt dashed that dream by waving her off and her nebulous alternate plan to invite her cousin to hang out with them vanished when Janna said she ached after her afternoon out. Macy didn't have any real hope Adam would disappear while she helped settle her cousin in their room, and sure enough, he was still lounging against the library/game room doorjamb when she came out a short while later. Sighing, she decided only the direct approach would do and walked up to him.

In the rec room behind him she saw Gabe bending over Grace as he showed her how to line up a shot on the pool table and got a funny pang in her chest.

Irritated, she shoved it aside and, pulling her gaze away from the couple, looked at Adam. "What do you say we go out on the porch?"

"Sounds like a plan."

On the covered porch that wrapped around two sides of the house, he moved in on her, bending his head with the clear intention of stealing a kiss.

She stepped back. "Not gonna happen, pal."

He straightened up. "I suppose I didn't really expect it would. Still, a guy's gotta try." He studied her in the dappled light filtering through the wisteria leaves. "You've changed a lot since high school."

"I certainly hope so. It's been ten years."

"I think it goes deeper than that, though. And has to do with more than your MTV success. You seem . . . happier."

She blinked at his insight, surprised in no small part because she hadn't expected any from a guy who'd go to his son's game and flirt with another woman in front of the kid's mom — a situation she would've had no part of, had she realized up front that's what was going on. But she shrugged. "That happens when you remove yourself from a place where people either hate your guts or treat you like a slut."

After her reputation went down the loo with a big, resounding whoosh, she'd decided if you can't beat 'em, give 'em what they expect. She'd discovered the protective covering of a really good costume and in-your-face flirting. She'd also put herself out there on the dating front for a while, hoping that more guys would tell the truth about their so-called experiences with her than the ones who'd lied through their teeth.

That latter thing hadn't panned out so

great. But it'd taught her a lesson that she retained to this day: keep your relationships brief and fun, then move along before they can bite you in the butt.

She shot Adam a genuine smile. "You didn't." He raised an inquiring brow and she added, "On our one and only date, you were one of the few who didn't treat me like a slut."

"Yeah, well, I had a fairly strict upbringing." He shot her a wry smile. "I sort of hoped you'd turn out to be one, though."

The belly laugh exploding out of her felt good, and she was still laughing when Grace and Gabe came out of the house. Wiping tears of mirth from her eyes, she turned to the teacher. "Are you leaving?" The other woman tended toward quiet and had a refined, good-girl air about her. But she possessed a sweet smile and a good sense of humor and had been ingenuously open about getting a kick out of hanging with her and Janna.

"Yes." Grace came over and took Macy's hands in her own. "Thank you so much for including me in your party this afternoon. I had a blast."

"It was fun, wasn't it? I really enjoyed getting to know you a little. We'll have to do it again sometime."

Gabe jingled his keys in his pocket and she gave the teacher a nudge. "It looks like your date is getting impatient. He must have a hot necking session planned down at Buzzard Canyon." Mentioning the spot, however, dimmed her humor considerably.

It resurrected when Grace turned pink and stuttered, "Oh, no, I don't think —" while Gabe shot her a look.

"You'll have to cut Ms. O'James some slack, Grace," he said coolly. "She has sex on the brain. Must be the L.A. influence."

"Only with you, sugar," she said, and Grace and Adam laughed, obviously believing it was just another example of her flirty ways. But she admitted to herself that there was more than a grain of truth to the matter. It had been a fairly long dry spell since she'd thought of having sex with anyone. But every time she clapped eyes on the big fire chief it seemed to be the first thing that popped to mind.

Well, she'd just have to do something about that. One, because she didn't poach on other women's turf, and two, the guy was far from a lighthearted player, which was her usual type.

And face it. Being back in Sugarville is challenge enough.

Wasn't that the damn truth. A challenge,

squared. The last thing she needed was some sparks in the dark sexual chemistry with a man she suspected just might burn her alive.

When it came to Gabriel Donovan she intended to keep her distance . . . and then some.

CHAPTER SIX

Gabe heard war whoops and the sound of boys laughing as he let himself out the kitchen door and headed for his car. Tracking the noise, he spotted Tyler and Charlie taking turns stalking each other through the fruit orchard beyond the small parking area. They dodged in and out of the trees and behind the shed at the end of Bud's enclosed garden, popping out from behind cover long enough to shoot streams of water at each other from long-barreled, pump-action soaker guns. It was over ninety today, so he thought their activity had a helluva lot more appeal than climbing into a car that had been cooking in the sun since he'd stopped home at noon. Opening the vehicle, he watched the boys over its roof as he gave the heat trapped inside a minute to escape.

But in the abrupt that's-so-last-minute-this-is-*now* way of kids, Tyler suddenly lowered his gun and, dragging it behind him as if it equaled his body weight, trudged in Gabe's direction.

It soon became clear, however, that the boy hadn't noticed him. "Mom," he said in an aggravated voice before he and Charlie even reached the parking area. "We've been waiting for*ever!* When are we gonna go to the pool?"

Gabe hadn't noticed the women until then, but now he homed right in on Janna sitting in a lawn chair under the oak tree with Macy on the ground at her feet. The dappled shade cast by the broad leaves was fairly deep, so they weren't exactly in high-def. But they were noticeable enough that he was surprised he'd missed them in the first place.

Macy turned her head to look at Tyler. "We'll leave as soon as your mom's toenails dry."

"I don't know why you hadda go paint 'em in the first place," the kid groused.

"Because she has her first physical therapy session in twenty minutes and when a girl's facing something difficult it gives her a lift to look her best." She flapped a go-away hand at him. "Besides, by the time you two've dried off, so will the polish."

"Whatta we have to dry off for?" Ty demanded indignantly. "We're just gonna get wet again at the pool."

"That's true," Janna said, extending her good foot to admire her paint job as Macy gathered nail stuff together and threw it in a little case. "But you're not climbing into my car like that."

"We wanna go in Aunt Macy's car!"

"Not going to happen, Ty," Macy said, climbing to her feet and brushing off her butt. "My car's a two seater and there are four of us."

"That sucks," he muttered.

"Well, I suppose your mom and I could always take my car and you and Charlie could stay home with Grandma."

Janna nodded. "That would work."

"Nuh-uh!"

Macy observed him with a stillness Gabe had never seen from her, since she was usually electricity in motion. "Then quit your whining," she commanded in a tone that didn't resemble her usual easy-breezy way of speaking. "Contrary to what you seem to believe today, it's *not* all about you. Now, go dry off and don't forget to ask Grandma for a couple of dry towels to take to the pool."

"Aw, *man!*" But he headed for the back door of the boardinghouse, passing Gabe without acknowledging him.

As the screen door slapped shut behind

the boys, Gabe watched Macy bend to lift her cousin out of the chair.

He went to help. "Kind of rough on the kid, weren't you?" he said as he hipped her aside and reached to gently raise Janna onto her feet. Okay, so he actually thought she'd handled Ty dead right. Yet somehow words he never intended to say seemed to come out of his mouth whenever he was around her. He narrowed his eyes at her for once again putting him in that position. "I had drill instructors in the army weren't as tough as you."

"Gee, why aren't I surprised you were a big, bad soldier?" she shot back. "The only shocker here is that *you* weren't the D.I. I can see you getting nose-to-nose with some poor, hapless recruit to yell in his face until his ego is paste beneath your boot."

I'll show you *nose-to-nose*. He took a hot step forward, then, catching himself, executed a bigger one in reverse.

Jesus. The woman turned him into someone he didn't recognize faster than you could clock a cheetah going from zero to seventy. But this was it. He was through falling into that trap. He was getting his Zen back and from now on keeping his mouth shut.

He shot a glance at his watch. What the

hell was he doing hanging around here, anyhow, when he'd scheduled a meeting with his volunteer firemen in fifteen minutes?

But his good intentions went up in flames when they all stepped out into the blazing sunshine and he took his first real good look at her outfit. "What the hell are you supposed to be today?" he demanded. "A belly dancer?" Okay, it wasn't quite that overt. But holy shit.

"I'm pretty sure it was her Wonder Woman Underoos back in the fourth grade that set her on the path to all things dress-up," Janna said with a fond smile at her cousin's animal-print bikini top and the crocheted bronze scarf tied low on her hips, its long, silky fringe shimmying with every breath she took.

"Hey," Macy said. "Do not mock my Wonder Woman underwear. I'll have you know I have fond memories of the white stars on those little blue pants and that great winged *W* on my chest." Her lips curled upward. "I totally rocked those undies."

Then she turned and pinned him in place with a level gaze. "As for what I'm wearing today, Donovan, it's called a bathing suit and cover-up. Women in the new millennium wear them when they go to the pool.

Deal with it."

"Or an almost-cover-up, anyway," he murmured, taking in the long, smooth stretch of skin between Macy's forehead and toes, broken only by the strings and two tiny triangles of the giraffe-skin fabric that almost protected the modesty of her high, sweet breasts and that peek-a-boo scarf that bared her stomach and one boyish hip before showcasing glimpses of those yard-long legs. Crap. Was he drooling?

He shoved his hands in his pockets and shrugged. "Well, hey, you're a big girl and you'll wear what you're gonna wear." He turned to Janna. "Good luck with your first PT session."

He walked away to the sound of Macy muttering, "For God's sake. Was there anything you *didn't* eavesdrop on?"

There wasn't enough time in the drive between the boardinghouse and town for the AC to catch up with the heat in his car, and his khaki shirt was stuck to his spine by the time he pulled up in front of the one-engine firehouse.

His six volunteers were already there, and he strode into the mini kitchen and joined them at the table where they were drinking coffee. "Sorry I'm late. I stopped off at the boardinghouse after my meeting with the mayor and got hung up."

Johnson, a strapping blond farmer, shrugged as he reached for the sugar container to add a heaping teaspoon to his cup. "I'm impressed you made it at all. I'd be hard-pressed to drag myself away if I had the opportunity to hang out with Macy O'James. Did anyone else see her in *Burn, Baby, Burn*?"

"Oh, yeah," Bundy agreed fervently, while Solberg said, "That one was hot, no question. But she was off the hinges in *Ain't No Talkin'*. Who can forget her in that little satin nightielike thing?"

It was touch-and-go for a second, but Gabe managed not to take his exasperation out on his men. But Jesus, wouldn't it be nice if he could go just one day, or hell, even a couple of hours, without having to listen to everything Macy? This was a small town, however, and apparently once word that O'James was featured in the provocative videos had gotten around, the entire town had started tuning in to watch.

Ignoring the comments, he nodded his thanks to Kirschner, who handed him a mug of coffee. Then he looked around the table at his men.

"I asked you to meet me here," he said, "because the upshot of my meeting with the mayor this morning was more budget cuts in the works. It won't affect your pay per fire, but there's no money for the non-emergency support person I'd hoped to hire. So I'd like to run something past you that I brought up with Mayor Smith."

"You actually got something past Mayor Tightwad?" one of his men demanded.

"Yeah, since it won't cost him much and has the potential for a big return. I don't know if you're familiar with the Fire Corps, but it's a volunteer program that provides support personnel, saving fire departments across the nation time and money. We're too small to have a branch in our area, but I'd like try recruiting for one. So if you all are willing to take a dunking for the cause, I did get Smith to unclench his wallet long enough to get us a booth and a dunk tank at the county fair in August. People seem to love those things, and with the chance to knock us into a tank of water comes an opportunity for us to raise some money, hand out literature and talk up the benefits of volunteering for the fire department."

"I'll do it," Johnson said, as others at the table nodded their agreement. "What the hell, it's a chance to meet chicks — something I don't get off the farm often enough to do much of. If you really want a turnout, though, you should talk Macy into being part of it."

His first inclination was to snarl, "Enough about O'James, already!" But applying cold-blooded logic to the suggestion, he had to agree the guy had a point. The way she'd laughed that night on the porch with West-ler popped to mind, as it had way too often. And picturing a wet Macy, laughing like that even once? Hell, they'd have men lined up the length of the fairgrounds, ready and willing to lay down their hard-earned cash for the opportunity to make her do it again.

So he nodded. "Good thinking," he agreed, congratulating himself that it didn't even sound grudging. "I'll run it past her."

"You mind the lifeguards now!" Janna called after Tyler and Charlie as they tumbled from the car and raced for the gate to the town pool.

Macy raised an eyebrow at her cousin, causing the other woman to make a face in return. "I know, I know." Janna said. "Wasting my breath."

"And so unnecessarily, too. Unless things have changed dramatically since my time, those lifeguards keep an eagle eye on the kids and expel anyone foolish enough to give them lip." Reaching across the console, she gave Janna's thigh a comforting pat. "That's one thing you *don't* have to worry about. I'll head back to supervise as soon as I get you situated with the therapist and make a quick stop at the Shop and Save to pick up some TP for Auntie." She glanced down at her pool wear, then shot Janna a sly smile. "Think the patrons there will be as scandalized as the fire chief was over my display of skin?"

"You know this town. Some will, some won't. But Macy, about Gabe —"

She grimaced. "I know, be nice, he's a good man, a righteous, upstanding member of the community, yadda, yadda, yadda."

"I'm sure he's all those things." Janna's lips tilted in a wry smile. "But what I was going to say was, what's with all the verbal foreplay between you and him whenever you're together?"

"What?" She pulled her gaze from the road to stare at her cousin in shock. "No verbal foreplay! We don't do that." Then, directing her attention back to the traffic, she admitted, "Well, at least he doesn't. He seems pretty into Grace. And if *that* shouldn't halt me in my tracks, I don't know what will, since I've never poached another woman's guy in my life. But *man*." She shook her head. "There's just something about him. He opens his mouth or, okay, just stands there giving me that cool, judgmental look and it's like he's catnip and I'm the cat, he's Mad Dog and I'm the wino, he's crack and I'm the —"

"I get it, Mace."

"Well, I wish I did. I'm not sure I even *like* him. But I sense all kinds of heat beneath that outer chill, and boy, am I attracted to him. I've never felt anything quite like it."

"I'm thinking he's pretty attracted to you, too."

"But don't you see? If he is, that makes him a pig. And me a guy-rustling pigette. Because there is Grace."

"Who is a sweetheart," Janna said.

"Yeah, she is," she agreed trying to ignore the sinking feeling in the pit of her stomach. "I really like her."

"So do I. But I gotta say, Macy, when it comes to sparks between her and Gabe? I see zip. Nada. None."

Not particularly liking herself for the satisfaction that hearing that gave her, she said as she wheeled the car into the clinic's parking lot, "Maybe their fascination with each other is something they prefer to keep private. They're both pretty contained."

"I suppose." But staring at the blue-and-white County Seat Sports and Spine sign, Janna didn't sound convinced.

Or even as if she were actually still paying attention to the conversation. Macy touched her arm. "You nervous?"

"Big-time. Which no doubt makes me a big fat baby."

"No, it doesn't. You've been through a lot, and this is something new added to the mix. But first times in everything are always the hardest. I think it's that going-into-the-unknown thing. I bet your progress will grow in leaps and bounds with the therapy, though."

"If it doesn't kill me. I'm tired of hurting and *I* bet this is gonna be painful."

"There is that possibility."

Janna's head snapped around and she laughed. "That's one of the things I love about you, Macy. You never sugarcoat stuff or try to placate me with false promises."

She shrugged and climbed from the car, circling the hood to help Janna out. "Not much point in promising you something I have zero experience with. But I'm hoping for the best for you, Janny."

She was thinking about her cousin ten minutes later when she strode into the Shop and Save and headed for the paper-goods aisle, her flip-flops slapping against the linoleum floor. Between her rat-bastard ex and the accident, Janna'd had an extremely rough six months, and Macy hoped like crazy the therapy would at least start her on the road to regaining her health.

It likely helped that Sean and his barely legal new squeeze had recently moved to Spokane. No longer having to risk running into him whenever Janna went out had to make things a little easier. She still had to deal with his parents, but the elder Purcells, who wanted a relationship with their only grandson and were embarrassed by their son's actions, treated her with scrupulous politeness.

Macy was hunkered down in front of the multiroll packages on the bottom shelf when a voice she could have gone the rest of her life without hearing drawled from behind her, "Toilet paper, Macy? How appropriate. You always did turn everything to shit."

Swallowing a sigh, she selected a twelve-pack, rose to her feet and tossed it in the basket. Stooping, she grabbed another and added it, as well. Then she turned to face her old high school nemesis.

From their first encounter Liz Picket had disliked her, but in the beginning it hadn't been personal. As the school beauty, a cheerleader dating Macy's crush, football star Andrew Mayfield, and the only child of one of the wealthiest men in town, Liz had been the undisputed female leader of the most popular group in school. Her sense of entitlement made her an equal-opportunity bitch to anyone she felt was her social inferior, which since Sugarville was largely a farming community, had pretty much meant all but a select few. What surprised Macy was how everyone had kept their heads down and let her get away with it.

Being the new kid in school too many times to count had taught *her* that allowing people to walk all over you simply invited them to trample you some more. So when Liz pushed her, she'd pushed back. But not nearly as hard as she would have if she hadn't been trying so hard to fit in in Sugarville.

Apparently no one had ever returned any of the crap the princess of Sugarville dished out, however, so when Macy did Liz went ballistic and what had been generic trash talk became personal. Then Andrew asked Macy out, after telling her he'd broken up with Liz. That turned out to be as true as the tales he wove of Macy's easiness, but had Liz blamed him?

Hell, no. She'd declared all-out war on *her*.

So here they were ten years later, apparently about to play out the same ol', same ol'.

Or not. Maybe, just this once, she'd take the high road and refuse to engage.

"Liz Picket. Long time, no see."

"Not long enough." Liz tilted her chin and shot Macy a supercilious smile. "And it's Picket-*Smith* now. I'm married to the mayor, you know."

Her good intentions dissolved. "Of course you are. You always were one for riding on a man's coattails instead of carving out a place for yourself on your own merits." She raised an eyebrow. "But then, I forget myself. You don't *have* any of those."

Liz flipped her expensively cut, exquisitely colored long-layered bob away from her face. "Unlike you, you mean, who makes her living in sex videos?"

She couldn't help it, she cracked up. And every time she attempted to regain her composure the ridiculousness of Liz's statement made her howl all over again. When she finally got herself together, she said, "Oh, God, thanks for the laugh." Swallowing a couple of snickers that still wanted to escape, she dabbed beneath her eyes with the sides of her fingers and shot Liz a grin that was likely a little demented around the edges. "You must be the only twenty-eight-year-old in captivity who equates rock videos with porn. You really are provincial, aren't you?"

The other woman's perfectly made-up face mottled with fury, and Macy realized she had inadvertently issued the ultimate insult. Because she remembered now the way Liz had always prided herself on being so much more worldly than the rest of the girls in their class. Back then it had even been true. The rest of them had gone to Long Beach or Ocean Shores for family vacations or spring break. Liz had gone to Paris.

The other woman leaned into Macy's space and said in a low, vicious tone, "I wonder if your aunt and uncle know you blew the entire football team?"

Fury drove a spike up Macy's spine, but applying the discipline she'd taught herself years ago, she stepped back from both it and Liz and gave the other woman a cool assessment. "I doubt it, considering that was always more your style than mine," she said mildly. In truth, it had been neither of their styles. But wherever girls gathered in a small-town high school — in locker rooms and restrooms — Liz could be found bragging of every sexual act she'd ever taken part in with her boyfriend of the moment.

"Tell you what, though," she said. "Why don't you trot over to the boardinghouse and ask them? I'd *really* enjoy hitting you with a slander suit. Wouldn't His Honor the Mayor love the publicity from that? Especially when it comes out — as these things have a tendency to do — that, while you were busy ridiculing *me* as the school whore, you were the one committing sexual acts I never even dreamed of. What was it you used to tell all the other girls? 'I may be a slut . . . but at least I'm a rich one?' *That* oughtta play well in court."

Then she moved closer and her voice lost its easygoing equanimity. "Get this through your head, Elizabeth. I'm no longer a kid without resources. And I'm only going to say this once. If I hear so much as a *hint* of that rumor making the rounds, I will have your ass in court so fast you'll make Linda Blair's little pre-exorcism head whirl look like an ordinary event. It doesn't matter if the whispers originate with someone else. I have lawyers who *live* for tracking false rumors back to their source."

The mayor's wife stared at her, breathing hard for a moment. Than she took a deep breath. Let it out. And ruined her pretty looks with the ugly expression that twisted her features. "You trailer-trash *bitch!*"

"Uh-uh-uh." She wagged her finger admonishingly. "Only the truth, remember? I freely confess to being a bitch. But the only trailers I've ever been in has been on location. And, honey, while you may not know this, never getting out of Sugarville and all, those are a *long* way from being trashy."

"Ooooh!" Liz stomped off and Macy pushed her cart toward the front of the store. Back in high school such an encounter would have had her stomach churning for the rest of the day. She hadn't been any more capable of penitently hanging her head or turning the other cheek while self-satisfied liars trashed her good name then than she was now, but she'd always felt sort of sick to her stomach even as she was giving back as good as she got. But now? Surprisingly, it had been downright cathartic to lay down the terms if Liz was considering picking up the same old gauntlet. And she actually felt . . .

Pretty darn good.

"You've got your nerve showing your face."

Her short-lived pleasure popped like a balloon meeting the business end of a pin. Stopping her cart, she looked at the woman standing a few feet in front of her, her heart

107

beating a sickening rhythm. "Hello, Mrs. Sorenson."

"Don't you hello me, Missy! Look at you, sashaying into a God-fearing store half-naked. How dare you go on with your life as if you didn't ruin my Jimmy's?"

For a second Macy was thrust back into the chaos of That Night at the post–football game kegger in Buzzard Canyon, where the senior class had been celebrating a victory over their arch rival, the Pateras Billy-goats . . . until a slip of the foot from the brake pedal of Auntie Lenore's Buick had destroyed the football careers and scholar-ships of three of the players. Jerking herself out of it, she drew a deep breath and shak-ily exhaled it.

"All I can say now, as I said then, is I'm sorry," she said quietly. "It was an accident, Mrs. Sorenson, not anything I ever, *ever* intended to happen. I felt horrible about it at the time and I feel horrible about it now."

"You *should* feel horrible," the older woman said fiercely. "I hope you take that guilt straight to hell with you when you die." And ramming forward with her cart, she ricocheted off Macy's as she stormed past her.

God. Macy rubbed her forehead where a headache was brewing. Had this been the busiest-beaver day or what? And it wasn't even three o'clock yet. It felt as if it ought to be midnight, she was suddenly so exhausted.

Well, get over it, girl. Squaring her shoulders and putting on her game face, she pushed her cart up to the checkout stand. Life didn't stop because of a couple unforeseen encounters. She had to get over to the pool to keep an eye on Tyler and Charlie the way she'd promised Janna she would do.

But man. Wasn't *that* just bound to be one big barrel of giggles. Who knew how many more people who hated her guts might be there?

CHAPTER SEVEN

Gabe stepped out onto the wraparound porch after dinner, the wooden screen door slapping softly closed behind him. The scent of Bud's barbecue lingered in the evening air and the homey clatter of Lenore cleaning up drifted from the kitchen window at the back of the big farmhouse.

He'd come out specifically to find Macy, and he located her sitting in the swing at the short end of the porch's L. Shoving his hands in the pockets of his jeans, he gave her a nod while keeping his gaze on the post over her right shoulder. "Hey," he said, feeling somewhat at a loss. He was accustomed to sparring with her, not having to hit her up for a favor.

It didn't help that she hugged her knees to her chest and demanded in a don't-get-comfortable tone, "Something I can help you with, Fire Chief?"

"Yeah. I want to ask your help on something."

Her bark of laughter was not amused. "Trust me," she said flatly, "that's the last thing you want. Any cause near and dear to your heart will *not* benefit from having me be part of it. Not in this town."

He'd been avoiding looking at her too closely for fear of getting sucked into that vortex of heat and temptation he'd been dodging ever since he'd first clapped eyes on her. But the matter-of-fact way she put herself down made him give her a good, hard look.

And he discovered she didn't look like she usually did. He'd noticed before that she didn't dress provocatively around her aunt and uncle yet still managed to look dolled up, if in a more girl-next-door way than the ramped-up sex-squared look she adopted whenever she went to town. But it just went to show how assiduously he'd *not* looked at her at dinner tonight, because until this moment he hadn't noticed that her hair had been pulled back in a plain braid, her lipstick was chewed off and she was wearing a baggy pair of shorts with a loose T-shirt that should have been tossed in a ragbag a long time ago.

"Whoa," he said. "Who are you and what

have you done with Macy?"

She curled her lip at him. "You're a laugh a minute, Donovan."

"You're saying that *is* you?" He made a rude noise, then narrowed his eyes at her. "Unless . . . You on your period, or something?"

"What?" She jerked upright, setting the swing's chains to creaking. Her bare feet slapped against the porch decking and put an end to the seat's sudden off-kilter wobble. "No!" she snapped. "What kind of question is that, anyway?"

A dumbshit one, he mentally acknowledged as heat crawled up his neck. Jesus. He didn't say stuff like that to women!

But before he could assemble even a half-assed apology she abruptly laughed. And turned back into, well, not the complete Macy he knew, but at least someone more closely resembling her usual self.

"You know what, Gabriel?" she said. "I take back what I said to Janna today. I think I *do* like you, after all. You're pretty much a call-'em-as-you-see-'em kind of guy, aren't you?"

"Too much so, apparently, if *that's* what comes out of my mouth."

She shrugged. "You say what you're thinking. And despite getting an overdose of that today, I generally prefer to know where I stand. Although I can't say I understand what prompted that particular remark."

He must have given her a quick once-over, because she looked down at her ratty attire and said, "Ah." Then pinned him in place with her gaze. *"And?"*

"And . . . I'm an insensitive clod." Because, big deal, she'd dressed down for once and let her makeup wear off. Putting his fore- and index fingers to his temple, he pulled the trigger of his thumb. And felt the corners of his mouth curve up in satisfaction when she laughed out loud. "You had a rough day, I take it?" he said.

"I've had better, but it wasn't all bad. Being at the pool with Ty and Charlie was pretty cool." Waving the subject aside as if it had no importance, she propped one bare heel on the edge of the swing's seat, wrapped her arms around her shin and rested her chin on her kneecap. "So, what's the cause you're pushing?"

"My fire department. My crew is all volunteers — they get paid for the fires they go out on, but that's it, and my budget doesn't allow for much more than their stipends and my salary. The mayor agreed to sponsor a booth at the fair for us, as well as a dunking tank, so we can raise some funds. You'd be a huge draw."

"You've been in Sugarville *how* long now?"

He hitched a shoulder. "Since February."

"Long enough to be familiar with my reputation, then."

"Which one?"

Her lip curled in disdain. "Don't go coy on me now, Donovan."

He sank onto his haunches in front of her, his forearms propped on his thighs, his hands dangling. "I'm not trying to be — I've heard two separate things. That you're a hot mama in the sack and not particularly selective about who you sleep with. And that you single-handedly destroyed the high school football team's shot at the state championship in — I can't remember what year — and cost two players their college scholarships."

She sighed. "The first is crap," she said. "Which I'm sure you have a hard time believing." Without giving him the chance to refute the charge or agree, she added, "The second, unfortunately, is true. It was an accident, but I still hit three football players with my aunt's car. And there are a lot of people around here who are never going to forgive me for that."

"There's also a lot of people around here who think your music videos are the pinnacle of cool. So will you give the fire department a hand?"

She studied him for a moment, then shrugged and nodded. "Sure. Why not? But if the citizens of S-ville stay away in droves, don't say I didn't warn you."

"That's not gonna happen." He rose to his feet. "Thanks. My guys argue over which video of yours is the best, so they're going to be pumped." He heard a car turn off the road onto the long drive and said, "That's probably Grace. I'll get out of your hair."

She was looking beyond him. "I doubt that's Grace," she said, rising to her feet, as well. "I mean, I'm sure you're hot as all get-out in the sack, yourself, and I know we aren't exactly rife with privacy around here. But Grace strikes me as much too classy to show up hauling her own trailer."

He pivoted to see a red pickup truck towing a classic bullet-shaped silver Airstream up the drive, then glanced back at Macy, raising his brows. "Are Bud and Lenore expecting a new renter?"

"Not unless somebody's moving out, which I haven't heard. And wouldn't bringing your own trailer to a boardinghouse be kind of redundant anyway?" Her eyes first narrowed on the approaching truck, then snapped wide. "Omigawd. Oh. My. *God!*"

115

Her face lit up and just like that the Macy he knew reemerged with a vengeance. Screaming with laughter, she shot down the porch steps and ran toward the truck, her hands waving crazily overhead.

And Gabe realized it wasn't the sex-infused clothing or crazy-ass wigs or artful makeup that made Macy Macy. It was her lack of self-consciousness, her bone-deep joy, or some shit like that, that lit her up from the inside out, bringing a light to her eyes and giving her cheeks that peach-skin flush.

He loped down the steps in her wake as the screen door banged open behind him and some of the boarders barged out onto the porch, demanding to know what all the fuss was about. The truck had rocked to a stop, and Gabe rounded the back of the sleek Airstream in time to see the driver door opening. A lean, medium-tall man in a muscle shirt that showcased the tattoos covering his arms climbed out of the cab.

Macy took a flying leap at him.

Gabe watched, narrow-eyed, as the guy caught her and hauled her in with the long-fingered hands he'd clamped on her butt. She wrapped her hands around his neck and her legs around his waist, leaned back and grinned at him.

The man laughed. "Hello, luv," he said. "Miss me much?"

"Holy shit!" Gabe heard newlywed Tiffany gasp from behind him and glanced back to see most of the boarders and Lenore not far behind him. "Do you know who that *is*? That's —"

"Jack freakin' Savage," Brian Dawson breathed reverently. "From Aussie Kiss."

"Aussie Kiss?" Lenore said, perking up. "Isn't that the band our Macy's done videos for?"

"They're like the *hottest* band since the Rolling Stones," Brian told her. "And Savage is their Mick Jagger." When the older woman merely looked at him, he elaborated. "That's the Stones' lead singer."

"Yes, I know who Mick Jagger is," she agreed dryly. "And it's very nice that Mr. Savage is an important celebrity. I'm just not sure I'm wild about him having his hands on Macy's rear."

Gabe seconded that.

Oblivious to the crowd they'd attracted, Macy studied the familiar buzz-cut dirty-blond hair and the tiny silver barbell piercing the eyebrow of her best friend in the entertainment industry. Then she gave him her highest-wattage smile. "Not that I'm not totally jazzed to see you . . . but what the heck are you doing here?"

Jack gave a theatrical sigh. "Well, now . . ." He put her back on the ground. "As it happens, I needed a break from the L.A. madness and this is closer than Ireland. And I've got business reasons. I need your input on our next video."

"Ooh. Did you bring me the music for the new album?"

"It's in my rig. Speaking of which, what do you think the odds are of your relatives letting me camp on their property?"

"Well, I dunno. Let's get one over here and ask." Twisting around, she noticed the gathering for the first time. "Auntie Lenore, could you come here?" Her attention was snagged by Gabe — or more accurately, by his long denim-clad legs — disappearing around the end of Jack's trailer, but she pulled it back where it belonged. "Everyone else, please go inside. I'll introduce you to Jack later."

Her aunt strode up to them. "This young man is a friend of yours, I take it?" Her voice was mild, but she gave the hands still resting on Macy's butt the gimlet eye.

Macy laughed when he promptly released her and took a step back.

He sent her a brief scowl, but his trademark charm flashed in the smile he gave her aunt. "Jack Savage, ma'am," he said, offering his hand. "I've known Macy for several years now. We met when we were both starting out in the business."

"There you go being generous," she said, elbowing him in the side. "Jack was a bit further beyond 'starting out' than I was when we met," she told her aunt. "Which was at the audition for Aussie Kiss's first video. He's the one I told you about who picked me for a bigger part than I auditioned for."

"Sure, and weren't you exactly the girl I'd written *Burn, Baby, Burn* about?"

"You obviously have excellent taste," Aunt Lenore said. Her eyebrows furrowed. "You don't sound Australian."

"Because it's an Irishman I am."

"Well, for goodness sake." She studied him a moment. "Why call your band after another country?"

"It's not, really. Aussie Kiss is a slang term in my country."

"For?"

"Uhhh . . ."

To Macy's delight, he actually blushed — something she'd never witnessed before. But taking pity on him, she leaned forward and whispered, "He doesn't want to say, Auntie, because it's dirrrrrrty."

"Then it's probably best you don't," her aunt agreed. "I'm already subtracting points for the tattoos and the stickpin through your eyebrow."

"Yes, ma'am," he said politely, but Macy watched her friend retreat inward a little. "Well, it was nice finally meeting you after hearing all Macy's stories of her aunt and uncle. But I'd best get to town to see if I can find a place to park my trailer."

"Don't be silly," Lenore said crisply. "There's a perfectly good spot behind the chicken coop for your trailer. I imagine Bud can even jury-rig some kind of hookup for electricity and water."

Jack looked at her a little uncertainly. "You wouldn't mind then?"

"Of course not. I might be old-fashioned about your body decorations, but Macy's friends are always welcome in our home."

"Thank you. I appreciate that, as I'd like to be close. I need to pick her brains for the first vid from my new album."

"Jack gave my career's new phase instant credibility when he listened to my suggestions for his last video — then acknowledged me in the credits. Because of him, other artists started asking me to come up with concepts for them."

"No, that was strictly on the merits of her

talent," he told Lenore. "She's a natural. Not only does she have an eye for the aesthetic of music videos, she imbues them with her own unique perspective. But regarding letting me park my rig, Mrs. Watson. I want you to know I realize you run a business. I'll pay you, of course."

She waved a dismissive hand. "We'll discuss that after we see what effect you have on my utilities bill. Meanwhile, you could use some fattening up. Come in the kitchen and I'll fix you a plate."

He dove into the meal Lenore set in front of him. Macy could have told her aunt that for all he was heroin-chic lean, Jack could put away an amazing amount of food. Instead she simply enjoyed Lenore's pleasure at watching him eat.

"I see I'll have to charge you for your meals," Lenore said dryly as she slapped another dollop of potato salad on his plate and filled up his milk glass for the third time. "As it's plain you'll otherwise eat me out of house and home."

"It's just so *good*." He dabbed barbecue sauce from his lips with his napkin and shot her a crooked smile. "We don't get much home cooking in my business, and this is fierce spectacular. You eat like this every night?"

"Nah," Macy said. "Usually we eat better."

Jack made a rude noise. "You're havin' me on. Food doesn't get much better than this."

"I'm telling you, it's a phenomenon. Every meal Auntie makes just seems to taste better than the one before. Give her a week and you'll see what I'm saying."

Uncle Bud joined them as Jack was finally pushing his plate away. They talked for a while, then he directed the rocker to drive his trailer around behind the chicken coop. While they positioned it and got it leveled, Macy went back to the house to fetch Janna so she could introduce her to Jack. But her cousin was clearly worn-out by the day's therapy session, for she was sound asleep in their room. So she went back out and explored the trailer's interior as the men circled the vehicle outside, discussing the finer points of running utilities to it.

"You won't have sewer hookup," she heard her uncle say, and glanced out the window over the little round stainless sink to see him and Jack squatting down inspecting she didn't know what. "But you can always clear the holding tank at a dumping station when needed."

"Water's not a problem," he added, pointing to an outdoor faucet. "We can get you hooked up with that in no time." He proceeded to do just that as she snooped freely through the sleek, well-appointed trailer. "Electric's a little trickier. With the fire chief living here, it's probably not a good idea to just drag out an extension cord."

"I heard that."

Macy immediately lost interest in the sleekly compact interior and made a beeline for the door. But, embarrassed that she might have exposed more of herself to him than she should have before Jack showed up, she found herself acting like a twelve-year-old with her first crush when she stepped out into the cooling evening air and promptly pretended she didn't notice Gabriel. Still, that was better than her first impulse, which was to jump down his throat for making more work for her uncle.

Because that wouldn't do. Janna had already figured out her animosity toward him was partly hormone-driven. She'd just as soon her uncle didn't cop to it, as well.

"Slick little trailer, Jack," she said as she joined the men. "But why didn't you just bring the tour bus?"

"The lads are off to Jackson Hole in it to do some fishing." He gave the Airstream a fond look. "She's a sweet little bird, isn't she? Much smaller and easier to maneuver than the bus."

Macy made a rude noise. "Like you've ever driven a bus."

"I'll have you know I drove the band's first one all over the U.K." He gave her a cheeky smile. " 'Course that was a VW camper van we picked up on the cheap in Dublin."

"Hey," Gabe interrupted without heat. "You want to jaw with Macy or get your rig hooked up sometime tonight?"

"Sorry, mate. I haven't seen me little luv here in a bit, but I'm all yours. I appreciate your willingness to figure out the hows of this wiring stuff. If I had to come up with a plan, you can be sure I'd make a complete bag of it."

She'd missed the part where they'd been introduced, but clearly it had happened somewhere along the line because the three men conversed with ease. The conversation, in fact, soon turned to posthole diggers and trenches and plastic tubing and electrical feeds. She felt her eyes start to glaze, but she perked right up when Gabe picked up a dual-handled device with two shovel-like blade thingies on the end.

"Ooh. Men with tools," she murmured and suppressed her juvenile satisfaction when those intense gray eyes fastened on her for an electric moment.

Then he looked away and, keeping the handles together, drove the apparatus's blades into the ground. Pulling the handles apart, he raised the digger out of the embryonic hole he'd made, emptied the dirt he'd excavated, then repeated the process.

She was fascinated by all the small muscles that bunched and lengthened and shifted beneath his skin and under his T-shirt. Well, so did Jack's, she saw as he used a shovel to start a shallow trench, and *he* had the added attraction of all those tattoos undulating with every movement. But he was *Jack,* so her appreciation for the view he provided was more in an ooh, buff-statue-in-the-museum sort of way.

Bud joined her. "This is the advantage of having young bucks around," he said jovially. "Someone else to do the heavy lifting."

She tore her gaze from the view and grinned at her uncle. "Want a chair to enjoy the show in comfort?" she asked. "I saw a couple in the little closet in the trailer. There's also some Guinness in the cupboard. Jack's got that Irish fondness for warm beer, but if you can tolerate it room temperature . . ."

"You're pretty familiar with the boy's

habits — never mind not shy about making yourself at home in his Airstream," Bud said in a low voice. "You two — ?" Pink crept up his cheeks even as he wagged grizzled eyebrows.

"Nah," she said. "I love him to pieces. But like a brother, you know?"

"Gotta confess I'm relieved. From the little I've talked to him, he seems pretty grounded for a famous sort. But I can't say I'm wild about the idea of him dragging you from pillar to post any more than I was when it was your mother doing the dragging."

"Yeah, touring's definitely not for me. You know I've been in the same little condo in Redondo Beach for more than eight years. I guess I'm a nester like you and Auntie." She flashed him an affectionate smile. "So, about that chair and beer?"

"I'll take the first, but pass on the second." He inspected the tube that ran parallel with the top of the trailer. "I'll just get this awning set up while you fetch the chairs."

But Macy had barely spun around to go into the trailer when a car pulled into the parking area, sounding a cheerful beep as it rocked to a stop. Turning back, she watched Grace climb from her little Ford Focus, then observed Gabriel's happy-to-see-ya smile and the poleaxed expression that crossed Jack's face before he quickly covered it with his public persona, that slightly cool, slightly aloof rock-star shell that was a world removed from his actual warm personality.

And she didn't get it. She liked Grace, she genuinely did. But the girl dressed primly and was hardly loaded with man-eater do-me-daddy mannerisms.

"So, what the hell?" she murmured, then fought a blush and shook her head at Jack when he raised an eyebrow at her.

But, really. What was it about Grace that made her such a man magnet?

Chapter Eight

Grace hesitated next to her car before heading for the group by the silver trailer. Holy crapoly, was that who she thought it was? *Dear Lord.* She'd assumed Macy was the height of cool. And now *Jack Savage* was in the Watson's backyard?

Don't let me act like a stupid groupie. Please *don't let me do that!* Putting on her calmest teacher face, she slowed her walk to a stroll.

And still arrived before she was ready.

Heart beating a frantic tattoo, she sidled up to Gabe, smiled at Macy and snuck a look at Savage.

Only to find him staring back at her. When he caught her peeking, one side of his mouth curved up.

"Grace, this is my friend Jack," Macy said. "Jack heads —"

"I know who he is," she said and — yay — actually sounded fairly composed.

"Oh. Sure." Macy laughed. "I guess you'd

have to be raised in a cave not to, huh?"
She dug an elbow in the rock star's side.
"Jack, this is Grace. She's Gabe's girl, my
nephew Ty's teacher and my new friend. So
be nice."

"I'm always nice." He turned to her, flashing an easygoing smile. "Pleasure to meet
you, Grace." He thrust out his hand.

Hoping she wouldn't swoon like a rabid
fan-girl at her first concert, she reached out
to shake it. Savage's callus-tipped fingers
wrapped around hers, and an electric shock
streaked through her system, followed by a
wave of lust.

She swallowed a snort. Because, please.
As if *that* would ever be satisfied. She had a
rich and varied love life, although unfortunately only in her head.

It was her curse that men rarely saw her
as a sexual being. They seemed to like her
well enough, but because she didn't dress
or talk or, okay, behave in *any* way remotely
like the hottie she fantasized being, they apparently thought she wasn't interested in
sex.

Oh, she was interested. And not just in
the plain old vanilla variety, either; she
dreamed of out-of-control throw-caution-
to-the-wind, Desire with a flaming capital *D*
sex.

Instead, her way-too-few lovers had treated her with lowering care. And Gabe, whom she'd been dating fairly steadily for the past six weeks and had thought might be her guide into the world of strip-me-naked-and-hold-me-down screaming orgasms, hadn't even slapped any real moves on her. When he'd first asked her out, she'd thought for sure that *finally* she had a shot at the fantasy sex she'd been dreaming of since her teens. There was just something beneath his surface calm that made her know he'd be wild or — even better — dominant in that order-a-girl-to-do-the-unspeakable-in-bed kind of way.

But although they got along famously and had fun together, he'd never done more than kiss her good-night at her door. And to her surprise, as fantastic as he was in the smooch department, maybe she didn't feel that out-of-control chemistry she'd hoped for with him, either. But would it hurt him to at least *try?* Just once she'd like to be treated less like a lady and more like a tart.

She sure as heck didn't fool herself that a famous rock star with densely tattooed arms and a lovely accent would be the one to suddenly sniff out her inner sex kitten and itch to release it. That didn't stop her, however, from tingling right down to the bone when

Savage looked at her with those heavy-lidded amber-brown eyes as if she had his full, absorbed attention.

Unfortunately, it also didn't stop her from blushing to her hairline. Because that was Part Two of her curse: her outer good girl was aeons stronger than the self she wished to be. A self who was fearless like Macy.

Jack's gaze drifted lazily to the front of her blouse. Oh, God. Could he tell her nipples were hard? Which bra had she put on this morning, anyway? Please let it be the slightly padded one.

But when he gave her that one-sided knowing smile again and licked his lips, she knew. It was the skimpy, lace-trimmed number.

The heat in her face was so scalding she was surprised her features didn't melt right down her neck onto her firmly buttoned ecru blouse. She hated the fact that, as a teensiest-bit-repressed schoolteacher, she was already a cliché. Did she really need to compound it by reacting like a thirteen-year-old? He was a rock-and-roll god, for goodness sake. Probably every woman he met had this response.

"You wanna get this done sometime tonight, Savage?"

Gabe's sardonic demand made her start

skittishly. But Jack flashed him a smile that was surprisingly boyish. "Yeah, sorry, mate," he said. "I just got sucked in for a minute by your pretty little bird here."

Fury shot up her spine and she forgot all about her schoolgirl blushes. "Listen," she said in a low, stiff voice. "You might be a big hotshot rock star, but that doesn't give you leave to mock me."

He'd started to turn away, but pivoted back to look down at her. "Oh, I'm far from mocking you, luv. I've had a thing for shiny-haired girls in Peter Pan collars since Caitlin Doyle led me around by my —" he cleared his throat "— uh, nose at Kill o'the Grange in County Dublin."

"What is that — Kill o'the Grange?" she demanded, her teacher's interest piqued.

"School I was in my sixth class. What you'd call an elementary, I guess." His gaze drifted over her shirtfront again. "I had it bad for Caitlin when I was twelve."

"Savage!" Gabe bellowed.

"Yeah, yeah. Keep your cacks on, guv. I'm coming." He ran a finger down her nose, then strolled back to pick up a shovel.

Macy came over. "A bit overwhelming on first meeting, our Jack."

"I'll say." She shot the tall blonde a glance. "I had this overpowering urge to throw my

132

panties at him."

Macy laughed. "I like you, Grace. You've got depths I think a lot of people overlook."

"Absolutely. Because shedding one's underwear for a rock star is so profound. Not to mention original."

"Oh. Well. He *is* Jack Savage."

"He certainly is." She studied Macy's fond smile as the other woman watched Jack work. "So, are the two of you — ?"

"No." Macy's attention returned to her. "But he is one of my best friends. Jack's one of the good guys. For all the perks and attention his fame brings him, he's generous and down-to-earth." She flicked fingers toward where he was putting his back into digging the hole and spoke a little less softly than she'd been doing. "I don't know many Hollywood types who would do their own work. Most of the ones I've met would be on their cell phones trying to hire someone — or better yet, getting their agents to do it. And never mind that it's closing on nine p.m. in a farming community that rolls up its streets at six."

She waved her hand. "But enough about men. I was thinking we oughtta have a girls' night out one of these evenings."

From the corner of her eye Grace saw Gabe suddenly raise his head from where he was bent over the posthole digger to glance over at them.

"You, me, Shannon and Janna, if she's up to it," Macy continued, reclaiming her attention. "Maybe hit the Red Dog, throw back a shot or two and shoot the breeze. Or we could go to a coffee shop if you'd rather, although I'm not sure any are open in the evening."

She gave Macy a shy smile, feeling as if she'd suddenly been singled out to sit at the cool kids' table. "Either sounds fun. Count me in."

"Good. Your schedule and Shannon's are probably more complicated than mine or Janna's, so why don't you guys pick a night that works for you and we'll go from there."

She was about to agree when she heard the beep of a pager. Glancing at the two men working alongside the chicken coop, she saw Gabe on his phone.

A moment later, he snapped it shut. "Fire," he said to no one in particular, already striding for his SUV. "Gotta go."

"Dude definitely needs to work on his social skills," Macy muttered, but Grace doubted he heard her, since his long legs were eating up the distance to the parking area.

Bud shot his niece a wry smile as he

passed the two women, fishing a pair of leather gloves from his back pocket and pulling them on as he walked over to the discarded posthole digger. "Guess I'm not going to escape the heavy lifting after all."

Grace turned a questioning brow on Macy, feeling as if she'd come in on the middle of a conversation.

"He was pretty pumped at having two strong backs to do the hard work," Macy explained. She was quiet for a minute, then said, slowly, "I guess I never really thought it through before, but Gabriel's really on call 24/7, isn't he?" She gave her a searching look. "That's gotta complicate your dating life."

Grace made a noncommittal noise, feeling it disloyal to admit that they'd had several dates cut short. In any case, she glanced from Gabe's car reversing from its parking slot in a tight U to Jack wiping sweat from his forehead with the back of his hand and leaving behind a smear of dirt she had a ridiculous urge to wipe clean.

And thought to herself, *I have a feeling that's the least of my problems.*

The hell I've got a problem with my social skills. Gabe pulled onto the highway, hit the siren and sped east away from town. He might not be the life of the party or some big world-renowned rock star, but he got by just fine. And he sure as hell wasn't some middle schooler who had to have a girlfriend's undivided attention.

But first Savage had made Grace blush like a schoolgirl saying God knows what to her, or, to be fair, merely paying attention to her, and now Macy was going to take her out for a girls' night? The first was understandable: it wasn't exactly every day your average citizen was introduced to a celebrity. But the Macy thing — that was just plain wrong. Grace was wonderfully calm and easy on the blood pressure. What if Macy went and turned her into someone more like herself?

But as he tried to imagine Grace all tarted up, strutting her stuff at the local honky-tonk and setting men on fire, it wouldn't gel. Grace was her own woman, not one filled with flashy, edgy, in-your-face sexuality like Macy. Guys tended to respect her precisely because she wasn't the kind of woman to flash cleavage. Although that probably didn't mean she wouldn't like to have a little fun. And he had to admit The Flirt could probably provide that in spades.

Still, he was tense over the strange-ass evening this had turned into, and wrestling a fire into submission sounded like just the antidote.

But not one he'd find tonight, he saw moments after turning off Highway 2. There was a spot ahead lit up like high noon with the truck's halogen work lights, and when he pulled over to the side of the farm road running through Art Bailey's spread he saw that Johnson and Solberg had the flames under control. They must have caught the small storage barn before the building was fully engaged. It had sustained some damage and still smoldered, but he had no need of the turnout gear he kept in the back of his ride. Solberg was inside with the hose taking care of the last of it. Climbing from the SUV, he cast a curious glance at the old pickup truck full of split wood he'd parked behind even as he assured himself that the fire being out was a *good* thing.

And, hell, it was; his men had done their job. Too bad it didn't stop him from feeling a little let down. For as he'd already noted, the evening had left him feeling strangely tense, and he would've welcomed the chance to blow off some steam. God knew his opportunities in that direction were limited these days.

He'd given up his old standbys — enonstop, indiscriminate fighting and fucking —

eat seventeen. That's when a caseworker had helped him see past his rage long enough to realize he was headed down a one-way track to early death or incarceration if he didn't get his shit together. So he'd climbed aboard the Straight and Narrow Express, set a course for himself and, except for a few backslides early on, had pretty much stuck to it from that point on. He thought before he spoke now. He never used his fists. He even expressed most of his obscenities internally.

Okay, he hadn't given up sex — even if it felt that way sometimes. He was, however, a whole lot more selective than he'd ever been at seventeen. But, hell, what grown man wasn't?

Still, fighting fires was one of the few outlets he had when things got tense, and the only one that was guaranteed to relieve whatever ailed him. Yet the chances to pit himself against an inferno, to feel the muscular pulse of the fire hose in his hands, the spike of adrenaline rushing through his veins — not to mention outwitting that brutal bitch in full conflagration — were fewer and farther between since he'd traded in his job in Detroit for this county fire-chief gig. Being chief instead of crew meant more supervising and less getting to throw himself in the thick of things.

But he had a job to do here and no time to dwell on matters he'd already decided on. Going up to Johnson, who was guzzling a liter bottle of water, he said, "What've we got here?"

The blond volunteer capped his bottle and swiped the back of his hand across his mouth. "Good Samaritan driving by —" he nodded toward a middle-aged man standing a short distance away talking to the farmer who owned the property "— saw smoke rolling out of the shed and called 911. He found the water hookup and hose and did what he could until Solberg, who was nearest the station, got here with the truck. I showed up maybe two minutes later."

Gabe was suspicious by nature, and his years on the Detroit arson squad predisposed him to look twice at the Good Samaritan. He didn't have any real reason to believe it was arson, but given the recent garbage-can fires he couldn't rule it out. And if it was, it would leave him with three options. Either the garbage-can arsonist was escalating, Bailey was in financial trouble, or he was dealing with a vanity firebug. He'd seen his share of the latter in his career: arsonists who liked to set fires, then be a hero by "catching" them before they got out of control.

"First impressions?"

"Of the man — seems solid. The fire . . . ? At this point there's no obvious indication of arson," Johnson said, and Solberg, who arrived stripping off his turnout coat, nodded his agreement. "None of the doors or windows appear to have been opened for more oxygen and there's only a single point of origin that I've been able to establish so far."

"Take a look and see if you can determine how it started. I'll be over to give you a hand in a minute." He walked over to the farmer and the Samaritan.

"Hey, Mr. Bailey," he said, shaking the farmer's hand. "I'm sorry about your barn." He turned to the other man. "Good thing you were here to stop it before it was fully engaged." He extended a hand to him, as well. "I don't believe we've met. I'm Fire Chief Donovan."

"Dick Ames." He shook with a firm, work-roughened grip and Gabe took a cautious step back from the vanity arsonist theory as he studied him.

The man had a fit, farmer's body and made level eye contact. Most vanity firebugs had grandiosity issues — security guards who'd failed the police-academy entrance exams, soldier wannabes without the actual discipline for the military life. This man didn't appear to fit the mold.

All the same . . .

"Can you tell me what happened?"

"I was on my way home from my son's orchard near Peshastin. He'd cleared a section to put in Honeycrisps and we cut up the Red Delicious trees he'd thinned for firewood." He gave his head an impatient shake. "But that's not what you're asking. I was heading back to my spread down Two a piece past this cutoff when I saw a column of smoke rising from over this way. Twilight was just turning to full dark, so I wasn't sure at first it was even what I thought it was. But this isn't the time of year you wanna chance fire. Well —" he shrugged "— I don't need to tell you things are getting dry, and the last thing we need is a runaway brush fire."

Gabe questioned him about the color of the smoke and the flames when he'd arrived on the scene. He asked whether he'd smelled anything unusual and if any of the doors or windows had been open or looked as if they'd been forced. Ames gave thoughtful responses and Gabe decided he probably was exactly what he appeared to be: a

141

neighbor helping a neighbor. Didn't mean he wouldn't make a few discreet inquiries to check the farmer's story, but for now he turned to Bailey to ask about the contents of the building. Then, noting the nearly full moon had risen, he sent both farmers off to catch up on what they could of the chores that had been shuttled aside in order to deal with this.

After seeing them off, he wrote up his notes, then went over to give his men a hand sifting through the burned section of the small barn.

"Coulda been one of Bailey's hands smoking in here and not disposing of his butt properly," Johnson said. "They all know better, but it still happens more often than it oughtta." His jaw hardened. "My men can whore, fight and kick up a fuss and I don't give a good goddamn. But they know if I catch them smoking in a nondesignated area their asses will get the boot so fast they'll be lucky to touch down before they hit the county line." He went back to sifting through the debris at his feet.

"The material in here appears properly stored." Gabe worked his way away from the fire's source. "And Bailey doesn't have any small kids who might have snuck in to play with a book of matches. Solberg, check the wiring — make sure nothing obvious is wrong with it."

"Got it, boss."

He had no idea what time it was when he next rose to his feet, but the moon had shifted quite a way toward the west. Slapping his hands to the small of his back, he arched to stretch out his muscles. "Doesn't look to be arson." He shook his head. "So much for my gut, 'cause I had an itch that said it was. Nothing here indicates it started spontaneously, but I sure as hell haven't found an obvious accelerant or ignition device, either."

"I think I may have, chief," Johnson said, looking over his shoulder. "You might want to come over here and take a look at this."

Gabe went over and squatted down. He looked at the patch of ground Johnson had carefully cleared of debris. In the light that his volunteer moved closer, he saw a faint, tubular shiny spot on the scorched barn board floor, and Gabe scratched up a thin strip of wax with his fingernail. "Oh, yeah," he murmured. "The gut *doesn't* lie."

He gave his men a nod. "Someone used a candle as a timing device. Guess we've got us another arson, after all."

CHAPTER NINE

Macy couldn't sleep. The room was stuffy, but it wasn't that; Bud and Lenore had installed central air-conditioning a few years ago, and although they didn't set it to hotel standards of coolness the house was worlds more comfortable than it had been in her teenage years. No, it was the way her mind kept spinning as it busily sorted and re-played the events of the day in an endless, restless loop that was the problem. And rather than flop from side to side until she woke up Janna, she might as well get up.

Tossing back the sheet, she sat up and swung her legs over the edge of the bed, wondering what time it was. O'dark thirty, certainly; beyond that she didn't have a clue.

Grabbing her watch from the nightstand, she carried it over to the window and saw by the light of the moon that it was twelve forty-eight. It felt as though she'd slept much longer than an hour, but it must have been one of those deep, suck-you-to-the-bottom-of-the-sea slumbers, because now she was wide-awake.

Gathering up her iPod, which Jack had loaded with the music from his upcoming album, she headed for the door. She'd listen to a song or two while she raided the kitchen and see if any concepts popped to mind for corresponding videos. If something really good occurred to her she could always go see if Jack was still up. *Or not,* she thought, looking down at the hip-hugger boy shorts and skimpy tank top she slept in. She wasn't exactly dressed for visiting.

Inserting the earbuds as she made her way down the darkened hallway, she thumbed on the music, humming appreciatively as the first song purled through the wires. By the time she entered the kitchen her hips were already moving to the beat. She made a beeline for the industrial-size refrigerator.

Its interior light nearly blinded her in the dim room. Blinking, she bent to look inside, moving items out of her way as she searched for the blackberry pie Auntie Lenore had served tonight.

Swallowing her disappointment when she came up empty, even though deep down she'd known the odds were against any being left, she studied her other options.

"Sweet view," a deep voice said from behind her.

Emitting a squeaky screech, she whirled, yanking the earbuds from her ears.

Gabriel sat at the worktable in the moon-dappled dark, a fork in his fist, the pie dish and a tall glass of milk in front of him.

Music whispered out of her iPod and she switched it off. "You bastard! Not only did you scare five years off my life, you're eating *my* pie!"

"Yeah?" He made a production of enjoying the bite in his mouth, then swallowed. "I didn't see your name on it."

She grabbed a fork out of the drawer and stalked over to the table, rounding it to flop down in the chair next to his. "Gimme a bite."

"Forget it." He wrapped a blocking arm around the pie pan. "There's plenty of other stuff in the fridge. This is mine. Go find something else."

"C'mon! Just a bite." She reached over with her fork, but he hunched his shoulder and her forearm skidded across his, skin to skin.

His inner arm felt like hot sanded silk over marble. Her heartbeat kicked up its pace, and all thoughts of food vanished. She had an almost uncontrollable urge to scoot closer and trace the velvety veins that snaked down his inner forearm with her fingertips — then maybe her tongue.

She jerked her arm back. What the hell was that all about? She wasn't a particularly sexual woman — or at least she hadn't been before clapping eyes on this guy. But looking at him, all solid shoulders in that thin old-fashioned tank-style undershirt, she had a crazy urge to touch him again — this time on purpose. To rub herself all over him.

Appalled at her wayward thoughts, she muttered, "Fine, be that way. I'll find something better."

But he was already pushing the plate toward her. "Have a damn bite if it means so much."

Her throat felt dry as ashes, rendering her ability to swallow uncertain, yet she could hardly say she no longer wanted the pie after making a fuss about him sharing it. So, cautiously, she extended her fork and broke off a bite, making sure that no skin made contact this time. But she was hotly aware of his hard physique, sullen lower lip and uncharacteristically rumpled hair. Conscious of the male scent of him, even though it was nearly buried in an acrid smoke overtone.

Huge and shadowy, with that scent and

aura of heat, with the pale gleam of gray irises through dark lashes, he was Lucifer after the Fall, beautiful and primal.

Or — hello! — a fireman after the fire he's been called out on. She shoved back her chair. How idiotic could she *get?* "Keep the pie," she said lightly. "I'm going to see if there's any ice cream."

She found a hand-packed tub of vanilla in the freezer and scooped some into a cone from the box above the freezer. For about two seconds, she considered taking the coward's way out and trotting her treat back to her room. By the time she'd rinsed off the scoop and returned it to its drawer, however, she'd buried the urge. She had spent her entire senior year in a town whose populace thought the worst of her and had never hesitated to let her know it — and she hadn't run away. She sure as hell wasn't running from Donovan just because he made her feel inexplicable yearnings.

Defiantly, she came back to the table and, folding one leg beneath her on the seat, sat down. She did, however, choose a chair across the table from Gabriel so there would be no more inadvertent brushing of arms.

She could be pigheaded, yes. But she wasn't stupid.

Gabe leaned back in his chair, watching

Macy. He'd been moodily eyeing her long legs and round butt as she'd scooped ice cream atop her cone.

Especially that butt — he was an ass man from way back, and he should have known hers would lead to trouble the minute she'd strolled in wearing that skimpy tank and next-best-thing-to-spray-paint shorts. All he'd had to do was keep his mouth shut and she might have grabbed something from the fridge and left without even noticing he was there. Had he chosen the smart route, however? Hell, no. He'd watched her bend to peruse the contents of the refrigerator, and the sight of that round, subtly gyrating booty had evaporated every scrap of good sense he possessed. It was one fine view, and instead of keeping his mouth shut, he'd had to go and say so.

It was now safely out of sight, so his rebellious body ought to be settling down. Yet covertly eyeing her as he ate his pie, he had to admit that, aesthetically speaking, the chick had no bad side. God knew the head-on scenery wasn't shabby. Macy was far from stacked, but she had a perky, eye-catching rack all the same, and he could see the faint, shadowy outline of her nipples behind the thin stretch cotton of her tank top. Even as he watched, they hardened, peaking the material in a way that was impossible to ignore even in the dim room. His dick stirring to attention, he forgot covert and stared, riveted.

She shivered. "I didn't think it was possible on such a warm night, but this ice cream is giving me the shivers." Swirling her tongue along its side, she gathered in a lick. "It sure tastes good, though. I love ice cream." She took another lick, looking at him across the table. "So, that fire you went to tonight. Is everything okay?"

"Yeah. There was some property damage to a shed, but a passerby called it in before it got out of control." He looked at her bedmussed hair and heavy-lidded eyes. "You go over to Savage's trailer in that getup?"

"What?" She froze with her tongue flattened against the ice cream to stare at him. Reeling in the confection she'd been in the midst of lapping, she lowered the cone and swallowed.

And her eyes blazed across the table as she shoved to her feet. "What the hell business is that of yours? Who are you, the sex police?"

Good question. Why was it any skin off his dick what she did with the Irishman?

Yet he was seriously bugged by the thought.

Macy knew she should let it go and walk out the door. Yes, she would remain steamed and probably not get a wink of sleep. It was still the smart thing to do.

So, sue her. She wasn't going to be smart.

Her heart pounded with what she'd tried to tell herself was rage. But she wasn't one for self-delusion, and inhaling through her nose, she acknowledged the feeling for what it was: excitement. Because she'd caught him eyeing her boobs — and liked it to the extent that her nipples had come to attention. She looked at his mouth and big hands . . . and liked those, too.

But he didn't get to treat her as if she breathed, therefore she put out. She did not, she never had, and the time was long gone when people could say whatever the hell they wanted about her. Just as she'd refused to take her ice cream and retreat to her room, she wasn't about to let this go unchallenged.

Exhaling quietly, she tossed her cone in the sink and rounded the table, not even slowing when he rose to his feet. Coming to a halt a scant foot away, she thrust her chin up at him, getting as close to in-his-face as she could manage, given the disparity in their heights.

His big shoulders blocked the moonlight

filtering through the window over the sink, but enough illumination remained to make out the thick brows bunched together, the proud thrust of nose and chin and the full curve of his lower lip. A wall of heat pumped off his supersize body and, resisting the urge to lick her lips, she raised her brows at him.

"You sure seem interested in my sex life," she said. Her voice came out huskier than she'd intended but she refrained from clearing her throat. "Why is that, I wonder? Not getting any yourself these days?"

Okay, probably not her brightest move to introduce *that* topic. 'Cause nothing like handing him the perfect opportunity to regale her with his sexual exploits — which she didn't doubt for a second were a gazillion times more interesting than hers would ever be. Not that she cared that his experience outstripped her own.

Really, she didn't. Still, as much as she disliked admitting it, she did *not* want to hear the details of what he did with Grace.

And to her surprised relief, he refrained from supplying them. Instead, he leaned down until his big Roman nose practically mashed her own and growled, "I warned you about playing your games with me, O'James. But you just won't listen, will you? Because this —" his hands sketched the outline of her body, which was maybe a little closer to his than it ought to be "— looks like an offer to me."

She knew she was playing with fire. Her heartbeat pounded in her throat, her fingertips, her nipples and between her — well, *every*where. But although it didn't take a genius to guess where this would lead if she didn't throttle back on the attitude and beat feet while the getting was good, she didn't back up so much as an inch. "Yet I'm not the one who brought up my sex life. I was minding my own business, having a civilized conversation about the fire you went out on tonight, when *you* started making comments about my sleepwear."

She could feel his gaze like a touch, minutely inspecting her tank and boy shorts. And clearly her eyes had adjusted to the shadow he cast, for she saw a muscle tic in his jaw. "What little there is of it."

Bent out of shape at the unfairness of his attack, she slapped her hands on his chest and shoved. Hard.

He arched back a little from the waist, but otherwise didn't budge.

That made her angrier yet and she shoved again — with identical results. "It's the middle of the damn night and I thought I'd have the kitchen to myself. Not to *mention* you'd see more goods at the town pool! But hey. If I'd known Prudezilla was going to be in the kitchen waiting to sit in judgment of my sleeping duds I would have swaddled myself from neck to toes."

"Prudezil— ?" Dark brows snapping together, he towered over her, and this time it was she who leaned back. "You think I'm — ?"

"Prim. Proper. Pedantic." She loved seeing the insulted outrage on his face. *Not so much fun when the label's on* you, *is it, Bub?* *"Pris*-sy," she added for good measure and shrugged. "What can I say, big boy? If the strait lace fits . . ."

"Prissy?" His eyes went dangerous and she knew she'd gone too far. When was she going to learn to quit doing that? Hastily, she took a step back.

But Gabe obviously had other ideas, for whipping an arm around her waist, he yanked her flush with his body and thrust his big mitt into her hair, hard fingers tangling in the strands as he scowled into her eyes. "I'll show you prissy!" he growled.

And stamped his mouth over hers.

It took merely that for her to ignite — and the flash point was blinding. Or maybe that was simply her eyelids dropping like a curtain the instant his mouth claimed hers.

Because, oh. God. That *mouth.*

It was hot. Full-lipped yet firm. And knew exactly what it was doing. It opened over hers. Applied pressure. Rubbed. Sipped.

Sucked.

And when that didn't immediately garner the reaction he was looking for, he raised his head and growled, "Open up." Then returned to his task, concentrating on tantalizing first her upper lip, then her lower lip. Then her entire mouth. Demonstrating conclusively why she should obey his command.

She opened up.

A satisfied sound rumbled in his throat. Releasing his grip in her hair, he slid his hand around to cup her face. Thumb stroking fire along her cheekbone, he held her softly, almost tenderly. But his kiss was hard, his tongue stealing in to stake dominion over hers in no uncertain terms.

Hooking her fingers through his Hanes's armhole and U-neck openings, she rose up onto her toes, applying some dominion-wannabe action of her own. The silky fan of hair over the hard plane of his chest brushed the backs of her fingers, and releasing her grip on his undershirt she wrapped her arms around his neck. Her breasts flattened against the solid wall of his chest.

The sheer heat of him felt as though it should melt the clothes right from her body, and she made a needy sound.

He ripped his mouth free. "Shit," he whispered, then cocked his head and came at her from a different angle. His kisses grew hotter, deeper, wetter, driving her head back. Leaning into her, he arched her over his supporting arm. Then he suddenly removed the hand lightly grasping her face and used that arm to sweep his pie plate aside. And still kissing her, he lowered her to the table. Easing atop her, he propped himself up on one elbow to keep from crushing her.

With a deep-throated groan, he raised his mouth from hers and pressed open-mouthed, suctioning kisses down her throat. His hand lifted the hem of her tank and slid beneath.

"Oh," she sighed as his fingers burned a path up her diaphragm. Callused fingertips pressed the underside of her breast and she arched, wanting closer, rougher handling.

He obliged her, smoothing his hand up to cup her breast and give it a firm squeeze. Catching her nipple between his thumb and the side of his index finger, he compressed it and tugged.

"Oh, God, Gabriel!" Her chin tipping ceilingward, she arched until only her hips and the back of her head remained on the scarred wooden surface.

He suddenly went very still above her. Then his mouth abruptly lifted from her neck, his hand slid out from under her tank top and he pushed back, climbing to his feet.

Leaving her to collapse back onto the table, feeling suddenly cold and exposed. Pushing up onto her elbows, she blinked up at him. "Gabe?"

He pulled his gaze from her tank front, his face expressionless when he met her eyes. "This never happened," he said definitely. His eyes narrowed. "You get me?"

She flinched, his words a sharp slap to the face.

Then anger blazed through her. Anger at him for making her want him, then acting as if wanting her back was somehow beneath him or something to be ashamed of. Anger at herself for letting down her guard, for trusting him enough to allow things to get to this point. She might have been willing to keep quiet about such behavior from the horde of stud wannabes during her high school years. But that was ten years ago, and her tolerance was all used up.

She raised her chin. "Do I get you? As much as I can get anyone who would start something like this only to suddenly change his mind mid . . . whatever. If you were a woman there'd be a name for you." She sat up and scooted off the table.

She looked Gabriel in the eye. "But don't worry, Donovan. It's not something I'm anxious to spread around, myself, and you're dead right, bud. This never happened. And you can be damn sure it will never happen again."

And beating him to the punch, she turned and walked out on him before he could on her.

CHAPTER TEN

Thwack!
  Thwack!
  Thwack-thwack-thwack!

The report of Gabe's nail gun echoed in the clearing surrounding his starting-to-come-together house as he framed in the mudroom addition he'd just decided he needed to add to the back. By rights he should be working on drywall inside, as the last-minute addition to the already framed and shingled construction could easily wait. But taping and mudding took precision. And God knew with the shitload of aggression needing to be worked out of his system, he was in no mood for taking that kind of care.

The way he felt at the moment, in fact, he'd just as soon take a sledgehammer to the drywall he'd spent the past couple of weeks screwing in place. So, yeah. He was definitely better off outdoors getting a start on the enclosed back porch. He should have included it in his plans in the first place.

"Don't worry, Donovan. It's not something I'm anxious to spread around, myself."

Thwack!

Thwack!

Then his finger stilled on the trigger. Because her lips had been swollen and reddened from his kisses, her hair mussed from his hands when she'd said that.

From the goddamn kisses and hands he should have kept to himself.

"You're dead right, bud. This never happened. And you can be damn sure it will never happen again."

He set the nail gun down before he could hurl it across the clearing. Which made zero frigging sense. Because that what-happened-between-them-never-happening-again shit? Hell, that was a good thing. A *gooood* thing.

So why did it make him feel like howling every time her edict replayed itself in his head?

Tires crunched in the gravel drive, and Gabe rubbed the incipient headache growing between his eyes. Great. Company. That's what was missing in this fucked-up afternoon after his sleep-deprived, fucked-up night.

But some of the tension went out of his

shoulders when he saw it was Johnny Angelini. For a minute there . . .

No. Straightening, he set down the nail
gun and reached for the shirt he'd tossed
over a nearby sawhorse. Of course he hadn't
thought it was Macy. Having her show up
on his doorstep would not only be unwelcome; it'd be pretty damn improbable. He'd
seen the way she'd recoiled from his less-
than-smooth handling when he'd jerked to
an awareness of what he was doing — and
with whom — last night. The wounded look
that had flashed across her face was yet
another thing that kept popping up, unbidden, to play and replay itself in his mind.

So no, he hadn't expected her. But he had
half feared to see one of the guys from his
unit. Not that he didn't enjoy their company. But he wasn't in the mood today for
the slight gulf forever between them — a
result, no doubt, of him being their boss.

Johnny pulled his cruiser to a stop, shut it
down and climbed out. "Hey," he said with
an easy smile. "Sounded like a war was being waged back here . . . if everyone was
armed with pussy-boy twenty-twos."

"I beg to differ, bro— that would be my
finishing gun. This one sounds more like a
Remington hunting rifle." But he had to
swallow a snort. Because like he would

know — he'd never been hunting in his life. Still, flinging the bull with Johnny made him feel as if he just might get through the day without doing something stupid after all, a first since watching Macy storm out of the kitchen a dozen or so hours ago.

He was wondering which would be stupider: picking a fight with someone so he could throw just one satisfying punch or going sniffing around O'James's door again, when Johnny broke into his internal debate.

"What the hell are you doing here?" The deputy stared up at the scabbed-on framing. "I thought you were done with the exterior."

"I decided I needed a mudroom and it's too nice to be working inside anyhow." The rationale slipped off his tongue easy as butter from a hot knife.

"Wouldn't it have been easier to include it in the plans to begin with?"

"Hell, yeah, it would." His shoulders twitched in a shrug. "But I've never lived in a house before. I'm learning what I need as I go along."

Johnny, who'd been lowering his butt onto the other sawhorse, paused mid-sitting. Then he sat the rest of the way down. "You kiddin' me — you've never lived in a house? Having been raised in the same farmhouse until I was — I don't know — twenty-two, twenty-three, I find that hard to visualize."

"Growing up, it was just me and my old lady and we lived in apartments, duplexes, in a trailer or two and, once, in a Quonset hut. But no houses." He gave the equivalent of a facial shrug. "So this is all new to me."

The deputy scratched his lower lip with the edge of his thumbnail. "I've never heard you talk about your family. Your mom all you got?"

A sour laugh escaped him. "I don't have anyone." Not wired to open a vein in order to satisfy someone else's jones for blood and thinking he'd said too much, he reached for the nail gun once again.

And yet . . .

His hand came away empty, and he glanced at Johnny. "Mom was a party girl," he heard himself say impassively. "When I was fourteen and starting to gain my current height, she decided I was cramping her style. So she turned me over to the system."

Johnny jerked upright. "She dumped a fourteen-year-old kid, her own *son,* in the —" His eyes, usually filled with humor, went hard and flat. His voice dispassionate, he said with quiet conviction, "That goddamn. Son of a fucking. Bitch."

"I see you've met my mom." Amazingly,

having his friend know the truth — that his own mother had cared more for her good times than she had for him — didn't make Gabe feel like the loser he'd always assumed it would to have his private intel become general knowledge. Instead, Johnny's unemotional yet unequivocal condemnation of Heather Donovan's actions soothed something he hadn't even realized still pinched deep in his soul.

Swiveling to lie on his side along the length of the sawhorse, Johnny bent his elbow, propped his head in his hand and studied Gabe. "Did you at least land in a good home?"

"I was in a couple that probably would've been pretty decent if I hadn't been too enraged to let anyone close enough to help me. I got in so many fights between fourteen and sixteen that I finally landed in the Creighton Boys' Home, which was basically an institution for incorrigibles."

"Damn, dude."

He laughed. "It actually turned out to be the best place for me. I met a counselor there who helped me with my anger-management issues."

His friend raised an eyebrow. "I have a hard time picturing you with those."

"Oh, trust me. I was one angry kid." And

he needed to pull himself out of this current wrath-on he had going and shape up fast, because damned if he intended to go back to those out-of-control days. Not to the fury *or* the joyless fucking.

Okay, he had a feeling he would've gotten a helluva lot of joy out of fucking Macy, but —

No. Dammit, everything was all screwed up — and all because he couldn't keep his hands, his mouth, off of her. He'd had such a great thing going with Grace, had felt so mellow and easy with her, and —

Shit. He was going to have to break things off with Grace. That was the last thing he wanted, but a man didn't string a woman along when he was spending half his time jonesing for someone else. Not that he didn't plan to quit doing that, pronto. But he couldn't ignore the fact that even before Macy had come along, he hadn't felt more than a random, easily ignored urge to take matters with Grace to the next level. So yeah, it wasn't fair to either of them — and he needed to break it off.

He tried to put aside the matter of how the hell he was going to do that as he shot the breeze with Johnny. But the instant his friend climbed back in his cruiser to get back to his rounds, his mind returned to the problem.

Maybe Grace wouldn't be surprised. He hadn't made much effort to push the sexual envelope with her, and she was sweet and gentle and probably didn't care all that much about sex anyway.

Still. He'd never given her an indication that there was even a problem, so it was going to hit her out of the blue. He hated the thought of hurting her — or, oh, crap — maybe even breaking her heart.

Thwack! Thwack! Thwack-thwack-thwack!

Jesus, women were a lot of work.

"Men are one big, freaking mystery," Grace said over the clack of pool balls at the Red Dog three nights later.

Looking up from digging through her purse for her lipstick to see Ty's teacher owlishly regarding her, Janna and Shannon, Macy sternly admonished herself not to jump all over the other woman's remark. This stupid craving she had for Gabriel had to stop. It was so damn unhealthy — not to mention disloyal. She didn't need to know every little word he'd said to Grace, whose — jeez — friend she was supposed to be.

Locating the tube by feel, she pulled it out and rolled up the lipstick as she agreed with quiet fervor, "I'll drink to that, sister."

Grace pitched her voice to be heard over k.d. lang's full-throated lament purling out of the jukebox. "I don't get guys at all half the time." Then she pointed her glass of house white at Macy. "And before you all tell me my language in that last sentence was neither specific nor concrete for someone who purports to be a teacher, let me just say, I know."

Shannon scratched her red curls. "It wasn't?" she asked at the same time Janna said, "Oh, yeah, that was the first thing I was going to mention."

Macy simply looked at the brunette, noting the loose smile and slight befuddlement in her eyes. "How many wines have you had there, Gracie?"

"Two and a half."

"Cheap drunk, huh?"

Grace nodded amicably. "Yes, I am. I guess I should probably switch to Perrier." She blinked at the neon beer signs that provided most of the illumination in the dim, low-ceiling building. "Do you s'pose they even have Perrier here?"

Shannon nodded. "Since they dropped their tavern status and became a bar, they have just about everything."

"Okay, good." Setting down her wineglass, Grace planted her chin in her hand and regarded Macy. "I want to be you when I grow up."

Macy smiled, tickled. She could honestly say no one had ever said that to her before. "You do?"

"Yes. You're no Barbie doll. If Mattel made you, you'd be a kick-ass action figure. Now me —" She rolled her eyes and Macy reached out to keep her resulting wobble from tipping her off the side of her chair.

"Easy there," she advised and signaled for the waitress. "Let's get you that Perrier."

"Good idea. You get what I'm saying, though, right? If I were a doll I'd probably be the namby-pamby sidekick."

"You're pretty hard on yourself," Shannon commented, then narrowed her eyes. "Does this have anything to do with why men are a big freaking mystery?"

"Nah. I always knew I'd be the sidekick doll. Still, it prob'ly doesn't help that Gabe dumped me."

"He what?" Macy snapped upright, her heart pounding. Oh, God, oh, God. She didn't know what she felt. The "good" her longed to bitch-slap the man for hurting Grace.

The "bad" her did a few secret hand-springs and thought, *He's no longer another woman's man.* Crap. She hadn't felt this fixated on a guy since her horrendous crush on Andrew Mayfield in high school.

And just look at how well *that* had turned out.

Obviously not sharing her conflicts, Shannon spat, "That *pig.*"

"Well, see, that's the thing," Grace said. "He really isn't. We had a lot of fun together, and I consider him my friend, even now. But as much as I hate to admit this, there wasn't any spark."

Macy damn near blurted, "Are you *serious?*" Luckily her brain kicked in. Because she of all people ought to know that sexual attraction was subjective. Look how everyone thought she and Jack were an item when, as much as they enjoyed teasing each other as if it were so, they'd never even gone through a phase of feeling that way about each other.

"Well, well," a voice sneered. "Would you look at what the cat dragged in."

Macy shifted her focus beyond their table and inwardly sighed. *I suppose it was too much to hope for one lousy evening without confrontation.* For, as if her vagrant thought of a moment ago had summoned him, Andrew Mayfield, the author of her reputation as a tramp, strolled up to the table, trailed by what looked like the same coterie of sycophants he'd had in high school. God, things changed slowly in this town, and she had a feeling the narrowness of their minds topped the list. "Oh, goody. Asshole Andy and the Toady Team. My night is complete."

"Slept your way through the baseball team since you rolled into town?"

"Not yet. But I did play a round of golf with your daddy. He said I was the son he never had."

Andrew's face flushed, since everyone and their brother knew he'd been chasing his father's approval his entire life, to mixed results. He gave her a scathing once-over, taking in her blue bobbed wig, feathered headband, single long strand of beads and fringed flapper dress. "You're as fucking weird as ever, I see."

For a second she was thrust back to a time when she'd been the oddball outsider, scorned by her peers. But she shook it off, because the days when she would allow idiots make her feel like a loser were behind her.

And if the shaking off took several seconds longer than it should have, well, that would remain her secret. Hooking an arm over the back of her chair, she studied the man who had once taken her rejection of his sexual overtures so poorly he'd convinced an entire school she would roll onto her back for any guy who asked. "There are worse things. I could be a stone liar like you."

The woman at his side made indignant noises and, transferring her attention, Macy noticed for the first time that it was Dawn Thurborg, Liz Picket-Smith's best bud. The woman glared at her as if she'd flashed her boobs at the crowd in the bar. What *was* it with this group? The rest of the world got that ten years had passed, but this clique still seemed stuck in the archaic attitudes forged in high school.

Well, she'd attempted to play nice with Liz, and it hadn't gotten her anywhere. She wasn't wasting her breath here. "Hey there, Twilight."

"It's Dawn!"

"Oh. Sorry. You're looking perky as ever. Let me guess. Reunion committee chair, am I right?"

The other woman's chin shot up. "Second chair."

A snort escaped her. "Not a joint position, huh?" She waved an indolent hand. "But what was I thinking? Like Liz would ever share top billing."

She saw resentment flash across Dawn's face for both the truth of her statement and the fact that Macy would say it aloud where others might hear. "*You* are not invited," the other woman said coldly.

"To the reunion?" As if she had some huge burning desire to attend *that* to be vilified for three or four hours straight. Still, who elected Dawn the reunion monitor? And apparently she was no more capable now of turning the other cheek than she'd been in her Sugarville High days. "So the ten-year reunion is just for your friends, huh?" She gave the other woman a crooked smile. "Small party."

The two young women at the table next to them laughed, and one leaned back in her chair to look at her. "You can come to ours."

She grinned at them. "Why, thank you. I just might take you up on that."

Janna raised her eyebrows. "You rescinding my invitation, too, Dawn?"

The other woman blinked but then shook her head, looking as if she wondered where Liz was when she needed her. "Um, no. You can come."

"Well, lucky, lucky, me."

Dawn nodded. "*You* didn't ruin three guys' lives."

Eyes narrowed, Janna shot upright in her chair. "*Listen,* you —"

Macy gripped her cousin's arm to hold

her in place and leaned down until Janna met her gaze. "Let it go," she said quietly. "That, at least, makes more sense than riding me about so-called sexual exploits from ten freaking years ago."

"*Neither* thing makes sense," Janna said fiercely, then turned to give Andrew and Company the stink-eye. "Time for you to scoot along, Mayfield."

"Yes," Shannon agreed. "You really could use a course at the Thumper School of Charm. If you can't say anything nice, then why don't you go find your own table where you can slam each other to your heart's content?"

"Stay out of this, Chunketta," Andrew snarled. "It isn't your fight."

"No, *you* stay out of it!" Grace surged to her feet. She swayed slightly, but bracing her hand on the tabletop she faced Mayfield like a fierce little cat. "What are you, twelve? Boy, Macy was right — you are still stuck in high school. But I'd like to know where you get off insulting my friends like that. We were sitting here minding our own business — nobody invited you to come over here and start acting like a braying ass. Your father must be so proud. In fact, forget twelve — that's an insult to that age group. My gawd, I know nine-year-olds better-mannered than you."

"Is there a problem here?"

Grace collapsed back into her seat as if she'd had her legs chopped out from under her, and Macy looked past Andrew's group to Johnny Angelini. She didn't respond, and neither did her friends. They all merely raised their collective brows at the Idiot Brigade.

"No," Andrew muttered, his cheeks flushed. "No problem. We were just leaving." And he turned and walked away, his posse trailing behind him.

Johnny remained where he was, looking down at them inquiringly. Maybe that was the reason Macy jumped when she heard Jack's voice say, "What the bloody hell was that all about, luv?"

But the shock factor of seeing her friend with the deputy was nothing to the way her heart started to hammer when Gabe strode up, a pitcher in one big fist, the handles of three mugs clutched in the other. He thumped his load down on the table, threw a long leg over the chair next to hers and dropped down, one muscular thigh wedged against her seat.

"Excellent question," he said. "What the hell kind of trouble have you gotten yourself into this time?"

CHAPTER ELEVEN

Raised male voices in the pool room shouted in victory at the same time that Gabe heard an indignant "Hey!" at his own table.

Pulling his attention from Macy, he looked past her to see Janna leaning forward to glare at him.

"Don't put this on Macy," she snapped. "I'm tired of everyone automatically assuming she's to blame for every little thing that happens around here."

"Yeah, because trouble sure as hell doesn't follow her," he agreed with amiable sarcasm.

"Were you here, Gabe?" Grace demanded, and he looked across the table to find her regarding him without her usual warmth — which up until this moment not even his gently breaking up with her had managed to chill. She'd been so sweetly understanding, which was more than he'd deserved and for which he was eternally grateful.

Yet there was something funny about her

that he couldn't quite put his finger on. Then he snapped upright. Jesus. Was she trashed?

Guilt hammered him. Only . . .

If she *was* loaded, and it was due to him calling their relationship quits, she wasn't letting it slow her down any.

"We were minding our business, having a nice girls' night," she said in her I-mean-business teacher's voice, "when that buffoon strolled up with his gaggle of goons and started acting like a jackass, accusing Macy of absurd sexual doings and calling Shannon a rude name."

Say what? A muscle ticked in his jaw. No one accused Macy of absurd sexual doings — except maybe him. He did wonder, though, what constituted absurd.

"But Gracie here gave him a come-to-Jesus talk," Macy said, shooting the brunette an affectionate smile. "You're way more action figure than you give yourself credit for, girlfriend."

Gabe didn't know what the hell that was supposed to mean, but he watched it paint Grace's cheeks pink with pleasure.

"You think so?" she demanded with patent delight.

"Definitely," Macy said, and Janna and Shannon chimed in their agreement.

"Oh, my. If that's not just one of the nicest things anyone's ever said to me —" Still smiling her enjoyment, she turned her attention back to him. "But as Janna said, Gabe, don't put this on Macy." She regarded him with big eyes that weren't fully focused. "What are you doing here, anyway?"

Beats the hell out of me. One minute he'd been sitting around shooting the breeze with Johnny and the next thing he knew he was here, sitting next to Macy, way too aware of her scent, which was heady like musk and citrusy like oranges.

At least he was spared having to limp out an explanation. Jack grabbed a chair from another table and plunked it down next to Grace. Propping his elbow on the table, he braced his head in his hand and flashed her his rock-star smile.

"I got tired of my own company and found Gabe and the Garda here on Miz Watson's front porch, knockin' back lemonade. When I discovered you birds were out having all the fun, I talked them into accompanying me on a — what did you call it, mate?"

"A reconnaissance mission," Johnny supplied with an unapologetic grin as he wedged his own chair between Macy's and

Janna's. "None of us have ever been on a girls' night before."

"Do you suppose that could be because it's — hel-lo! — *girls'* night?" Janna demanded.

"That might explain it. All the same, we were curious, y'know? But not without apprehension. I mean —" he waved a hand at the three women "— all chicks, no guys. What if we get caught in the crosshairs when you decide all men are scum?"

"Oh, trust me, deputy, that was discussed and decided years ago."

Gabe's attention wandered from the conversation, his gaze drawn to Macy's hair or wig or whatever the hell it was. The thing was *blue,* for God's sake, and should have made her look ridiculous. Instead she looked edgy and exotic. Eye-catching.

Compelling.

Still, it bugged him, and he leaned into her space. "Blue?" he demanded, staring into her darkly made-up eyes. "What's with you and the costumes? You're a pretty woman —"

"Pretty is boring," she said.

He blinked. "No, it's not. Pretty's . . . appealing. Nice."

She yawned in his face and, scowling, he leaned closer. "Why are you so compelled

178

to play dress-up all the time?"

Because it's armor when the assholes are trying to drag me down. But Macy couldn't say that aloud. So she simply gave him an insouciant smile. "Because it's fun."

"Not to mention she looks cute in costume," Jack added from across the table.

She gave him a crooked smile. "Yes, not to mention that." But it was as though the pull of the large man at her side was the moon and she was the damn tide. She had a near irresistible urge to turn back to him, to get in his face and make him feel as on edge as he made her. Instead, she casually leaned back in her chair and looked around until she got the waitress's attention. Once she had it, she flashed the woman a sunny smile.

"Another round here, please?"

Grace was highly conscious of Jack Savage at her side. Not that her awareness was a big surprise. Not only was the man hot and a celebrity, he wasn't the least bit shy about checking her out.

She knew darn well how she stacked up against his usual *Playboy* Bunny types. It didn't prevent a shiver from snaking down her spine when he suddenly leaned closer and murmured, "Lace or sheer?"

Politely, she turned to face him. "I'm sorry?"

"Your knickers, luv. I was just wondering if they were lace or sheer?" He looked at her as if he had X-ray eyes. "My guess would be lace."

Certain she was going to stutter and not be able to stop, she was proud to instead manage a haughty, "You'd be wrong." *They're sheer.* "This conversation is so inappropriate I don't even know where to begin." Exciting, though. It was exhilarating not be treated like a lady for a change. "My underwear is certainly none of your business. But I'll satisfy your curiosity just this once. They're cotton. White. To the knee."

He laughed, and she had to turn away, because he made her feel so, God, just so . . . *So.*

Either people didn't ignore him, however, or he wasn't one to take a hint. He leaned right back into her space and breathed, "It's like a verbal wall-bang, isn't it?"

The spot deep between her legs clenched and she nearly gave herself whiplash turning her head to stare at him once again. *"What?"*

He indicated Gabe and Macy with a thrust of his chin. "I can't hear the specifics over the eejits in the back room, but if that conversation between Donovan and my friend Mace isn't a verbal eff, I don't know what is."

She knew her jaw was agape, but she couldn't seem to do anything about it. She didn't even glance at the subjects of this bizarre conversation, but simply stared at Jack. "You're certifiable."

"No, lass. I've seen it when a man gets that look." He reached out and hooked a strand of her hair behind her ear and goose bumps cropped up from the point of contact clear down to her ankles. "I imagine I get the same one when I look at you."

"Now I know you're punking me!" Angry that he assumed he could just mock her with impunity, she turned away once again, leaning into the table to compliment Janna on what a nice, bright kid Tyler was. But her ire rose all the while — this time directed at herself. Because she suspected Jack had every reason to believe he could get away with toying with her. If she didn't call him on his bull she was pretty much giving him permission to persist.

Equally as galling was that Savage was right about the other stuff, too. The tournament or whatever was going on in the poolroom did make conversation iffy unless you were right next to the person with whom you were attempting it. And looking at Gabe and Macy, she had to admit he might have a point about them as well, damn him.

From the little she could hear, it sounded as though they were trading their usual slings. But Gabe's posture defined sexual awareness as he leaned in, towering over the blue-haired bombshell. And although Macy didn't look as intense — she lounged in her chair with her usual insouciance — Grace couldn't help but notice, even in this dim lighting, that her cheeks were stained with color.

She felt as if she should be a little indignant — but she just couldn't work up the steam. She and Gabe simply had better-friend-than-lover chemistry.

And wasn't *that* the sorry story of her life.

Grace reached for her wine, only to murmur a swear word most people wouldn't dream she even knew when her hand encountered the Perrier. *Picked a helluva time to go back to your boring, sober ways,* she thought sourly, even as she wondered about Gabe. Had he ever looked at her that way? And if he had, how had she failed to notice?

Feeling Jack's rough-tipped fingers brush her nape, she jumped, twisting toward him. She might be cursed with nice-girl manners, but the knowing slant of his mouth, that barbell piercing his flesh just beneath the curve of his eyebrow and his heavy-lidded eyes watching her as if she were a timid mouse to his swaggering cat made something inside her snap.

She swatted his fingers away. "You think you can just make fun of me and I'll sit here and take it? Think again, Savage. I don't care if you are some hotshot rock star — I'm not nearly as mealy-mouthed as you seem to think I am —" *occasionally, anyway* "— and darned if I'll sit here listening to you ridicule me!"

He had the gall to shoot her a lopsided smile that displayed white, slightly crooked teeth. "Ooh, there's a temper under that mild-mannered exterior. I *like* it when you get all feisty — it makes me wonder what else I'd get if I scratched that silky surface. Although, just for the record, I'm not —"

"Excuse me," a female voice interrupted. "But aren't you —"

Breaking eye contact, Grace looked up and could practically *feel* her heart plunge. The young woman staring down at Jack was everything she was not. Now *that* was *Playboy* material, what with the woman's bottled red maximum-volume hair and shrink-wrap minimal clothing. A hummingbird tattoo rode the generous swell of the other female's cleavage just above her low-cut neckline.

"Omigawd," the redhead breathed reverently. "It *is* you. Can I have your autograph?"

"Sure thing, luv," Jack agreed amiably. "Got a piece of paper?"

"No, but here." Handing him a pen, she leaned forward, running scarlet-tipped fingernails along the edge of her top before tugging it farther down her breast. "Sign this."

Grace pushed back from the table.

Jack said her name and reached for her wrist, but she whipped it out of range and dodged between the tightly packed tables, just wanting to get away.

Once she'd put enough distance between herself and Jack, however, she hesitated, unsure where to go. She could head for the Ladies' but that was bound to be packed with women gossiping and freshening makeup. Shannon had driven, which was just as well, since she was probably in no condition to climb behind the wheel, anyhow. That's all she'd need to round out her night — to end up in a jail cell for driving under the influence.

"Crap," she whispered and made her way

to the front entrance, where she let herself out.

The noise level decreased dramatically as the Red Dog's front door closed behind her. The night air had cooled a good twenty degrees from the day's high eighties, and she picked her way across the crowded blacktop, weaving between tightly packed pickup trucks, American-made sedans and the occasional foreign car to the edge of the lot. It was dark and quiet and she wrapped her arms around herself, leaned against the trunk of a misshapen alder tree and stared out at the stars and a neon slice of moon.

She didn't know how long she stood there. Occasionally she'd hear laughter and music as the bar door opened, but then it would fade as it closed again, until the only sound left was the crickets in the wheat fields stretching out behind the Red Dog.

The soft slide of a shoe whispered against the blacktop behind her, and she whirled, thinking that seeking out the darkest, most isolated section of the lot maybe wasn't the brightest move she could have made.

But it wasn't some drunk looking to relieve himself or the Mad Rapist. It was Jack.

Which, come to think, wasn't a huge improvement. She pressed her back harder against the tree trunk.

He walked straight up to her, not stopping until he was less than a foot away. Gripping an overhead branch with both hands, he considered her, his usual easy smile missing.

"I only meant to tease you, Grace. Nothing I said was intended to mock or ridicule you." The densely patterned tattoos on his right arm were briefly illuminated in the meager moonlight as he lowered his hand as if to touch her. But if that was his intention, he changed his mind, for he reached back up to grip the branch again.

She blew out a sigh, because, really, this guy was so far out of her sphere it was just stupid to get all bent out of shape over not being *Playboy* material in a world where tens of thousands of women were. "You don't have to try to make me feel better," she said without heat. "I get that I'm not your type."

"Do you, now? And what would my type be?"

"Girls who yank down their tops so you can autograph their boobs."

"Are you daft?" Pushing off the branch, he took a step back, shoving his hands in his jeans pockets. "Birds like that are a dime a dozen — there ain't feckall unique about

186

'em. I wasn't kidding when I said I go for you Peter Pan–collar girls. Women with conversation to them, not just a set of tits on display."

A little throb pulsed deep inside and being a half glass of wine less circumspect than usual she said, "Congratulations. You have the distinction of being the only man to have ever said 'tits' to me."

"I'm sorr—" Looking at her, he cut himself off. And gave her a crooked smile. "You like it."

She raised her chin. "I do not."

"Yeah, you do. I'm thinking blokes treat you like Royal Tara fine bone and maybe you're a little tired of it."

She licked her lips. "Maybe."

"I know a whole raft of nasty words, both American and Irish. Want me to whisper a few in your ear?"

A laugh burbled out of her throat. "No."

"Probably just as well. I don't poach other men's preserves."

"Ignoring for the moment your charming chauvinism — other men's preserves, my fanny —"

A huge guffaw exploded from his throat and she gave him a narrow-eyed look. "What's so darn funny."

He grinned. "In Ireland, a fanny —"

"Yeah, yeah, is a butt. Big deal. I do know that word."

"Uh, not exactly. In my country a fanny is a bit farther forward."

"What the heck are you talking about, farther forw— oh. *Oh!* You mean — ?"

"Uh-huh." He seemed to get a huge kick out of the way that flustered her but then sobered a bit and said, "So, my chauvinism aside, what?"

"Huh?" She was still hung up on the differences in American and Irish slang. Then she caught herself. "Oh. Gabe and I broke it off."

"No shite?" Stepping forward, he gripped the branch again and leaned into her. "Then you sure you don't want to hear some dirty words?" His breath, lightly scented with beer, wafted against her lips. "I know some bleedin' deadly ones."

"You know words that will kill me?"

She felt rather than saw him smile. "No, luv. Brilliant, that means. I could impress you, dazzle you, even, with my fine grasp of smut speak."

"Maybe I'll say some more to you."

"Ah, no." He closed the gap between them to press a gentle kiss on her lips. Pulling back, he whispered, "This mouth is much too sweet to pollute with filthy talk." Then he grinned at her. "At least on the first date."

He might be playing her, but with her heart banging in her chest and lips throbbing, she decided she didn't care. Sublimating her natural inclination toward sexual shyness, she tentatively unleashed her inner hottie. She wrapped her hands around his neck, hauled herself up onto her tiptoes and kissed him.

And apparently did a decent job of it, because Jack made a sound deep in his throat and took control, his hands hauling her against his body, his mouth growing hard, avid, against hers. This was no she's-a-lady kiss he laid on her. This was let's-get-down-and-dirty, all tongue and teeth and Jack's-in-command.

She went up in flames. Climbing him like a kid on a Big Toy, she wrapped her legs around his waist and tangled tongues with him, letting loose her inner slut for real.

He backed her up against the trunk of the tree, his body as it pressed her breasts, her hips, her belly, every bit as hard as the bark against her back. A needy moan escaped her.

"Step away from her, Savage."

Shock jolted through Grace at the sound of Gabe's voice, and she stared into Jack's eyes as he lifted his mouth from hers and stared down at her. He didn't look happy.

"I thought you said you and Donovan were through."

"We are!"

It bugged her that he looked to Gabe for confirmation, but to be fair she supposed a man in his position might hear a lot of lies.

Gabe nodded. "We are," he agreed. "But she's put away more wine than she's used to tonight and I won't let anyone take advantage of that."

Jack looked at her. "That true, darlin'? You fluthered?"

"No!" Then honesty compelled her to admit, "Well, maybe." She held up her hand, showing him her thumb and index finger held so infinitesimally apart you'd be lucky to fit a cat's whisker between them. "A tiny bit."

"Damn." He stepped back. Running his fingers over his buzz cut, he regarded her. "Go on home, Gracie. We'll try this again when you're sober."

She was frustrated, embarrassed and feeling downright sulky. "Maybe I won't be in the mood then."

He just regarded her silently for a protracted moment, then nodded. "That's what

I'm afraid of, luv. But come see me if you are."

And turning on his heel, he strode off across the lot.

CHAPTER TWELVE

"Sonofa— !"

Gabe's sudden chopped-off expletive in the midst of dinner made Macy jerk in surprise — then slap splayed fingers to her chest as he exploded from his seat, sending the solid-oak chair tumbling to the floor with a resounding crash. All around the table, the boarders, like her, similarly flinched, yelped or leaped to their feet.

But Uncle Bud's uncharacteristic blasphemy as he, too, got up, sliced through the racket. He tossed his napkin toward his plate and didn't notice when it fluttered to the floor. "Fire!" he barked, jabbing a thick finger toward the dining room window behind her.

"What?" Shock had her recoiling all over again. "Where?" Then, swinging around, she saw what Gabe and her uncle had seen: a thin, oily column of smoke rising from the adjoining property on the other side of the

small rise. "Is that the Driscolls' place?" she demanded as she rose, but her voice was merely one in a cacophony of exclamations and questions.

Gabe ignored them all. Already thumbing his cell, he was halfway to the door, but paused to look over his shoulder at Bud. "Do you know where I'll find water over there?"

Bud shook his head. "From the color of that smoke, I'm guessing it's the shed Driscoll keeps his roofing supplies in, but I'm not sure where his water connection is in relation to it. There's a creek running through his property that might not be too far away, though." He trained a steady gaze on the younger man. "Tell me what I can do to help."

"You can —" Gabe turned away to growl instructions into his phone. Snapping it shut a moment later, he looked back at Bud. "One of my men is already on his way to the fire truck and another will meet us on the property." His glance encompassed everyone milling around. "All of you grab as many containers as you can find and meet me over there. If we can find a faucet or if that creek is near enough, maybe we can do some damage control until the truck gets there."

They scattered in all directions in search of buckets and dishpans. Macy corralled Ty and Charlie and went with Jack out to his trailer, where they emptied it of anything that would hold liquid. They threw their finds into the bed of his truck, loaded up the boys, climbed in and roared off, Macy providing terse directions to the neighbor's driveway.

Pulling up behind Gabriel's vehicle moments later, they saw old man Driscoll frantically aiming a garden hose emitting a stream of water that looked woefully puny at the burning outbuilding. Gabe was hastily pulling on bulky beige pants with neon-yellow stripes circling the hems, then catching their dangling suspenders and hauling the padded straps up over his shoulders. He stamped his feet into big boots, then shoved his arms into a jacket that matched the pants as he strode over to relieve Driscoll of the hose. Macy jumped out of the truck in time to hear him instructing the farmer to wheel his irrigation sprinkler over.

Other vehicles rolled in, and the Experimental boys arrived on foot, having raced across the field. Gabe turned to the gathering. "Driscoll tells me the creek is over that rise about seventy-five feet." He pointed to Bud. "Organize a bucket brigade — let's get as much water up here as we can until my truck gets here."

They did as directed, Tyler squatting in the creek, scooping water into containers that Charlie then took and passed to Lenore who passed it to Bud and on up the line. It seemed to Macy that she twisted, grabbed, turned and passed for a long time as choking smoke filled the air around them. It was probably less than ten minutes, however, before they heard the dissonant horn of the pumper truck sounding from the highway. Then it was there, wheeling into the Driscoll property.

Gabe was at its side even as it rocked to a stop, and she watched him pull a hose from its berth as a pump switched on. It pulsed from flat and inanimate to round and alive in his hands. One of his firemen swung out of the cab of the truck at the same time another screeched into the yard, threw his vehicle into Park and leaped out. They started unfolding two additional hoses.

Macy knew the rest of them were no longer needed. Realizing as well that Ty and Charlie were bound to be overly excited and that Janna, left behind at the boardinghouse, was equally likely to be beside herself with anxiety and curiosity, she went to collect the boys to take them home. But she turned, walking backward as she watched Gabriel wield the hose.

He was standing close enough to the fire to singe his eyebrows, sucking smoke and handling a hose that would probably send her whipping around like an out-of-control buckaroo — and a big grin shone white in his increasingly sooty face. With an odd little start, she realized he had been . . . amazing tonight. Clear and concise. Focused and in charge.

She watched as he disappeared inside the shed. *God.* Not to mention *that.* There was something mind-blowing about seeing someone voluntarily enter a burning building when everyone else's instinct was to flee as far from it as they could get. It was hard to tear her gaze away.

But she did so, because the last thing she needed was to develop a thing for Gabriel Donovan. She had a lousy track record when it came to men. She had yet to pick herself a winner, and there was sure as hell no reason to think her ability in that arena had suddenly improved.

So she shoved the fire chief right out of her head and, whirling, went to find Jack and her family. From now on, she was back to playing it smart.

She was giving Gabe the widest berth she

could devise.

"Oh, excellent timing, sweetheart," Lenore said a few days later when Macy strolled into the kitchen. "You're the answer to my prayer. Here." The older woman thrust a small cooler at her. "I need you to deliver this for me."

Macy took it before its rounded corner could poke her in the chest. "Deliver where? What is it?"

"Gabe's lunch. He's working on his house out near Buzzard Canyon, at the end of Coulee Road. Take it to him."

"What? No." She tried to hand it back, but Lenore turned away.

Her aunt did deign to direct a gaze over her shoulder, however, as she picked up a cleaver and whipped a raw chicken onto the chopping board without so much as glancing down at it. "Why?" she demanded. "You have plans with Tyler?"

"Noooo," Macy admitted. "He's at Charlie's today."

"Janna need you?"

"You know she's at PT until four-thirty."

"Are you and Jack working on that video thing?"

She shook her head. "Not right this minute."

"Then haul your skinny behind over to Gabe's property and deliver that lunch. I told him I'd send it over, and no one else is around right now to take it." Her voice went cool, developing that neutral tone it only got when she was displeased with or disappointed in someone. "Unless you're too important to run a simple errand for me."

Macy *hated* having that tone directed at her. "No, ma'am. I'll get right on it." She slammed out the door, missing the crooked little grin her aunt directed at the chicken carcass.

She was tempted to tool around the back roads for a while instead of heading straight over to Gabe's place. Blowing out a breath, however, she decided to act like the grown-up she liked to pretend she was. It wasn't his fault, she supposed, that she had this stupid fascination, or whatever the heck it was, for him. So she'd just drop off his lunch, then jet.

Easy peasy.

And perhaps her luck had turned for the better, she thought as she drove up the approach to a close-to-finished house and didn't see another vehicle. Maybe Gabriel had run into Jacob's Hardware to get something for his job here. Whoo-hoo. She grabbed the cooler and climbed from the

'Vet, slamming the door behind her. She'd just leave this for him on the front porch and be on her way.

"Yo! Around back."

Crap. Well, there was no dodging her obligation now. She stalked around the side of the house, heading in the direction of Gabe's voice.

Rounding the back, she caught sight of him, standing on a scaffold rigged between two sawhorses, putting up siding on an enclosed porch, and stopped dead. *Hell, hell, hell.*

He was stripped to the waist, all sweat-sheened skin, hard shoulders and long silky spine, a leather tool belt riding his hips. He lifted a long narrow board and fitted it beneath others of its kind atop a weatherization wrap. The overhead position made the muscles in his arms and shoulders bunch and flex and afforded her a glimpse of black armpit hair and a white stripe of skin where the small of his back lifted out of his waistband. Holding the board in place with one hand, he reached for a nail gun atop a nearby step ladder and — *thwack! thwack, thwack, thwack!* — the board was tacked in place. He walked the length of the scaffold, adding nails to finish securing it.

Setting the gun back atop the ladder, he

wiped his hands on the worn seat of his jeans. "Is it beer break time already?"

"No, it's lunchtime." She walked up and set the cooler on the sawhorse opposite from where he stood. "I'll just leave this here."

Gabe whipped around so fast one foot swept space, his heel barely regaining its purchase on the edge of the plank. The sudden swoop his gut took, however, owed nothing to the misstep. "I thought you were Johnny."

She regarded him without her usual flirtatious smile. "As you can see, I'm not."

No shit. Oh, she wasn't all sassed up for once, no lipstick — or makeup of any kind that he could tell, for that matter — and her amber-ale hair was piled atop her head in a haphazard knot. Her skinny-rib yellow tank and navy rubber flip-flops looked Wal-Mart ordinary, and her cutoffs were a mess of raggedy strings straggling down her thighs. But there was no mistaking her for the deputy. And, unaccountably, it was a look that made him hotter than those fuck-me costumes she usually favored.

She waved a hand at the cooler in a gesture strangely elegant. "So, there's your lunch, courtesy of Auntie L," she said. "Enjoy." She turned away.

"Not so fast." *Let her go let her go.* But he didn't want to. He was tired of pretending he didn't look at her and want to slide her shorts down her long legs, thumb aside the crotch of her panties and bury himself hard and deep inside of her.

And why shouldn't he do just that, if she was similarly inclined? He was a long way from seventeen. For years he'd been careful to stay away from anything smacking of excess passion, and it had given him the restraint, the discipline, he'd so sorely needed at the time. But the truth was, slipping-the-leash sex wasn't going to turn him into the angry, foulmouthed kid he'd been back then. Hell, he'd now been a hard-working, responsible adult for as many years as he'd been alive at the time he'd decided on the course that had turned his life around.

And he didn't want to watch her walk away, which she was doing even as he thought it. "As long as you're here, why don't you make yourself useful."

"Excuse me?" She turned back. "I'm not your lackey, Donovan."

"C'mon. These boards take a lot longer when I'm handling them on my own — we could get the mudroom sided in a snap if you'd lend me a hand."

201

"And that's supposed to matter to me why?"

"Beats the hell outta me." Sparring with her always made him feel somehow lighter, and a big laugh rolled out of his chest. "Because you're a decent woman who hates to see Sugarville's overworked, underpaid fire chief spend his few free hours working in the broiling sun?"

"Pffft. That doesn't bother me at all. Now a grown man whining like an eight-year-old, on the other hand —"

"A big fire could burn something to the ground because I'm way out here when it starts." Okay, it was hard to keep a straight face with that one, since his guys took turns staying within a reasonable distance of the truck. And she had to know it, given the other night.

But it worked. She blew out a sigh. "Oh, all right. Whatever."

Her sulky tone tickled him and he shot her a grin. "You're a doll."

"Damn straight. So what is it, exactly, that you want me to do?"

Oh, mama. He looked at those lips, those legs. There was a lead-in if ever he heard one. But having learned a thing or two over the years, he merely hopped off the work bench and reached for a new length of HardiPlank. "Climb up on the other end. Here — let me get you something to bridge the gap." He thunked a pier block in front of the scaffold at her end and offered her a hand up, shrugging when she snorted and stepped up unaided.

He climbed on with the board, showed her how he fit it beneath the already-applied siding and had her hold it in place while he worked his way down the wall with the nail gun. His shoulder and arm brushed hers as he leaned in to tack her end of the board.

"Ty hasn't stopped talking about the fire the other evening," she said. "I think his current plan is to be a fireman when he grows up." She shrugged. "Well, that or a rock star like Jack. He told me, though, that you said Driscoll's fire was arson."

"Yeah. One more in a string of them."

"Whoa." She looked at him. "That doesn't sound like Sugarville."

"So everyone keeps telling me." And it burned his ass that not only were the fires happening on his watch but apparently escalating in seriousness. "I mean to put an end to them."

He reached her portion of the plank again and she leaned back when he leaned in front of her to finish securing the very end. There was only so far she could go on the narrow bench, however, and that simply made his biceps brush her breasts this time instead of her arm or shoulder. Heat shot down his spine and he didn't stop to think. Turning to her, he reached out to turn her toward him, as well. "God, you make me crazy," he said hoarsely. "I've got to —"

She came up onto her toes and kissed him.

Yes. He closed his eyes in sheer pleasure, absorbing her addictive flavors. His hands tightening possessively, he yanked her to him, making body slap body, his heat to her cooler skin, nothing separating them but a scrap or two of cotton and denim.

Her hands tightened on his shoulders as well, nails flexing and retracting like a cat's as he spun them a half turn until her back touched the wall of the porch. Releasing his grip, palms flattening against the boards on either side of her head, he leaned into her, rubbing chest to breasts, hard-on to belly, while his tongue stroked and twined around hers. Then he bent his knees, aligning his sex with hers.

She moaned deep in her throat and savage satisfaction flared through him. *Yes. Like that. Mine.*

The thought jarred him. *No.* He tore his mouth from hers, staring down at her for a second while confusion roiled in his gut.

What was he thinking? He didn't do posses-
sive. He was just looking for a nice uncomplicated fuck. Yeah. Uncomplicated. None
of that flowers/chocolates/lovey-dovey shit.

He lowered his mouth to hers once again.

Yet even as his mouth ravaged hers, even
as the rock, the press, the rub of his body
against hers drew forth more soft sounds
from her throat, his thoughts jumped to the
kiss he'd caught Savage giving Grace outside
the Red Dog. Which made him wonder just
what the hell Macy's relationship was with
the guy.

He shoved it out of his head. Because
what the freaking hell did he care what their
relationship was? It wasn't as if this was
leading to anything exclusive. But the sweet
heat of Macy's mouth, the soft compliance
of her body moving against his, made ignoring it pretty much out of the question. He
tried. But the deeper he kissed her to make
himself forget, the more he *wondered.* Had
she moved like this, moaned like this for
Savage? No matter how hard he worked to
push the question away, his mind kept
circling back to worry it like a puppy with a
knotted rag.

Until finally he tore his mouth free and
demanded, "Does it bug you that Savage
was kissing Grace the other night?"

"Wha?" Licking her lips, she blinked at him as if she were in a fog. Slowly her eyes focused. "Jack kissed Grace?"

Oh, hell. "Yeah. I thought you knew."

No, she didn't. And wasn't that interesting, Macy thought. She'd spent several hours with Jack this week, arguing over which song should be Aussie Kiss's first release from their upcoming album and thrashing out the finer points of her concept for its video. And Jack, who wasn't usually shy about discussing the women who interested him, hadn't said boo about locking lips with Gracie.

But that was something to consider later when her body wasn't throbbing with unsatisfied lust. Now, she looked up at Gabe. "What do you care if he was or not?" she demanded. "You dumped her, but nobody else can kiss her?"

"I didn't dump her! And that's not the point —"

Her heart dropped. "Are you two still together?" Oh, crap, that wasn't what Grace had said.

"Well, no, but —"

She narrowed her eyes at him. "But nothing, bub. Unless . . . Did *she* break up with you?" Although, again, that wasn't what —

"No, but —"

"Then you *did* dump her, Donovan." And yet here he was, less than a week later, putting the moves on *her.* Not that she hadn't liked every moment of it. But still, he was kissing her but thinking about *Grace?* "Jeez! Men are such dogs." Shaking her head, she stepped back from him, careful to watch her step so he'd have no reason to touch her again. "And what the hell am I doing here, anyhow, helping one of your species?"

She jumped down. "Do your own siding. And don't forget to bring Auntie's cooler back!"

"Dammit, Macy!"

She stormed off, refusing to acknowledge that her anger might have less to do with Gabriel's interest in Grace than it did his effect on her. Everything about him lit her up: the way he looked — all that heat and muscle and smooth, taut skin. The way he moved, so lithe and powerful. And then there'd been his laugh — God, that *laugh.* It had turned her inside out every bit as much as his scorching kisses. It had rolled up from his belly and stopped her heart — then set it thundering again.

The man made her just plain stupid, and she didn't like it. She didn't like the thumping pulse, the kiss-me, do-me, *kiss*-me impulses that sparked through her veins, along her nerve endings, simply because he was near. This wasn't her. She'd learned a long time ago to slap on a front, to laugh and flirt and call the shots. But Gabe left her feeling all out of control. Every damn time.

Well, screw that. Stalking over to the 'Vet, she climbed in and cranked over the engine with a roar. Slamming it into gear she backed in a tight circle, then threw it into First and roared back down the drive.

Screw it, screw it, screw it. That crap stopped *now.*

CHAPTER THIRTEEN

Gabe heard Macy talking to Lenore in the kitchen and came to a halt out in the hallway. He had to rein in his first impulse, which was to march in there and demand to know what her problem was. He'd asked one pertinent, perfectly reasonable question the last time they were together and her response was to get all bent out of shape and storm off? Not to mention that for the past week and a half, ever since that day, except for the occasional well-chaperoned glimpse at dinner, he'd barely clapped eyes on her.

For someone so red-hot conspicuous, she sure as hell had a knack for disappearing when the mood hit her.

"Isn't he cute, Auntie?" he heard her say now. "He followed me home. Can I keep him?"

"Depends on how house-trained he is," Lenore replied dryly.

She'd allowed a dog to follow her home? What was the story on that?

He snorted. As if he'd be the first one she'd rush to tell. But he'd bet the farm it was a male critter she'd flirted with until it'd had no choice but to dog her footsteps.

With a shrug, he continued into the dining room to take his seat, absentmindedly returning greetings to the AAE boys and Mr. Grandview. What the hell did he care? It was nothing to him what Macy did, and besides, he was bound to hear the entire story at dinner, anyway. Still, if she had picked up a stray mutt somewhere, he'd put money down it wasn't a real dog like a golden retriever or a Weimaraner. She'd probably adopt one of those bug-eyed little ankle nippers that seemed to spend their lives wearing weird-ass outfits and riding around in chicks' purses.

It turned out he was wrong — and he came halfway out of his seat when a geeky-looking guy, staring at Macy as if he'd won the Mega Millions Lotto, trailed her into the dining room. Then Gabe resettled. Gave his shoulders an impatient roll. So, again, big deal. No skin off his stones.

"Hey, everyone, meet Jeremy. Jeremy, this is . . . everyone. Grab a seat," she urged him, grasping his scrawny wrist and hauling him over until they were directly across from Gabe. "Here's a couple together." She grinned at the guy, plopped down next to him when he sat, then quickly went around the table solicitously identifying everyone for him.

Since she and her pet nerd were the last to arrive, the platters started around the moment she concluded introductions. Gabe watched as she fussed over the weedy little guy, helping him select the choicest piece of fried chicken from the platter and picking the plumpest biscuit for him.

Today she wore her hair puffed at the crown and her eyes more thickly lashed than usual, as well as dramatically outlined in black. She had on tight black capris, high-heeled sandals and a black polka-dotted white bra — or so the latter garment appeared to him.

"Christ," he muttered. "I guess if it's Tuesday, it must be sex-kitten day."

Jack grinned. "Macy likes to channel her inner Brigitte Bardot occasionally."

"You'd know." Gabe glowered at him, too, because . . . hell, he didn't know why. Just for drill.

"Don't bark at Jack," Macy snapped.

"You're right. Sorry, pal," he said without taking his gaze off her. "I'm just wondering why it doesn't bother you she's wearing her underwear in public." The two of them being so tight and all.

"Probably because he knows the difference between underwear and this," she retorted in a tone suggesting he was an idiot.

And he must be, because given its underwire cups and lingerie straps he sure as hell couldn't see the distinction. Brows furrowing, he gave Jack an *Is she serious?* look.

Jack merely shrugged. "Don't ask me, mate."

Bud leaned forward to look down the table at Macy's date. "So, Jeremy, you new in town?"

The geek tore his gaze from Macy's cleavage. Squinted at the older man. "I'm just visiting my cousin Henry."

"And yet instead of hanging with him," Gabe muttered, "here you are. At our table."

Macy slapped her hand down on the table. "Listen, you ass —"

"Where you visiting from?" Janna asked.

"Spokane."

"Nice town. What do you do there?"

"He's an accountant," Macy said, giving the back of Jeremy's hand a brotherly pat. "Don't you just love a cerebral man?"

Gabe's cell phone rang and he said a heartfelt, "Thank you, Jesus," because for some damn reason he felt seconds away from snatching her hand off Mr. Cerebral's arm and dragging her out to the porch for a little . . . discussion.

Why he couldn't exactly say. Still, he was grateful for the interruption. The screen showed it was Bundy, one of his volunteers. *Please,* he thought, hitting the button with his thumb. *Let this be a nice big fire.* "Talk to me."

"I'm at the Feed and Seed, Chief," Bundy said. "Got a possible lead on the arsons."

"I'm on my way." Shoving his phone back in its holster, he tore a hunk of meat from the chicken breast on his plate and stuffed it into a biscuit as he surged to his feet. "Sorry about disrupting your dinner, Lenore," he said and loped from the room.

What the hell's the matter with you? Scowling, he climbed into his rig, shoved his key in the ignition and, firing it up, slammed it into gear. *Now you're wishing for fucking* wildfires *to cancel your own lack of control every time you get near the woman?*

Jesus. For over a week he'd been obsessing over that damn kiss. It had been hot and fierce and sweet — and he couldn't seem to get it out of his head. He prided himself on being an in-charge kinda guy. But she was making him just flat-out crazy.

Not in charge at all.

He pulled into the feed store a minute later, happy to shelve the subject. Happier yet to whip his cloak of professionalism around him. The Closed sign was up in the entrance's sidelight, but the door was unlocked and he found Bundy and Joe Mc-Fadden, the proprietor, in the back. "What've we got?"

Bundy gestured for McFadden to talk.

"This may be nothing, Chief," McFadden said, "But I was hauling some pallets out back when I saw Colin Atkins and the Kaufman boy not far from my Dumpster. Colin had a box of matches he was tossing up and catching. Not that I saw him actually use them. Neither did the boys run away or anything when they saw me. They strolled off easy as you please, so it may be that they were just looking for a place to sneak a smoke. Only —"

"There're better places to do that," Gabe said. "Places where they'd be less likely to be seen."

"That was my thought. Plus, something about it just made me think of all the odd fires we've been having this summer."

"Daylight and business hours, however, doesn't strike me as the best time to chance starting a fire."

"True. Although I did stay late to clean up the pallets the feed shipment came in on instead of going home after I closed the store. But that just strengthens the argument for them thinking it'd be safe to smoke a cigarette or maybe do a little weed back there." He rubbed the back of his neck. "I'm probably being paranoid."

"Maybe so, maybe no." Gabe gave the store owner a level look. "I tell you what, though, Mr. McFadden, I'd rather be called in to discuss your concerns beforehand than try to save your store after it's already been set on fire." He turned to Bundy. "I'm not familiar with either kid. What are the odds of their parents letting us question them?"

"Without actually catching them in the act? Not great. There's maybe a chance with Colin —"

McFadden made a skeptical noise and Bundy nodded. "Yeah, you're right, probably not. And Jake's old man is Gus Kaufman. No way in hell he'd allow it."

"Damn." He eyed the two men. "Either of you know whether the boys have access to a car?"

"I don't think so," McFadden said. "Or if they do, it's not very often. I don't recall seeing either of them driving around town."

"So if they're out and about at night, it'd

likely be around the neighborhoods or the retail area."

The merchant nodded. "That would be my guess."

Gabe turned to his fireman. "Any chance you'd be willing to do a little surveillance with me this evening?" he asked. "I have to tell you up front that the mayor probably won't authorize payment."

"Hell, I'm in." The beefy fireman shrugged. "It's not like I got myself a hot date tonight. And unlike you, I don't share the same roof with the world's hottest video queen — so there's no huge incentive to rush home."

Gabe flashed on an image of bra-clad Macy fawning all over the nerd, and his teeth clenched. But he managed a wry smile for his crewman. "Maybe I can score you an autograph. You can't spend it, but I suppose it's better than a poke in the eye with a sharp stick." Turning to McFadden, he thrust out his hand. "Thank you for calling us. We'll do our best to follow up on your information."

Outside, he turned to his man. "As well-thought-out schemes go, this one is pretty half-assed." Opening the door of his rig, he looked at Bundy over its top. "But hop in, anyhow. I get the impression you and Mc-

Fadden consider these kids players, punks, or at least largely unsupervised kids?"

"Yeah." They climbed into the SUV and Bundy turned to look at him as they buckled up. "Both families have a history of letting their kids run wild. The Kaufman and Atkins kids don't have *Brady Bunch* home lives and tend not to spend a lot of time there. They're known to get into trouble, but mostly it's been petty stuff."

"Let's track down Johnny Angelini. If anyone has experience with the town's troublemakers, it'll be him. Maybe he can shed some light on where we're likely to find these two."

When they found Johnny twenty minutes later, he gave them places to look where the boys usually hung out. Gabe and Bundy spent the next couple hours checking out the kids' haunts but failed to run across them.

Finally, Gabe blew out a breath, pulled a U-ie and headed back to the Feed and Seed where Bundy'd left his vehicle. "It's going to be full dark in about five and we're going in circles. Let's call it a night."

"Sounds good to me," Bundy agreed. "Who knew you could get so played out just driving around?"

They were approaching Cedar Street

where the Feed and Seed was when his passenger suddenly said, "Holy shit. That's them."

Gabe's head whipped around. "Where?"

"They just turned down Hemlock."

Cutting the lights, Gabe let the SUV drift over to the curb, where he shut down the engine. "I'd like to see what they're up to. Let's try to follow them without them making us."

It was easier than he'd imagined, since the boys failed to even glance behind them. They bumped and shoved each other as they ambled down the street, laughing and exchanging rowdy ripostes.

Then, at the mouth of the alley separating A-1 Garage from Morgan's Rent-A-Car, they paused and did shoot furtive looks over their shoulders. Gabe and Bundy melted back into the shadow of the retreads stack in the side yard of Kelly's Tires. When Gabe eased his head back out to chance a look down the street, the boys were gone.

"Must've gone down the alley," he breathed, and he and Bundy cautiously emerged from their hiding place. Without discussion they sought whatever concealment they could find as they approached the mouth of the alley. Standing to one side, he craned his head around the corner of the building and was in time to see the boys toss burning twists of paper into a Dumpster. It ignited with a whoosh.

"Shit. Call in the truck." He started down the alley, but concealment here was zero. The boys, who'd been staring at the flames, spotted him and raced for the other end of the alley. He sprinted after them.

Bundy pulled abreast seconds later. "Truck's on its way. I'll take the one on the right."

The boys looked over their shoulders but must have thought the men on their tails posed no threat, because they laughed and put on a burst of speed. It wasn't for nothing, however, that Gabe had spent umpteen years humping hoses weighing over a hundred pounds empty — and considerably more when water pumped through them — up smoke-filled flights of stairs. It had conditioned Bundy as well, clearly, since the younger man pulled ahead of him.

The kids shot out of the alley and hooked right. Gabe exited in time to see them scaling a chain-link fence into the lumberyard. Bundy was scrambling over it in their wake and Gabe cleared it twenty seconds behind his crewman. They began closing in on the teens.

Casting ever-more frantic glances over

their shoulders, the boys weren't laughing now as they dodged between fragrant stacks of two-by-fours.

One foot skidding on something, Bundy went down, catching himself on his hand. Gabe slowed marginally as he came abreast. "You good?"

"Yeah, go, go!" The fireman was already pushing himself upright.

Gabe caught up with one of the teens at the far fence. The boy was near the top, about to swing a leg over, when Gabe pushed off with the ball of his foot and took a flying leap, catching a toehold in one diamond-shaped link and grabbing hold of a couple of others with his fingers and thumb. The fence rattled as, reaching up with his free hand, he grabbed a fistful of the kid's waistband and jerked. The teen started to fall sideways and had to scramble to find purchase for the foot still in the air.

Without relinquishing his grip, Gabe dropped back to the ground, popping the boy's grip from the links and hauling him down with him. Through the fence he could see the other punk racing down Cedar toward McFadden's store.

He transferred his grip from the youth's Levis to a fistful of T-shirt as Bundy ran by and hauled himself up and over the fence.

His crewman dropped to the other side and raced off after the fleeing adolescent.

"Hey, perv, lemme go!" The sandy-blond boy in his grasp twisted and turned like a worm trying to avoid being threaded on a hook. "You gotta go into Wenatchee you want some that action," he sneered. "I don't swing that way."

"Kid, I doubt you have the balls to swing either way."

The teen put some extra muscle into trying to escape and Gabe gave him a shake. "Knock it off. I don't want to hurt you — but I will if I have to. So which one are you, anyway, Atkins or Kaufman?"

The boy went still, as if it had never occurred to him that Gabe might have tumbled to his identity. He snapped his mouth shut.

Gabe gave him a don't-screw-with-me look. "We can make this easy or hard — makes no never mind to me. So what's it gonna be? You want to play games or are you going to tell me if you're Atkins or Kaufman?"

"Atkins," the boy mumbled.

"Well, Colin, you're in some deep shit." Fishing his cell from its holster, he thumbed in Johnny's number. "Got me a bona fide arsonist," he said when the deputy answered. "And Bundy's seconds from laying hands on the kid's partner in crime. We've got a Dumpster fire in the alley between Hemlock and Cedar just beyond A-1 — my truck's on the way. Clear out a room for me to interrogate them."

"You got it," Johnny said, the same time as Colin said, "Dude, you ain't no cop — you can't interrogate us!"

He snapped the cell closed. "Hate to burst your bubble, kid, but the county hired me because I'm licensed to do just that. They got a fire chief and investigator rolled into one."

In less than a half hour, Bundy had corralled the second boy, the fire had been put out by Kirschner and Johnson, and Gabe was ensconced in the sheriff's department's sole interrogation room with the two boys and Johnny, who had asked to sit in.

Pulling out a chair and taking a seat, he clicked his pen and looked across the table at the teenagers. "First thing we need is your phone numbers," he said, pushing the pen and his notebook over to them. "We'll have to get your parents in here."

"No!" They said in unison.

"You can't tell them," Jake added, sounding horrified.

"I have no choice if you're a minor."

"But we're not!" Colin said. "Jake turned eighteen in June and I just had my eighteenth birthday last week."

"Yeah? Let's see some ID."

Jake pulled out a driver's license and Colin a Washington State ID card. Gabe studied them and nodded. "All right, then." Sliding them back to their owners, he shrugged. "That's kind of good news/bad news for you," he said. "It means you can refuse to have your parents present. But if I find cause to ask the prosecutor to charge you, you could also be tried as an adult." He looked at Johnny. "You have a Miranda card?"

The deputy handed him one and he read the boys their rights. "Knowing and understanding your rights as I've explained them to you, are you willing to answer my questions without an attorney present?"

They exchanged a glance, then gave a jerky nod.

"I need that verbalized for the record."

"Yeah," Colin mumbled and Jake Kaufman added his sullen agreement. "Like we got a choice," he muttered.

"You're eighteen. That means you do have a choice. So if you're changing your mind, call your attorney and we'll wait until he gets here. Or you can talk to me now and

223

see if we can straighten this out."

"I said no attorney, didn't I?" Jake said.

"Okay, let's get down to it, then. Considering I witnessed you setting it, we have you dead to rights for tonight's fire. What I'm more interested in are the others you've set this summer."

He could see the lie already forming in their expressions and hardened his own. "Do not give me any bull about this being your first, because I know better. We've had four garbage-can and three Dumpster fires in various businesses here in town this summer. We've also had to put out sheds that sustained serious property damage on two separate farms outside of town."

"What the hell?" Colin said indignantly. "We didn't set no sheds on fire!"

Jake gave his friend a shot to the shoulder. "Shut up, Colin!"

Gabe looked at the slightly older boy. "Are you saying you did?"

"Hell, no!"

"Look, if you're trying to avoid incriminating yourself in the can and Dumpster fires, it's too late to pretend you didn't set them, because we know you did. You watch *CSI*?" At the young men's sullen nods, he said, "I rock arson forensics, kid. I can establish a pattern that ties you to them." *If this were a*

TV show. "But the Dumpsters are fairly small spuds and we can probably work something out. The sheds, on the other hand —"

"You gonna let them throw the book at us for something we didn't do?" Colin demanded of his friend.

"Okay, okay, it wasn't us," Jake said. "Those sheds. We didn't touch 'em."

Gabe was skeptical by nature. But he was beginning to think that might be the truth. "But you concede the can and Dumpster fires, yes?"

Jake looked at his friend, stared down at his hands, then flipped his shiny brown hair out of his eyes and nodded. "Yeah."

Gabe thought it over. His working assumption had been that the firebug was escalating, because what were the odds they'd get two separate arsonists in a town that until this summer had never seen one? Yet thinking about the lighted twists of paper he'd watched the kids use to set today's Dumpster on fire and the more sophisticated candle-as-timing-device they'd found at the shed fires, he now had his doubts. He looked at Jake. "You've got your license. Do you have a car?"

The kid made an *as if* noise.

"I'll take that as a no. How often do you

get to drive your parents'?"

"Goddamn never."

"Where were you on the tenth and the twenty-sixth?"

Jake jumped to his feet. "Fuck I know?" he demanded. Then his eyebrows furrowed. "Wait. The tenth? I had a date with Hayden Stewart. We saw that chick flick with whatshername — Katherine Heigl — at the Majestic."

"Matinee or evening?"

"Dude. It was a date. Evening."

And Colin didn't drive. He thought about the addresses he'd read off their IDs. It'd be a helluva hike out to Bailey's place. Doable, he supposed. But about a two on the Probability Meter.

"All right. You can go for now. The PA likely won't be charging you for the can and Dumpster fires. But you probably will be put in a program to determine why you felt compelled to set those fires in the first place." His theory was too much time on their hands, too little supervision and limited funds. "But know this. Set another and we'll toss your asses in jail and throw away the key."

He doubted they heard much beyond the "you can go now," but the prosecutor's office could catch up with them in a day or two to make the arrangements for them to enter the program.

Johnny moved to take one of their seats as they clattered through the door — which slammed in their wake. He raised his brows at Gabe. "You really don't think they set the Driscoll and Bailey fires?"

"I'm starting to seriously doubt it."

"It kind of begs the question then, doesn't it?" the deputy said.

"Yeah. If they didn't, who the hell did?"

CHAPTER FOURTEEN

That night Macy flipped from side to side in her childhood bed until Janna finally snapped, "For God's sake — would you just *do* the guy already?"

"What?" Rolling onto her side, she stuffed her pillow beneath her neck and, supporting her head in the crook of her elbow, peered through the darkness toward the other bed.

"Please," her cousin said. "Just do us all a favor and jump Gabe's bones. Get it out of your system." The bedclothes rustled as Janna turned toward her. "And what the hell were you thinking to troll Jeremy in front of him that way? The boy's a minnow — why not just throw chum in front of a shark while you're at it?"

"I know, I know," she agreed miserably, because she'd felt guilty about that — had known it was poor judgment on her part from the moment she'd seated Jeremy across from Gabriel. "He kissed me last Thursday — Gabe that is, not Jeremy."

"No duh. *And . . . ?*"

"And I nearly disintegrated from lust — but *he* was thinking of Grace."

"What? No. That can't be right. I've seen the way he looks at you. He *never* looked at Grace that way."

"Well, he sure as hell went out of his way to ask me if I knew Jack had kissed her outside the Red Dog the night we were all there. Right in the middle of the most intense, scorching —" She swallowed, because it still hurt. No, not hurt! It still pissed her off, that was all. "He dumps Grace, gets *me* all jacked up, then makes sure I know he's thinking about *her?* So, I guess when I met Jeremy I didn't think the matter through very well. I mean, he's really sweet and his admiration just felt . . . good, y'know? But you're right, I shouldn't have used him that way." And not long after Gabe had taken off, she'd found the gentlest way possible to send the younger man on his way.

She blew out a sigh. "If the situation were reversed and Gabe had dragged a woman back to the boardinghouse and rubbed my nose in her, I would've told everyone and their brother he was a pig. The fact that I'm

229

a woman doesn't make it more palatable."

"I wouldn't go overboard beating myself up about it if I were you," Janna said dryly. "I'd give odds nothing as exciting as being dragged home by a hot video star has happened to Jeremy in his life. You made the guy's day. Not to mention probably raising his status with his cousin and all the cousin's peeps."

The knot in her stomach was suddenly much more manageable and a small smile curled her lips. "He did have one of the Experimental boys take several shots of the two of us on his iPhone."

"There you go. But I stand by my advice. You and Gabe have got to quit dancing around each other and do the deed. There's so much sexual tension surrounding you I'm surprised cats aren't spontaneously yowling in the streets. As for the rest of us —" She heaved a sigh. "We need a break."

"Well, much as I hate to disappoint you, you're not going to get one. This is the second time he's kissed me only to turn around and shoot me down. I'm through. There's not going to be a third."

"Crap." Janna rolled over onto her back. "I was afraid you were gonna say that."

She rolled over, as well. "Sorry, Janna. But it's just an all-round bad idea."

■ ■ ■ ■

Gabe thought a lot during the next several days about hooking up with Macy and decided it was an excellent idea.

He acknowledged that, up until now, he'd had a pretty screwed-up way of showing it. For some reason, every time he'd had a solid shot at the gold with Macy, he had instead shot himself in the foot. But he was tired of being such an idiot. Hell, he couldn't even say why he'd resisted so hard. It was like a constant itch under the skin, he wanted her so bad. And it wasn't as if she hadn't fallen in with the program whenever he'd kissed her — she'd given, in fact, a damn fine impression of a woman who wanted him in return. Logically speaking then, there was only one conclusion to reach. He understood fires. Hell, he *specialized* in fires. And him and Macy?

Major potential to burn down the town without ever touching a match.

Having made up his mind, he was suddenly impatient to stroke her, kiss her, lay her down and bury himself deep inside her. Like now, if not sooner.

The thing was, though, she was slipperier than an eel these days. He knew she was in and out of the boardinghouse, but half the time he didn't even realize that she'd been there until she'd already left again. The only time he saw her was at dinner and then she was usually the last to sit at the table and the first to leave.

But tomorrow was the first day of the county fair, and she'd said she'd lend a hand at the booth. They might have their differences, but he didn't doubt that her word was golden. The woman had integrity. Just look at the way she'd put everything in her own life on hold to help her family.

He was proved correct the next day when she strolled up to the booth with not only Tyler and his friend Charlie in tow but her aunt and uncle. Her cousin brought up the rear, picking her way on a pair of crutches over the uneven ground.

"Hey." He pulled out a chair and waved Janna into it. "Sit down. How you doing?"

Swinging into the seat she smiled up at him. "Better. I'm finally starting to feel some real results from the PT."

"Janna's going to stay with us," Macy informed him. "Ty and Charlie have big plans for this fair and dragging Grandma and Grandpa around the grounds is their ticket to seeing all they can, isn't it, guys?"

"Yeah," Tyler agreed.

Charlie nodded enthusiastically. "We want to see it all."

"Good thing Lenore and I are spry," Bud said, giving his grandson a fond smile. "You want to head up to the rides?"

"In a minute." The youth watched as, to the groans of female voices, a softball hit the net behind the trigger target. "We want to do that first."

"Yeah, we wanna knock you into the tank," Charlie said, grinning up at Gabe. "Bet you'd make a big splash."

"I'll arrange to be your target if you don't mind waiting your turn in line." He indicated the row of mostly young women. "Our tank has been doing a booming business."

"Hmm. Wonder why," Macy murmured looking at the buff, wet fireman seated on the dunking platform.

Gabe shrugged. Playing up the beefcake-firehouse-calendar look — board shorts in the tank, turnout gear with bare chests out of it — had been selling tickets like crazy. And that was the idea.

But speaking of playing dress-up . . .

He inspected Macy's getup and shook his head. She was rigged out in a forties-style halter and tap pants, both of which appeared to be constructed from vintage floral curtains. Her amber hair was caught up in

233

some sort of black net drawstring bag and she'd arranged her bangs in one of those WW II–style swoops. "I take it getting wet is not in your game plan."

Jack Savage strolled up. "Sorry I'm late, luv," he said, bending his head to peck a kiss on Macy's lips. "I got hung up signing a few autographs." He turned to Gabe. "How's it goin', mate? We thought we'd be more effective to your cause acting as shills. Put our celebrity to good use by hauling in the paying customers."

Okay, hard to argue with that. Macy alone would have been a huge draw. Having Savage added the potential to finance extras for his crew for months — maybe even an entire year. So it'd be pretty damn small of him if he wasn't exactly thrilled to see the guy, wouldn't it?

He must have been unresponsive too long, however, because Macy said, "That doesn't mean we're unwilling to work the tank if that's what you need."

"No, you've probably got the right idea. And if you can recruit some volunteers while you're at it, that'd be pure gravy. If we can establish a Fire Corp in Sugarville, it will make us eligible for the Citizen Corp Affiliate program, which in turn will expand our resources and materials."

She raised her brows at him. "You want more volunteer firemen?"

"Oh. No. Sorry, I've had this in my head so long I tend to forget not everyone knows what I'm thinking. The Fire Corp is all about support personnel. We're interested in men, women, boys, girls — anyone we can involve for any amount of time that they're willing to give."

"What kind of stuff are you looking for them to do?"

"Any nonemergency task or role. Here, let me show you." Dropping into the folding chair beside Janna, he pulled over an open laptop and keyed in a couple of commands, glancing up at Macy when she bent over his shoulder to see. "This is their Web site. Take a look at it and use anything that seems applicable. Or feel free to come up with ideas of your own." He drew in a breath of her scent.

"Hey, Chief!" Charlie yelled. "It's almost me and Ty's turn. We wanna dunk you!"

He grinned. "Guess I'm up."

She stepped back. Gave him a cool once-over as he climbed to his feet. "That might almost be worth giving my own pitching arm a try."

He threw back his head and laughed. Eyeing her slender arms, he said, "Bet you throw like a girl."

She seemed to freeze for a nanosecond, but he must have imagined it because she flashed that smile she wielded to such effect. "News flash, sugar. I am a girl."

"Yeah." His voice went rough. "I've noticed." Knowing better than to expect a sudden demand to blow off his duty to join her behind the fun house for a little one-on-one, he strode off, peeling his T-shirt over his head as he walked.

"Holy shit," Macy murmured, watching him go. Dammit, he looked like that, *laughed* like that, and it was hard to remember her vow to keep her distance. Taking a deep breath, she tore her gaze off his muscular back, took the seat he'd abandoned and turned her attention to the Fire Corp Web site.

She hadn't gotten far exploring the ways other fire departments utilized their Corp volunteers before word spread about her and Jack's presence at the fire department's booth. Turning the computer over to Janna with a murmured request to continue the research, she slid across a pen and the tablet she'd been notating ideas on.

Then she focused on the crowd beginning to gather by their booth. A no-man's-land separated the gathering from her and Jack as if held back by an invisible force field. Unfortunately, it caused the people waiting in line for the dunk tank to be jostled, and she called out with a friendly smile, "Hey, it's good to see so many people turn out to support their fire department. Obviously you appreciate the importance of volunteer firefighters as much as Jack and I do."

"Bang on," Jack agreed. "Volunteer being the key word here."

"Which —" she lowered her voice and was satisfied to see it draw some of the crowd away from the ticket holders "— we'd love to talk to you about."

"Right. So form a couple of lines." Jack indicated the area in front of them. "Come talk to us. See what you can do to help your community."

To Macy's frustration, nobody moved. "Can you imagine what it must take to run into a burning building?" Macy said. She waved a hand at the firemen, who just happened to be razzing Gabe, who — omigawd — just happened to be wet and half naked as he sat on the platform.

She swallowed, forcing her gaze back to the crowd. "Look at them, ladies. Aren't they just. So." She patted her hand over her heart. "Big and strong? I mean, can you honestly look at them and *not* want to buy a ticket or twenty to support their cause? Even if you throw like a girl, like I do, where else you gonna get such a golden opportunity to ogle half-naked men?"

Clearly Gabe could hear them, because he shot her a grin over her purloined throw-like-a-girl line. Then a softball hit the target and the platform under him collapsed. He plunged into the water.

Simultaneously with him shooting back to the surface, his hands raising to slick his wet hair off his forehead, the curious paralysis that had held the crowd back suddenly broke, and its steadily growing mass surged toward them.

Hoping to stave off chaos, she used the authoritative two-fingered gesture of an air-ground employee guiding a plane into its Jetway. "Like Jack said, form a couple of lines, please, so the people who've already purchased tickets don't get trampled."

"And isn't it just a bugger when that happens?" he said with that wry Irish accent. "Puts a damper on a party, that does."

Which is exactly what they sold for the next couple of hours — a party atmosphere. They laughed and joked and sold a ton of tickets for the opportunity to knock a firefighter into the tank. They also gathered a respectable list of names and numbers from people who expressed at least a tentative interest in donating some time to the fire department.

Janna proved brilliant at presenting ideas she'd taken off the Corp Web site. They'd opened up a third line in front of her chair when they'd noticed they were losing a lot of the older people who didn't want to brave the crush in front of Macy and Jack to purchase a ticket. Macy tuned in at one point to hear her cousin say to the newly retired bank president, "I've heard my dad say more than once that you're one heck of an effective speaker. The fire department could sure use someone like you to speak to the community on a range of important safety topics."

"I'm not particularly knowledgeable on those topics," he replied.

"That's one of the things we're raising money for today," she said. "To train Fire Corp volunteers to speak knowledgably on things like CPR and first aid, fire prevention and proper use of fire extinguishers, motor-vehicle crash safety and, ohmigosh, too many things to even list. Or I bet you'd be dynamite at writing proposals for grants."

The man looked down at her for a moment, then gave her a slight smile as he bent to pick up the pen. "You're a pretty effective speaker yourself, young lady," he said. And signed his name to the volunteer list with a flourish.

"Way to go, Janna!" Macy crowed, high-fiving her cousin the moment the former bank executive walked away. She was pretty pumped over the afternoon's work. She'd feared her presence might be more detrimental than helpful to Gabe's cause. But except for the occasional dirty look or snide statement, people had been amazingly friendly.

Screams from the Loop-o-plane and Scrambler on the other side of the midway floated on the air, and her stomach growled when she caught a whiff of cinnamon sugar from the elephant-ear booth. "Man, I just realized I'm really hungr—"

"How 'bout getting some *real* action going in that tank," a loud voice suddenly demanded. "Let's see the MTV diva perch her little butt up there."

Macy sighed. *Congratulated yourself too soon, didn't you, girl.* Andrew Mayfield and a few of his coterie, including — oh, goody — Liz Picket-Smith, had muscled their way to the front of the line.

Jack started to rise, but she put a hand on his arm to stay him. "Ooh," she said, giving Andrew a big-eyed look. "You think my butt

240

is *little?*"

The crowd laughed.

Scowling, he yanked a hundred-dollar bill from his wallet and slapped it down on the countertop. "You'd be happy to accommodate me, I'm sure. Because this *is* for charity isn't it?"

Gabe caught the belligerent tone and looked over to see the same joker Angelini had chased away from Macy's table that night at the Red Dog. "Shit." Hauling the suspenders to his turnout pants up over his bare shoulders, he strode over to the booth. "We got a problem here?"

"No problem," the man snapped. "I've got a hundred bucks here for the fire department's cause. Just give me that bucket of balls over there and keep 'em coming. But I want *her* up there on the platform."

"She volunteered her time, Mr. —"

"Mayfield. Andrew Mayfield."

He said it as if Gabe should know his name. And Gabe had heard the name somewhere, but couldn't quite put a — aw, balls. Bud had mentioned it the night of Lenore's impromptu dinner following Ty's baseball game. He'd asked that Adam guy something about being one of those fools who'd believed Mayfield's lies back in high school. What the hell kind of history did Macy have with this jerk, anyhow?

Not having time to ferret out an answer, he shoved the question aside. "Mr. Mayfield, Ms. O'James volunteered her time to work the booth. She didn't sign up for the tank."

Rising to her feet, Macy essayed a delicate shrug. "I'll do it." She winked at the crowd. "Some guys just gotta get their kicks where they can, ya know?"

Gabe swore to himself, but signaled Johnson over to take her place at the booth. "You sure?" he asked in a low voice as he escorted her to the tank.

"No. But what's the worst he can do — get me wet? And like the man said, it's for charity. I will give you my snood to hold, though." She reached back to unhook the combs of the short black band that anchored the fishnet bag holding her hair. She handed it to him. "It'll never be the same if it gets soaked." Then she kicked off her shoes, climbed into the tank and perched on the platform. Crossing her legs, she struck a pose, grinning at the crowd when they cheered.

A softball hit the target and dropped her in the tank.

Surfacing a second later, she tossed her hair, which had lost its forties style, out of her eyes. "Good aim," she said dryly, and climbed back onto the platform.

She'd barely sat before a second ball hit the release trigger and dropped her back into the tank.

And so it went until the bucket was over half-empty. No sooner did she regain her seat than Mayfield knocked her back into the tank. Her clothes dripped and clung and her face began to grow pale beneath its light tan, but she continued to smile and toss off one-liners, talking to the crowd, ignoring Mayfield.

And except for one time when she said, "Here, I'm sure his pitching arm can use a rest," and did a cannonball from the ladder into the tank, she kept climbing back up onto the platform.

A couple of direct hits later, Gabe was stone-faced and feeling grim. He was ready, in fact, to go stuff the remaining balls up the guy's ass. Holding on to his composure, however, he strode over to Mayfield but merely picked the bucket up and handed it off to his closest crew member.

"Hey!" Mayfield protested.

"Fun's over," Gabe informed him flatly.

"Yeah, buddy, Jesus," a nearby spectator muttered.

"What a jerk," said somebody else.

"Jerk, hell. Guy's an asshole."

"What is the matter with you?" a woman said indignantly, stepping forward to speak directly to Mayfield.

"I'll tell you what's the matter," someone called from farther back in the crowd. "Ms. O'James was right — the guy *does* have to buy his thrills."

"By abusing women?" another demanded.

Mayfield whirled around. "What are you talking about, abusing?" he snapped. "I'm playing the same game the rest of you have been playing."

Gabe gave him a hard stare. "Everyone else has been playing in the spirit of fun. They haven't continuously knocked their target into the tank before she can even regain her seat from the *last* time she was knocked in. I don't know what your problem is, but there's nothing fun-minded about what you're doing here." He looked at Solberg, who was holding the bucket of balls. "Tally up what's left in there. We'll refund Mr. Mayfield for his unused balls."

"That'd pretty much be the two he's packin' in his pants, Chief," a male in the crowd drawled.

"Keep the money." Red-faced, Mayfield about-faced and shouldered his way through the crowd. His posse, Gabe noticed, had already melted away when it became apparent that no one else was finding Macy's predicament as amusing as they did.

He went over to the tank where Kirschner was helping her out. Grabbing a towel he looped it around her shoulders and looked down at her. "You okay?"

Bringing the towel up from her shoulders, she bent to wrap it turban-style around her hair. There were shadows in her eyes when she came upright once again, but she met his gaze, raised her chin and gave him a cocky smile that probably only he, standing so close, could tell cost her.

"Of course," she said, and shrugged. "Great day for a dip."

CHAPTER FIFTEEN

Okay, this is getting old. Gabe stalked over to Savage's Airstream the next morning but didn't pound on the door as his impulse urged. Because that would be fricking nuts. Man, what was it about Macy, anyway, that turned him into a . . . Hell, he didn't even know what to call the behavior he'd been displaying ever since clapping eyes on her. But it felt dangerously like his teenage self, and if he was smart he'd turn right around and get the hell away instead of chasing after her like a randy seventeen-year-old.

Currently, however, intelligence didn't rank right up there on his atta-boy meter. But he did knock on the lintel like the grown-up he was when Macy wasn't part of the equation. Melodic acoustic guitar drifted through the screened door.

"It's open," the Irishman said from the dimness within and continued playing. He looked up as Gabe opened the screen and entered the compact trailer. "Hey," he said, setting aside his guitar. "Do you believe that mentaller yesterday? A bigger bollox never put his arm through a coat." Waving a hand toward the galley, he offered Gabe a cup of coffee, then returned to his topic when it was refused. "Bloody good thing you stepped in when you did, Chief, because I was seconds from belting that ball-bag."

"I have a feeling we would have had people lining up for the opportunity to beat the crap out of him if we'd let them. The guy was an ass."

Jack's face went grim. "You don't know the half of it, mate."

No, he probably didn't, which didn't exactly improve his mood. He shoved his hands in his pockets. "You know where Macy is?"

"I think she took the boys to the baths."

He had to think about that for a second. "The pool, you mean?"

"Yeah." His brow furrowed. "Or, no, wait, that's tomorrow. Today she's headed over to check out a place she wants to use for the kickoff video for Aussie's *Vitamin G* album." He shot Gabe a wry smile. "I don't know how she does it, man. When we first sat down to talk about the video, I was locked on the title song for our first release. Then before I know it, instead of making 'G' a bleedin' deadly drinking song if I do say so myself, she's got me talked 'round to making 'Yesterday's Gone.' That song's a departure for us — less rock, more . . . well, not country, exactly, but a story ballad, y'know? I sure as shite never considered it for the launch song. Macy, though, she's got this grand way of visualizing exactly how a song should look on video, and I'm telling you, if we pull off feckin' *half* of what she envisions, it's going to be powerful."

Gabe knew he should care, but he was back to itching to run her to ground. "So where is this place?"

"Got me." Jack shrugged, picking up his guitar again. "She called it the old — what the hell was it? The Klemp — the Klim —"

"The old Kilimner place?"

"Yeah, that's it."

"Jesus, the joint's about one hot breath from falling down. She shouldn't be anywhere near it."

"Then you'd best go rescue her before she gets hurt, hadn't you?" Jack gave him a knowing smile and laughed when Gabe immediately turned on his heel and headed for the door.

Gabe heard him pick up the music where he'd left off before the screen door even slapped shut behind him.

Twenty Minutes Earlier

Macy hiked across two sagebrush-dotted fallow fields to reach the old Kilimner place. She'd borrowed Ty's backpack to carry her water bottle, digital recorder and a notebook, sketch pad and pencils.

Driving would have been faster, but it felt good to stretch her legs in the fresh air before moderate morning temps gave way to the less-forgiving afternoon heat. She loved the warmth of the sun on her shoulders. And the scent of the rolling wheat fields paralleling the ones she trekked, with their combined aromas of the shorn summer stubble and the green haze of barely sprouted winter wheat, had her drawing in deep, appreciative breaths.

It occurred to her that she hadn't missed L.A. once since she'd come home.

Maybe because, despite her last two years of high school, this *was* home to her. If someone had suggested that when she'd first come back she probably would've laughed in their face. But as long as Uncle Bud and Auntie Lenore lived here, it would likely always represent love, safety and stability to her.

Not that she regretted the time spent

away. She'd made a good life for herself in California. L.A. was everything Sugarville wasn't — something she'd particularly appreciated as a young adult. She'd grown into a person she could be proud of there.

But until this summer she hadn't realized that she'd never quite felt the same connection to it that she did to this sleepy little farming community.

That had been driven home yesterday in the midst of being continuously knocked into the tank. Andrew had done his damnedest to make her feel small or inferior, or whatever it was he'd intended — and to a degree he had succeeded. The sheer rapidity of being dumped in the water over and over again had shaken her right down to her foundation. It had literally stripped her of her armor and left her feeling naked and exposed. At first it was only sheer contrariness that had kept her climbing back onto that platform when she'd known damn well that she'd be knocked right off it again.

But before Gabe had put an end to the dunk-o-rama, she'd begun to catch glimpses of the crowd. And she'd noticed that no one except Mayfield's usual Idiot Brigade appeared amused by her predicament. They'd looked, in fact, royally pissed on her behalf, an impression that had proven true the minute Gabe commandeered Mayfield's bucket of ammo. Then, when she'd returned to the booth, dozens of people had gone out of their way to be neighborly. Several former classmates had been in the throng and all except one had mentioned the reunion, going out of their way to say they hoped to see her there.

Maybe she should reconsider her stance against going to the damn thing.

The wind was beginning to kick up when she cleared a slight rise and found herself almost to the Kilimner place. She got her first good look at it.

"Crap," she muttered, discouraged by its condition. It was much more dilapidated than the last time she'd seen it.

A self-deprecatory laugh escaped her. Because big surprise, considering how many years ago that had been. All the same it was disappointing. She was looking for a run-down farmhouse for Jack's video, not a place this far gone.

Hoping the interior might be more usable than its exterior, she climbed two steps to the creaky front porch. When she found the door unlocked, she pushed it open, laughing when it groaned like a cheesy sound track in a bad horror flick.

She stepped inside, sneezing at the cloud of dust she raised. In the bright wash of sunlight that poured through the open doorway and murkier light filtering through grime-encrusted windows, she gazed around.

It actually was in better condition inside than out. And maybe . . . just maybe —

She pulled out her recorder and notated possibilities as she subjected the first floor to a thorough, inch-by-inch inspection. When she reached the door to the cellar, she opened it but couldn't bring herself to go down the dark steps. It wasn't as if she were a big 'fraidy cat or anything, she assured herself. The cellar simply contained nothing she'd need for the video. Then she grinned and turned back to the kitchen.

Because a scaredy-cat was exactly what she was when it came to spider-infested cellars.

A spot in the kitchen floor felt spongy beneath her left foot and she was squatting to examine the entire surface for its ability to bear weight when the front door suddenly slammed. "Hello?" She surged to her feet, her heart thumping in her chest. "Is anyone there?"

No one answered, and the porch boards didn't give the telltale squeak she'd heard when she'd crossed them. Blowing out a breath, she gave her shoulders an impatient hitch. It was probably just the wind.

All the same, she went over, reopened the door and poked her head out. No one was in sight, and the overgrown drive showed no signs that a car had recently been anywhere near it. Besides, what were the odds that two people would choose the exact same time to hike to the same dilapidated old building? Zippo, that's what.

Shrugging aside the slight uneasiness that remained despite her logic, she went upstairs to check out the second floor.

The doorknob to the front bedroom twisted loosely beneath her hand, and she had to press it in and jiggle it a couple times before it finally engaged. Stepping into the room, she gave it a quick inspection.

And decided that while the farmhouse interior could be made to work with a great deal of elbow grease, why bother? She'd thought if this one turned out to be just right, it would be cheap and convenient for her friend. But the convenience factor went down the tubes if Production needed to find another place for the exteriors she envisioned, so they might as well look for everything they needed in one package. It would save a lot of time and energy for everyone.

Decision made, she left the room, but then paused as she smelled an acrid, smoky scent on the air. Going back in, she crossed to the window and pushed aside the grimy sheer, disturbing more dust in the process. Boards filled the glass-free expanse but were separated from each other by a couple of inches, and peering through a gap, she didn't see anything that posed a threat. She hoped, however, that a neighboring field wasn't on fire. It had been so god-awful dry this summer.

Behind her the bedroom door banged shut. "Oh, for God's sake!" she snapped, wondering where this sudden spate of poltergeist slammings was coming from. She tried to remember if she'd closed the kitchen door to the cellar but couldn't recall.

Pulling off Ty's pack, she retrieved her water bottle and knocked back a long gulp to wash the farmhouse's dust from her throat. Then she capped the bottle, shoved it back into the bag's outside mesh pocket and, swinging the pack onto her back, strode over to the door. It was time to go; her concept was a good one, but this wasn't the place she was seeking. Reaching out, she twisted the knob.

"What the — ?" She turned it harder. But

it merely rattled on the rod connecting it to the knob on the other side and turned loosely beneath her grip. She tried the same press and jiggle that had gained her admission into the room.

And still it didn't open.

"Okay. Deep breath here." Maybe she'd turned it the wrong way. Trying it in the other direction she discovered that wasn't the case. So, all right. Not far enough in the original direction, then.

But although the knob turned it didn't seem to be operating the latch, and she gave it an impatient yank.

It came off in her hand, its twin hitting the floor on the other side.

"Crap!" *Now what, genius?* Whirling around, she paced over to the window, then back to the door again, where she squatted to see if there was a way to jam the rod in there and somehow jury-rig it to work long enough to get her out of this room.

There wasn't, or at least nothing that occurred to her. Rising, she stalked away again, then stopped in the middle of the room, breathing hard, and tried to think.

Fine, then. She turned back to eye the hinges on the door. Going up on her toes, she grasped the balled head of the pin and tried to rock it free of the metal loops holding it.

"Damn!" Although rusty, it was solidly lodged, and without tools her odds of prying it out were slim.

She blew out a breath. Her odds were worse than slim. They were *zero.*

As she'd noted with the other interior doors, however, the paneling was flimsy. Maybe she could kick a hole in it big enough to climb through. She studied it. It really didn't look very substantial.

She could do this — so what if she'd never tried anything like it before? Grace had said that night at the bar that if Mattel made a doll, Macy's would be an action figure. So it was time to actually do something to earn the grade-school teacher's admiration.

She stepped back. Shook out her hands. Then, hoping to hell she didn't break her foot, she braced herself and took a deep, calming breath.

And coughed.

Looking down, her heart slammed against the wall of her chest. "Omigawd. Oh. My. *Gawd!*"

Curls of smoke wafted along the door's bottom edge, wisps drifting into the room.

"Shit!" Going over, she reached out to touch the wooden panel with the vague intention of getting an idea how near the threat was to the room holding her captive. But every time she tentatively extended her fingers to the door's surface, she snatched them back before she could bring herself to touch it. Finally mustering the courage, she slapped her palm against the door . . . then blew out a relieved breath when she didn't recoil from a hot surface.

That had to be a good thing, right?

So what now? Even if she could open the door to assess the situation she probably shouldn't, since all she could think of was some movie she'd once seen where opening a door had caused a big, hurking ball of fire to roar into the room, incinerating everything in its path.

She could hear the faraway crackle of the fire now, and seeing smoke begin to roll more thickly beneath the door, she raced across the room to rip the sheers from both windows. Coughing on a combination of dust and smoke, she rolled them up and squatted to stuff them in the crack between the bottom of the door and the threshold. Smoke then curled through the hole where the doorknob was supposed to be, and she removed her bra. Compressing the underwiring, she fit it into the opening, then wadded the delicate lace band and straps around it until the space was stuffed.

She drew another relieved breath when the smoke's entry into the room began to slow. Going back to the windows, she sucked a big gulp of clear country air deep into her lungs, then wedged her fingers into the space between two of the boards and tugged with all her might. When she stepped back a few moments later, her heart pounding and her arms hanging limply by her sides, the board hadn't budged so much as a centimeter. She'd managed to make the nails that held it in place creak slightly, but all she really had to show for her efforts was a broken nail and filthy hands.

She was rubbing the worst of the dirt off against her cargo shorts when she felt her phone.

"God, I'm so stupid!" Fishing it out of her pocket, hoping to hell there was reception out here, she punched in the emergency number, knowing that *that,* at least, would be correct. Nothing ever changed in Sugarville.

A sob broke in her throat when Becky Newith, who had been the town's crisis dispatcher for as long as Macy could remember, said a brisk, "Emergency." But she forced it down. She didn't have time to fall apart.

"Becky, it's Macy O'James." She had to clear her throat. "I'm trapped in an upstairs room at the old Kilimner place and the farmhouse is on fire. Smoke —" Her voice cracked and she cleared her throat again. "Smoke is coming in under the door."

"Stay on the line, Macy," the older woman calmly instructed. "I have to switch over for a moment to dispatch the truck and call Chief Donovan, then I'll stay with you until somebody arrives."

The amount of smoke getting through the sheers under the door began to escalate, and she crossed to the window, not only to put as much distance between it and herself but in hopes of seeing help the minute it arrived. But her view was limited at best and she didn't have a view of the overgrown drive at all.

She did, however, hear Gabe's voice roar her name from the other side of the house and, dropping the phone, she screamed his in return. Staring through one of the gaps in the boards, she strained to catch her first sight of him.

He charged into sight and even from up here she could see him methodically scan the building. But he was looking at the end nearest him. "Macy?" he called again. "You on this side?"

"Yes, yes!" She banged her palms against the boards and his gaze promptly homed in on her.

"Hang on!" he yelled. "I'll be right back."

"Don't leave me!" Panic licked at what little calm she'd managed to hang on to up until this point.

But he pinned her with that cool, steady gaze and she immediately felt herself regain some composure. "I'll be back in just a second," he called. "There's a ladder against the other side of the house and I'm going to get it so we don't have to wait for the truck to get you out of there."

She nodded and he loped away.

The panic threatened to return but then she heard her phone squawking and remembered Becky. She picked it up and, staring at the spot where she'd seen Gabe disappear and was fervently willing him to reappear, said, "He's here."

"Chief Donovan?"

"Yes. He said there's a ladder and he went to get it — oh, God, there he is! He's got it." She watched him stride toward her end of the farmhouse, the ladder clutched in his big hands.

"Okay, good," Becky said. "The truck is on its way, as well. So you're gonna be okay, Macy."

The top rungs of the ladder thumped against the windowsill and she nodded. Realizing the dispatcher couldn't see her, she whispered, "Yes." Heartfelt appreciation for the older woman's lifesaving voice on the other end of the line suffused her. "Thank you, Becky. God, thank you so much!"

"You're welcome. You held it together real good. Will you be okay if I hang up now?"

"Yes."

Seconds later, Gabe's gray eyes appeared one in of the breaches. "You okay?" he asked.

"No, I'm not okay! I'm trapped in a burning building!"

Lines fanned out from his eyes and she knew he was smiling.

Then he sobered. "Move to the side and stay against the outside wall," he said. "I'm going to break these boards."

She did as he commanded, and an instant later one of them cracked with an explosive sound. She jerked skittishly but stayed in place until he called an all clear.

She raced back to see him swiveling one of the remains of the board on its nail until it hung jagged-side-down from the window frame. Laying his ax on the floor inside the room, he climbed through.

The second he unfolded to his full height,

she launched herself at him, climbing him like a treed cat. Legs locked around his hips, arms clinging around his solid neck, she burrowed her head in the latter's warm curve, trying to absorb his strength. The wail of the pumper truck sounded in the distance, rapidly gaining volume as it drew closer.

"Much as I dig this," his voice rumbled over her head, "you've got to let go so I can get you out of here."

It took everything she had to relinquish her grasp. Then she squealed like a startled six-year-old when he promptly bounced her up and flipped her over his shoulder, his hand clamping her thighs to his chest. The next thing she knew he'd maneuvered them both out the big window and onto the ladder, and she was staring down at the ground about a gazillion feet below.

She grabbed the belt loops on his jeans waistband and slammed her eyes shut. Her stomach made slow, hinky somersaults as he climbed down the ladder.

A moment later they were on solid ground.

He lowered her to her feet as the truck rolled to a stop on the other side of the house and the siren trailed into silence. Doors slammed and men's voices called to each other.

"How's your breathing?"

She promptly fell into a coughing fit, but nodded as her throat cleared. It felt scratchy but not seared, and her lungs didn't have that pneumonia feel she imagined they would if they'd sustained real damage. "It's fine."

He made a *yeah, right* sound. "I'll take you to the clinic."

"No. I don't need it. Really," she insisted when he narrowed his eyes at her. "I was able to keep most of the smoke out."

A crooked smile tilted one corner of his mouth. "Yeah, I saw the rags under the door and your bra in the doorknob hole." For a second his gaze dropped to her lingerie-free breasts beneath her tank top, but in the next heartbeat returned to meet hers. "Excellent use of the materials at hand."

Taking her elbow he escorted her around the house. He settled her in the passenger side of the truck and handed her a bottle of oxygen. Showing her how to fit the face piece over her mouth and nose, he turned it on. "Stay here and breathe this. I'll be back as soon as I can."

But he didn't move. Instead, still leaning into the cab where she sat, he glided his fingertips down her cheek, brushed them against her temple and gently tucked her hair behind her ear. His gaze traced her features one by one before dropping to track his thumb as it rubbed over her bottom lip.

Then his hand suddenly dropped away and he straightened. "If your condition changes and you start feeling worse, hit the horn and we'll get you to the clinic. Or I can call your uncle — would you prefer that?"

"No." She probably should, but at the moment she just wanted to remain where she was, and given the choice, she'd have Gabriel get in with her.

But of course she'd never ask for anything so . . . needy. She wasn't the clinging type.

Still, she'd give her left pinkie to climb in his lap, wrap those strong arms around her like a protective shield and do exactly that — to cling like a barnacle. But that was simply reaction. Hell, she'd been trapped in a burning building and the man had saved her. No *wonder* she felt bonded and so, so grateful.

Making herself lift the mask from her mouth, she waved him away. "I'm shook up, but okay. Go fight the fire. I'll just sit here and catch my breath," she said.

And prayed she was the only one who

heard that pathetic little tremble in her voice at the thought of him leaving her sight.

Chapter Sixteen

"*Told* you I was fine," Macy said as they walked out of the town clinic a while later.

"Yes, you did." Over and over again. But Gabe kept his voice neutral because she'd been through the wringer and he knew she was probably still dealing with vestiges of a huge adrenaline spike. He'd sure as hell felt the effects of his own overload and he probably had ninety pounds on her.

Then there'd been the surplus of attention she'd received at the clinic. He'd admit it, all the exclaiming and fussing probably hadn't helped. So he kept his tone gentle when, for the umpteenth time, he said, "And I told you smoke inhalation can be a tricky thing and it's better to be safe than sorry."

He looked down at her wet hair, pulled back in a low ponytail, her bangs already starting to dry in the hot afternoon sun. Her face was scrubbed free of makeup and she looked soft-skinned and pretty.

He cleared his throat because he really didn't want to go there. Not after the helluva time he'd had turning away from her back at the Kilimner place. Usually, he jumped at the opportunity to fight a fire. But she'd looked so shell-shocked and forlorn as she'd sat in the SFD's truck that it had been all he could do to tear himself away.

It was uncomfortable knowledge and he promptly shook it off. "At least you got to get cleaned up," he said as they stopped at the passenger side of his SUV and he opened the door for her. That was the beauty of a small town; they'd let her shower off the acrid smoke smell, lent her a pair of purple scrubs, and one of the nurses had even scrounged up a tube of lip stuff to help Macy restore her girlhood or some equally incomprehensible shit. He tried to imagine that happening in any of the hospitals he'd been in and out of in Detroit and shook his head. Not likely.

He went around, climbed in the rig and started it up. Then he just sat there. He knew he should get Macy back to Lenore and Bud. Fearing her aunt and uncle might already have heard something through the town's always swift grapevine, she'd called them after the clinic staff finished examining her to assure them she was all right. But having watched their relationship with Macy, he knew the older couple were probably chomping at the bit to check their chick over for themselves.

The trouble was, he wasn't ready to take her back, to watch her getting sucked into the maelstrom of everyone's concern. *Why* that was so, he'd just as soon not study too closely.

This wasn't about him, though, and he put the SUV in gear.

They were silent as he pulled out onto the highway and remained so as they cruised slowly through town. As they neared the cutoff to the boardinghouse, however, Macy twisted in her seat to look at him.

"Could we not go there yet?" she asked quietly. "Could we — I don't know — just keep driving?"

Oh, yeah. He kept his sudden jubilation out of his expression, however, and casually rolled his shoulders as he glanced at her. "Sure. Where do you want to go?"

"I don't care. Anywhere. Let's just . . . cruise." Sticking out her lower lip, she blew a breath that fluttered her drying bangs. "The thing is . . . I don't think I can stand being fussed over right now. And I damn sure don't feel up to having to keep explaining what happened when I can't wrap my own mind around it." She peered at him. "Is that selfish of me?"

"Hell, no. You've been through an ordeal. Sometimes it helps to talk about it. But sometimes it doesn't."

She nodded vigorously. "Exactly. This is one of those 'it doesn't' times."

She turned back to stare at the wheat fields rolling into the distance outside the passenger window and Gabe went back to brooding over the same issue he'd been gnawing on ever since he, Johnson and Solberg had put out the Kilimner fire and he'd squatted down to examine its origin site.

If the candle residue he'd found in the rubble of the back porch was any indication — and it damn sure was — this fire, too, had been deliberately set, just like the ones at the Bailey and Driscoll places. And what he'd wondered then, what he had wondered in the clinic waiting room when the nurse wouldn't let him back in the examining room with Macy, and what he damn well wanted to know now was: had the arsonist known the farmhouse was occupied and started the fire anyhow? Or was it just freaking bad luck on Macy's part that she'd gone into a place where an incendiary device was burning down to a heap of tinder on that back porch?

"Can we go to your place?"

"What?" He whipped his head around to stare at her.

"Your house? Could we go there for a bit? I'd like to see what it looks like on the inside."

Oh, man, that was *so* not a good idea. He was on edge and he'd already had to fight his instincts to a standstill to keep from stripping her down and checking her over inch by inch to see for himself that she was okay. Her close call made him want to stake a claim, to celebrate that matters hadn't turned out as badly as they could have, to commemorate the fact she was *alive.* And the way he'd celebrate, given half a chance, was to bury himself inside her and fuck her to a screaming climax. So a secluded, if unfinished, house with just the two of them? That was the last place he needed to take her. Because she was in a pretty fragile state right now and he doubted she'd appreciate being slammed up against a wall the minute they cleared the door and having him go at her like a vampire scenting fresh blood. "Uh . . ."

"Never mind, forget I asked." She turned her head to look out the window.

But not before he saw the mortification that crossed her face. This from Miss Never-Let-the-Suckers-See-They're-Getting-to-You. "Listen —"

"No, really," she said. "I'm expecting a lot here. You've probably got things to do — like investigate that fire. You certainly don't have to babysit me." She turned back to him with that insouciant smile he'd seen her use time and again. "I'm sorry, sugar. I shouldn't have taken up so much of your time. Take me back to the boardinghouse."

Shit. "This —" he snarled, stabbing a finger in her direction then jerking his thumb back at his own chest, "— is not babysitting. You wanna see my house? I'll show you my house." Okay, that was less than gracious, but he was really struggling here to keep his paws to himself.

Then he took a deep breath and eased it out. Hell, what was he, a high school kid? Those no-control days were damn near two decades behind him. He was a grown man who could do any damn thing — *resist* any damn thing — he set his mind to.

"No, really, Gabriel," she said softly, and from the corner of his eye he saw her fingers twisting and untwisting the hem of her tank top. "It's not necessary."

Like the slight quaver in her voice when

she'd sent him off to fight the fire even though she'd clearly not wanted to be left alone, the trace of embarrassment he heard now got to him. So did her nervous fiddling. It made him ashamed of his surliness, and gentling his voice he said, "Actually I'd like to show it to you. The joint really is coming along. I've done a good part of the work myself and I'm pretty proud of it."

Her hands stilled and she flashed him a smile so open and sweet, he felt as though a fist had reached inside his chest, gripped his heart and squeezed. Making a U-turn, he pointed the hood of his rig back toward his place.

They didn't talk much in the ten minutes it took to reach the road to his property, but as they entered the wooded draw that left the high prairie to flow down a series of steep hills, she blew out a quiet breath.

He glanced over to see her still looking out the window. As if she felt his gaze, she turned to look at him. "This is where kids used to come to party in high school."

He hesitated, then said, "Those ball players you told me you hit back then with your aunt's car. It happened down the road a bit, didn't it?"

"Yeah." For a moment her eyes got a haunted look. "In Buzzard Canyon." She sat a little straighter in her seat. "Everyone assumed I ran them down on purpose because of the way they'd trashed my reputation, but it wasn't true. There was a *lot* of drinking going on that night and it was pitch-dark once you got away from the bonfire. Janna and I were sitting in the car getting ready to leave, arguing about —" Cutting herself off, she waved a hand. "Well, it doesn't matter what. The point is, the engine was on and the car was in gear. But the lights were off when my foot slipped off the brake. We didn't even see the boys staggering out of the woods." She met his gaze levelly, her chin jutting up. "It was an accident."

"I don't doubt it," he agreed and turned his attention back to the road. But catching her startled movement from the corner of his eye, he added, "From what I've gathered, the gossip that you lived to put out originated with Mayfield. So I imagine if you were going to run anyone down it would've been him."

A bubble of laughter escaped her and he smiled to himself. Then he turned his head to catch her eye again. "Plus, not even your worst enemies deny you stepped right up to accept the blame. Not every eighteen-year-old kid would do that. It makes me think if you'd done it on purpose you'd have led with that stubborn chin of yours and owned up to that, too."

She flashed him another sweet smile, and he had a quick glimpse of what she must have looked like as a little girl.

"Thanks," she said. "It's . . . nice . . . having someone not assume the worst."

A couple of minutes later they pulled into the clearing surrounding his house and she gazed at his Craftsman-style bungalow and sighed. It sat in a clearing surrounded by evergreens, two-story-tall boulders topped with more trees rising behind it. "This really is a beautiful spot. And your house is *very* cool. It's a nice size. I like that you didn't build one of those five-thousand-square-feet places."

He snorted. "What would I need with all that room?"

"What do half the people who build big need?" she countered, essaying a facial shrug. "It seems to be the trend, anyhow. You must be getting anxious to move in."

Not as much as he had been before she'd come back to Sugarville, he silently admitted. But he merely nodded and opened his door. "C'mon. I'll give you the nickel tour."

They climbed the steps to the covered front porch that ran the width of the house and he fished a key off his ring.

Macy slapped his arm. "Get out! You're in Sugarville, Donovan — no one locks their houses here."

He shrugged. "I've been here eight months. I spent the other thirty-three years in Detroit. I don't know anyone who *doesn't* lock up there."

"Old habits do die hard," she agreed as he opened the door. "I had a heck of a time remembering not everywhere is as low-crime as Sugarville when I first moved away. Oh! This is nice. I thought it might still be in the bare-studs-hard-to-tell-what-everything's-going-to-be stage, but it has walls and everything."

He nodded, looking around in satisfaction, the tension he'd felt upon closing the door behind them easing beneath her curiosity. The great room flowed from the door they'd entered to the granite breakfast bar that separated the kitchen area at the other end. In the middle of the front wall was the fireplace and a bank of windows that looked out onto the evergreens encircling his place. "I just got the last of the drywall up on this floor last week with some help from a couple of my crew. It's only taped — I haven't had time to mud yet."

"But you can tell what the rooms are going to look like. I like the open concept and I love that fireplace!"

"I like its openness, too. I was going to go with the classic bungalow interior, but I like this better."

She strode over to the fireplace and stroked the rocks that comprised it. "Did you do all this stonework yourself?"

He made a rude noise. "I was a big-city boy, O'James. We don't know from masonry. I had it done."

"It's gorgeous." Unabashedly nosy, Macy opened the door across from the kitchen and poked her head in. "A bathroom," she said, taking in the plumbing sticking out of wall and floor, then opened the door next to it. She glanced at him over her shoulder. "Bedroom or study?"

"I'm thinking office. There's going to be two bedrooms upstairs but that is still in the studs stage." He reached around her to open another door. "The walls for the rooms in the basement are done, though, if you wanna see that."

"Absolutely." The windows down in the partial-daylight basement admitted plenty of light to guide the way, and she preceded him down the stairs in response to his *after you* gesture.

The stairway culminated in a large area

that was anchored at one end by a fireplace matching the one upstairs, and Macy turned to him with raised brows. "Big space. Media room?"

He made a rude noise. "I have damn little time to watch TV, although I did leave space to mount one over this fireplace. I'm thinking more rec room, though."

She nodded approvingly. "What colors do you envision for the walls?"

"Huh?" He looked at her blankly. "I don't know. White?"

"Noooooo. This place cries out for earth tones. *White.*" She shook her head in disgust as she crossed to open another door. "How boring is that? Hello!" She craned her head around to grin at him. "Your den of iniquity?"

Crap. He looked past her at the air bed on the floor all made up with high-thread-count sheets and down-filled pillows. He'd forgotten about this or he never would have brought her down here. He'd arranged it with some vague intention of seducing Grace before acknowledging that would be too much like luring his sister into bed.

But he met Macy's gaze. "Nah," he lied with cool authority. "I put in a couple of late nights working here and thought it would be nice to have a place to crash. But when it came down to it I was always so dirty by the time I finished that all I wanted was a shower."

"So, it's never been used?"

"Nope."

"Good." She yanked him into the room, kicked the door shut and reached out to grip his T-shirt in both fists. He sucked in a breath when she rose onto her toes and plastered her curves against his angles.

She nipped his lower lip between sharp white teeth, then slowly pulled away, scraping over his sensitive flesh until it slid free. She looked up at him with an expression that sent his last good intention up in smoke.

He was firmly with the program even before she said in a throaty voice, "Let's break it in."

CHAPTER SEVENTEEN

For maybe twenty seconds Macy felt bold and in charge. Then Gabe took over. One minute she was leading this seduction, the next she was backed against the door with an aroused male pressing her into its wooden panels. His mouth, so hot, so damp, so commanding yet soft-lipped, ravaged her senses, and her only thought was an incoherent, desperately needy *more.* Wrapping herself around him, she gave back as good as she got.

The hard muscles of his chest flexed against her breasts as he reached up to untwine her arms from around his neck. Lacing their fingers together, he pinned her hands to the door beside her head. His thighs spreading, he bent his knees until his erection nudged the rapidly dampening notch between her legs. Swiveling his hips, he executed a slow grind.

Unprompted, her body performed the

do-me dance in response, her breasts rubbing against the solid wall of his chest, her stomach stroking his tight abs, her sex arching into the stiff thrust of his where he'd positioned it to hit her just right.

Breath exploding from his lungs, he ripped his mouth free and stared down at her blindly for a heartbeat as he rocked and rocked and rocked between her thighs.

Then his eyes regained a modicum of focus and with a groan, he stepped back.

"Nooo," she protested.

"Gotta stop or I'll go off like a thirteen-year-old kid with his first *Maxim* magazine."

She stalked his retreat. "Don't wanna stop."

He stared at her with hot, frustrated eyes. "You've been through the wringer today, and the last thing you need is me going at you like an orangutan on Spanish fly because I'm too horny to be gentle."

Ooh. She *loved* the idea of pushing him over the edge, of making him lose that ironclad control of his. She didn't need gentle or considerate or restrained right now. She wanted Gabriel wanting her as much as she wanted him. "The doctors said I'm fine, so don't treat me like some fragile flower. Let's finish what we started. Now!"

He reached her in one giant stride. "Don't

say I didn't give sensitivity a shot," he growled, pressing her back against the wall. Big hands slapping down on either side of her head, he leaned into his forearms, caging her in and clamping his mouth over hers in a kiss that was short on gentleness and long on heat-lightning–hot desire.

Macy instantly ignited. Wrapping her arms around his neck, she strained against him, rubbing against his solid, massive body as she tried to get close, closer.

He raised his head, his eyes burning down at her. "God, I want you — wanna be deep inside you feeling you come all over me." Catching her bottom lip between his teeth, he tugged, then slowly let it slide free. He bent his knees at the same time as he shoved her scrubs top up to bunch above the thrust of her breasts, then closed his mouth over a pebbled nipple and sucked hard.

She gasped, arching her back. Her fingers spearing into his dark hair, she held him to her even as she panted, "Feels good, feels so good. But I don't need foreplay. Want you in me now. God, please, Gabriel. *Now.*"

He reached between them and loosened the drawstring on her pants, then unzipped and pushed down his own jeans as she kicked free of her borrowed hospital bottoms. Wrapping his hands around her hips he lifted her up against the wall and stepped between her legs. Macy locked her legs around his hips as she felt the head of his penis, hot and broad, press against her slick opening.

"Condom?" she panted.

"Shit!" Gabe pressed his forehead against hers for a moment. What the hell was he thinking? With a low groan, he set her on her feet. "Don't move!" he ordered and took a long-legged stride to the air bed. He squatted in front of the little chest next to it and in a second was back, spitting out the top of the condom package he'd ripped off with his teeth. He rolled the protection on.

He picked her up again and muscled her legs apart, lined up his dick and pushed, hissing through clenched teeth as the head of his cock eased past the muscular ring protecting her entrance. She was tight. Jesus, so incredibly tight. Pressing deeper with cautious slowness, he grit his teeth as he felt himself sink inch by hanging-by-his-fingernails inch into a hot, wet satin vise that slowly parted against the steady pressure only to clamp around him like a lubricious second skin that had shrunk a size too small. He wanted nothing more than to pound into her but was afraid of going too fast, and it seemed like dog years before he was finally in her as deep as a man could go.

He dropped his head. "God, you feel good," he said and kissed her. He swiveled his hips, then pulled back.

"You, too," she whispered against his lips as he started pumping in and out of her with gentle, shallow thrusts. Slowly, the almost uncomfortably tight sheath grasping him relaxed slightly and her breath began to hitch. His thrusts promptly grew more emphatic until he was drawing almost all the way out of her before slamming back in. Drawing back and slamming in.

"Oh, God, Gabriel," she said hoarsely, staring up at him, all slumberous eyes and glowing, flushed skin. Using the grip of her strong legs on his hips to move, she angled her pelvis to meet each thrust. "I feel, oh, God, you make me feel so . . ." Her words trailed into a moan.

He watched the need flicker across her face as she moved in concert with him, then hunched to lightly bite one nipple. Raising his head, he demanded, "How? How do I make you feel?" Hands grasping her butt, he jerked her to him and ground in slow oscillations, wanting to stamp his ownership all over her.

Macy grasped his head and gave him a

fierce kiss that was all hot tongue and soft lips. Pulling back, she said, "Right. You feel so *right.*"

Yes. Forgetting every fancy move he'd ever learned, he picked up his speed even more, his hips pistoning him in and out of her. Deeper. Harder. Faster.

He must have found her sweet spot, for a frantic sound burbled out of her throat. *"Gabe?* Oh, God, Gabriel, *please."*

He clenched his teeth as she tightened around him, as he felt the preliminary clasp and unclasp that heralded her climax, his balls drawing up as his own release gathered at the base of his scrotum. Then she was coming and there was nothing preliminary about the hard, strong contractions gripping, tugging, *milking* his cock. Groaning deep in his chest, he thrust deep one last time and held.

Macy's voice climbed several octaves even as the top of his head threatened to blow off his shoulders. "Oh, Christ, Macy, I'm com— oh, Jesus, you're so fucking tight and I'm —" As the pressure grew more and more intense, his entire body tensed and he was so focused he forgot to breathe.

Then he roared her name as he came in hot, violent pulsations that went on and on and on as Macy clung to his neck and dug her heels into the small of his back.

He didn't have a clue how much time had passed before he finally collapsed against her, driving the breath from her lungs in a whoosh. "Sorry." He forced himself to lean back when all he wanted was to slump against her, to feel her cushioning him like the softest of beds. "You okay?"

Her lashes fluttered up, and a soft smile of fulfillment curved her mouth. "Oh, yeah. You could say that."

Satisfaction flashed through him. Satisfaction and something deeper, more primitive, something that whispered *mine* when it looked at her.

A sliver of alarm sliced through him, but he pushed it away. He wasn't letting anything wreck this. Not some caveman-possessive shit, not the tendrils of unease that plucked at him when he considered his loss of control.

Screw that. He felt good. Too good to analyze to death what had just happened. This was nothing like it had been when he was a kid, anyway. Then any willing female would have fit the bill — the girls had all been interchangeable. But today he knew *exactly* who was in his arms. It was Macy he desired, Macy who left him feeling as if he'd just ingested the world's best feel-good narcotic.

Which wasn't to say he couldn't show her how it felt to be sexed up by a guy in control, he thought as her legs slipped down his. He gently lowered her onto her feet and stepped back, steadying her. Watched, amused, as she primly pulled her top down, then admired that sweet round butt as she bent to grab her pants and pull them up her long legs. A hank of hair had pulled free from her ponytail to trail down her neck and her lips were swollen and pink, while a dark flush stained her skin when she turned back to face him.

He leaned down to kiss her in appreciation. She looked like a woman who'd just gotten hers, which left him feeling pretty damn good.

"That took the edge off," he said. "Let's see if I can't wreck you for other men in the next go-around."

Gabe's grin was all white teeth and satisfied male ego, and Macy snorted. "As if." Okay, that was weak, but it was the best she could manage since she was too busy thinking, *There's going to be a next go-around?*

"Ah. A challenge." Gray eyes darkening, he slicked his tongue over his lower lip. "I like that." And he swept her up in his arms.

In the time it took her to register his body

heat pumping through the fabric of her scrubs, he'd carried her the few steps to the air bed and laid her on its smooth sheets. Squatting on the floor by her feet, he leaned forward to stroke his hands down the purple fabric covering her thighs, her knees, her shins. Then, grasping the hems of her scrub pants, he abruptly surged to his feet, shaking her out of the pajamalike bottoms she'd just donned.

"What the — ?"

He shot her a cocky grin that made her roll her eyes. Yet she had to swallow a smile because, secretly, she got a kick out of this playful side of him. It was unexpected and charmed her pants off. She gave her bare legs a rueful look. Literally.

He climbed onto the air bed with her, eased her up into a seated position and peeled the top over her head with one swift, economical movement. Her hair was still drifting back to her shoulders when he let go, looking down at her with hot, satisfied eyes as she flopped, buck-naked, back onto the mattress.

"That's better," he murmured. "Every artist needs his canvas. And mine — ?" His heavy-lidded gaze followed his fingertip as it traced a path over her collarbone, between her breasts and down her diaphragm to her navel. Inserting the callused tip into the shallow swirl, he raised his gaze, letting Macy see his appreciation. "She's a beaut."

She should probably feel exposed, lying here without a stitch while he had on a shirt with a hem long enough to hide all but a peek-a-boo glimpse of the goods. Yet for the first time in she couldn't remember how long, she didn't feel the need for the protective covering of one of her costumes. "Let's see *my* canvas," she demanded, giving him a long, slow perusal. "I hope it's not one of those paint-by-numbers jobs."

Toeing off his shoes and stepping out of his jeans, he whipped his T-shirt off over his head.

"Ooh." She sat up, staring at his wide shoulders, at the black fan of chest hair that narrowed to a thin silky line down the defined muscles of his abs. "I remember this torso — although I do believe it may be the first time I've seen it dry. The other times I've seen you shirtless, you were coming out of a shower or a dunk tank." Then her gaze traveled lower. "I must say, though, that *that* —" she indicated his no-longer-rampant penis hanging between his thighs "Well, it felt a lot bigger." She snickered like a school-girl.

"You're such a card." He stood on first

one foot then the other as he pulled his socks off. Tossing them aside, he came down on one knee on the air mattress and threw his other over her thighs to straddle her.

He gave her a slow, carnal smile. "You females have it all over us poor guys with that multiple orgasm thing you've got going, so this is just for you." Pressing her hands back against the silky cotton sheet on either side of her head, his long fingers gently encasing her wrists, he slid down her body.

"Oh, but —" Her voice trailed off as his teeth scraped the skin on her throat and she surged beneath him, rotating her wrists to break his grip so she could hold him in return.

He didn't turn her loose.

She bucked. "Hey. 'Scuse me. Holding me down here."

"I know," he murmured between descending kisses, settling more firmly atop her. "I like it. I've thought about holding you down. Making you scream. That's my new goal," he whispered, stringing more of those kisses back up her throat. "I'm going to make you scream." Another openmouthed kiss, this one behind her left ear. "And scream." His teeth suddenly closed over the lobe, warm breath gusting down the whorls and making her shiver. "And *scream.*"

"I'd like to see you try," she said with weak defiance. But holy shit. She'd deny it with her dying breath, because it was sooo un-PC, but his words had her clamping her thighs together. Never having had a multiple orgasm, she'd assumed she was done.

But maybe he was onto something.

"Oh, I'll do more than try." He pushed up on his fingertips, keeping her wrists caged even as his palms lifted to avoid compressing them, and bent his head to kiss her.

"Lemme go, lemme go," she pleaded every time he lifted his mouth to change the angle. And she began to move beneath the newly resurgent need twisting through her system. She'd had sex before, of course. But never had she experienced the lack of control she always seemed to feel with Gabriel. She *wanted* another orgasm. Wanted *him* to touch her, take her, give her the reward these restless feelings promised. The way he had before.

"Soon." This kiss was deep and slow, and she arched, scraping her nipples against his chest hair. Raising his mouth, he shifted to once again kiss his way down her neck. He made his way down her chest but then halted his descent, his lips inches above her breast. His breath fanned her nipple and it tightened, grew longer. He studied it with intent eyes but didn't touch it.

She arched her back but . . . couldn't . . . quite . . . make it . . . reach. Panting, she dropped back onto the bed, her gaze locked with single-minded intensity on his mouth with its full lower lip and the hint of teeth showing beneath his sterner upper lip. The damn thing was *centimeters* from where she needed it and she raised her gaze to find him watching her with smoldering intensity.

Oh, God. Her lips opened and her tongue stole out to give them a lick. Extending its tip the tiniest bit farther, she curled a come-get-me gesture at Gabriel, then drew it back inside, shivering at the brush of moisture along the slick lining of her upper lip as it retracted.

He groaned. "Jesus. I can't believe how fast you can reduce me to a randy teenager without even trying." Bending his head, he rasped the flat of his tongue over her nipple. His gaze still locked on her face, he clamped his mouth over it.

An inarticulate sound exploded from her throat and she writhed beneath the attention he lavished on it with his lips, his tongue, his teeth. Not until she was nearly mindless did he let her nipple pop free and roll them onto their sides. At the nudge of his knee, she spread her legs, locking them around the thigh he immediately pushed into the newly opened space. He sank his long fingers into her butt to direct the movement of her hips, making her realize her hands were free. She gripped his shoulders and kissed him back when he rocked soft, suctioning lips over hers.

Feeling her last bit of control dissolve, she pulled back. "Again," she panted. "I want you in me again."

"In a minute," he murmured. Tipping her onto her back, he trailed his fingertips over her breasts and down her diaphragm to her navel. His fingers circled there for a moment before continuing their descent over the slight curve of her stomach to head south.

But then they halted and she arched her pelvis to encourage the continued downward momentum.

With a muffled chuckle, he complied, stroking his fingers into the golden-brown fleece between her legs, insinuating a fingertip into the creamy crease separating the plump lips of her labia.

One touch of that rough-skinned pad slicking over her clitoris and Macy's world exploded around her. A high-pitched keening purled from her throat as she thrust her hips high. Sensations flashed and pulsated and tiny pops of color burst behind her closed eyelids. "Oh, gawwwwwwwd," she moaned as he continued feathering his fingertip over the turgid little bundle of nerves. "OhGodohGodohGodohGod."

Gabe tore his mouth free and his gaze honed in on his fingertip, where it rubbed gentle circles in that sweet little slit.

"Not quite a scream," he growled as her hips collapsed back onto the mattress, leaving his hand high and —

Well, not dry, he thought with a crooked smile, lowering it to grip her smooth, lax thigh. "Still, a satisfying sound all 'round. And baby?" He grabbed another condom from the chest. "I guess this isn't just for you after all." Pushing higher on his elbows, he gave her another rough kiss, then rose to his knees and tore the wrapper open.

She cracked an eye open. For a second she merely stared, her gaze locked on the naked thrust of his cock. Then she slowly swallowed. "I take it back. Well, either that or the angle from here is creating an optical illusion. Because it's not really as big as it appears, right?"

"Hell, yeah, it is." Wrapping his hand around himself, he gave it a stroke, a get-real sound escaping his throat. "You're not looking at it through your sideview mirror, honey." He shook his head. "Like any guy would voluntarily cop to his dick being *smaller* than it appears."

She guffawed and her gaze, which had dropped once more to closely observe his hand action, returned to his face. "Good point." Pushing up onto her own knees, she looped her arms around his neck and stretched to press a kiss against the angle of his chin. Then she relaxed her posture, her hands sliding down to rest against his chest.

"Thank you," she said in a low voice. "For . . . you know." She twirled a vague hand at the sheets, avoiding his eyes as her cheeks, which had been regaining their normal color, turned pink once more.

Damn but she had pockets of sweetness in her. *Deep* pockets that he had somehow managed not to cop to until today. Crooking a finger beneath her chin, he raised it until she met his gaze and gave her a wry smile. "Trust me, sweetheart," he said wryly, "it was my pleasure."

"Mine, too." She laid her head against his heart and stroked the hair on his other pec. "This feels . . . good," she said around a yawn. "Safe. Have I told you I really like your chest?"

Something deep inside of him clenched

tight for a moment, something that had less to do with her admiring his chest than it did with her tender gesture and that *safe,* which grabbed him for some reason. Maybe because it implied a level of trust that would allow her to admit to the vulnerability of sometimes not feeling safe. He'd have expected her to fiercely guard what she no doubt considered a weakness.

Raising his hand, he stroked her hair from the part in her bangs to her low ponytail, which he slowly pulled through his fist.

He cleared his throat and his voice came out low and gruff when he said, "I'm pretty damn fond of yours, as well." But he didn't even glance at those perky round breasts.

She went abruptly still, but before he could figure out why, she raised her head and shuffled back a few inches on the mattress opening up a space between them.

She raked a gaze down his body, then back up again, and he was struck by the knowing smile she flashed him. Gone was the woman with her brief flicker of sexual shyness. This was the cocky chick he was accustomed to.

She rubbed the back of her hand down his abs, her lips curling up in a cat-in-the-creamery smile when he sucked in a breath as her palm brushed so close to the bob of his dick that he could feel the warmth it radiated. He was vaguely betting her moment of unguarded honesty had driven her to this sudden mood change when she raised a finger to bridge the gap. His cock jerked as if it had been electrified, and all cogent thought left his head. Wrapping her fingers around him, she squeezed.

He had her on her back in seconds, clever fingers slipping between her thighs to bring her back up to speed.

Thighs opening, eyes blurry with passion, she reached for him. "Hurry."

Falling over her, he stiff-armed himself away from her upper body with one palm, thumbed down his erection and lined it up. Planting both hands on the bed next to her head he tilted his pelvis and slid into her with one easy thrust.

The last time had been all flash and fire, so he took it slow, sliding in and out of Macy with long, easy strokes. Moaning, she raised her hips to meet each thrust.

But his effortless rhythm went to hell when, hooking the bend of his elbows around the inside bend of her knees, he leaned into her, driving her legs back toward her chest. Clearly the move had him reaching her buzzer, because Macy went ape on him. Bracing her feet against his shoulders, she writhed and ground at the apex of each thrust. Holding himself deep he reciprocated with a rapid grind of his own.

She went off, coming all around him just as he'd demanded. And just like that, so did he.

His first inclination when the last pulse and throb faded away was to collapse atop her like a felled ox. Only the knowledge that, given the position he'd put her in, he'd probably snap her back in two made him pull back and help her straighten her legs. Then he rolled onto his back, grasping her sweet ass to maintain their connection.

She did that lay-her-head-over-his-heart thing again and exhaled a shaky breath. "God, Gabriel. That was . . . amazing."

"No shit," he agreed. He'd never had sex quite like it.

And he had a bad feeling he'd been talking out his ass earlier. Because he wasn't wrecking her for another man. She'd just wrecked him for any other woman.

CHAPTER EIGHTEEN

When Grace answered the rat-a-tat-tat of the knocker against her front door, the last person she expected to see was Jack Savage. "Oh," she said, one hand going to the pale pink pin tucks of her gauzy Empire-waist blouse. She stared at him standing hipshot on her tiny stoop, his tattooed arms like living tapestries in the afternoon sunlight, his hands behind his back — and hoped to heck she wasn't gaping.

Or worse, drooling.

"You've been sober for a good, long stretch now," he said, checking her over from the top of her messy updo to her bare feet. "And yet you never came to see me."

Oh man, she had been so tempted. But when she'd sobered up she'd felt mortally embarrassed over the way she'd climbed all over him, then had been pretty sure he'd laugh himself silly if she actually took him up on his invitation. In the end she simply

298

hadn't had the nerve to present herself at his Airstream. "I didn't think you were serious."

He shook his head. "Jayzus, Gracie. You are one cynical bird."

"No, I'm not! I'm —"

"I kind of thought that might be your reaction, though," he interrupted, "so it's here I am, then, to woo you. I brought you something." Bringing his left hand out from behind his back, he presented her with a bedraggled stalk of Queen Anne's lace, a tall white flower that grew wild along the roads. "And of course, what are flowers without the always popular chocolates to go with them? Or in this case, it." He brought out his right hand to offer her a bag of M&Ms. "Me, I go for peanut, but in case you're allergic, I didn't want you thinking I'm out to plant you six feet under, when my real aim is to shag you."

She choked and heat flooded her cheeks — as well as areas much farther south. "You have *got* to quit saying stuff like that."

"Ah, well, now." He stepped forward and she retreated as the hard muscle beneath the soft cotton of his black T-shirt brushed her breasts. He kept backing her up until they were in her living room, then closed the door behind them. "Too late to come all-over prim on me now, luv. I already know how much you like it when I talk dirty." He looked over her shoulder. "This is a nice flat. What is that you're doing over there?"

Interest lighting his sunlight-shot-whiskey eyes, he skirted her to reach the spot on the floor where she'd rolled out a long length of green construction paper and arranged the snapshots she'd been taking all summer of her upcoming students. Glue and scissors and a stack of fall-colored paper leaves were positioned above the top edge around the midway point.

"I'm planning my classroom bulletin board."

"Hey." He squatted down to indicate a photograph. "That's Ty. And here's his friend Charlie." He turned a white smile on her. "This is bleedin' deadly, Grace. If I'd seen my kisser on my teacher's wall back in Fourth Class, I would've been one thrilled little bugger." His brows furrowed for a second, making the little silver barbell beneath the left one shift. "Seems like Ty and Charlie should be closer together, though. I haven't seen the two of 'em separated since I got here."

"Now that you mention it, neither have I." She sank down to sit cross-legged next to him and switched Zach Westler's snapshot with Charlie's.

Jack's left arm crossed her vision as he reached to pick up a leaf. She got a quick glimpse of a few of the individual tattoos that made up the whole: a Celtic cross, vines, a koi within a fleshy unfurling flower, an icon with an eye in the middle that looked East Indian or Aztecan. Then his thumb gently caressed the crumpled-then-smoothed orange tissue paper she'd glued atop a gold construction-paper leaf, traced its green string veins. "I like this. Where are you going to put it?"

She pointed to a spot, and he set it in place, then spent a moment finessing the angle. Picking up another, he raised his brows and she pointed out another spot. He arranged that one, as well.

As if her hand belonged to a stranger, she watched it reach out and trace the tattooed heart on his inner forearm, aware of the heat of his skin beneath the word *Mum,* which was written on a narrow banner that waved through the heart's middle.

He stilled and turned his head to look at her. Her intentions must have been clear on her face, for he raised that brow again and said, "Yeah?"

She wet her lips. "Yes."

"Just to be clear, you're willing to put

aside this brilliant art in favor of shagging?"

"I am."

"Thank you, Jayzus," he said fervently, and she grinned at him, expecting to be pulled to her feet and asked the way to the bedroom.

Jack had other ideas. Pulling her over to straddle his lap, he scooted out of reach of the bulletin board project and rolled her onto her back. Then he plastered himself over her, kissing her to within an inch of her life.

It was the first time in Grace's life a man had ever wanted her too much to wait for the nicety of a bed. The knowledge set loose her inner hottie. Igniting, she returned his kiss with everything she had. The next thing she knew, it was a full-fledged conflagration.

"Are you freaking kidding me? *Three times?*"

Color flowed up Macy's neck as she looked at her cousin's incredulous tone. Crap. She hadn't meant to say a word about that part of this morning's events. Only . . .

Making love with Gabriel had been like nothing she'd ever experienced, and she'd just sort of blurted it out before her inner censor could catch up with her big mouth.

"Seriously?" Janna demanded. Shifting on

the seat of the chintz chair in their room, her newly cast-free leg supported by the ottoman, she gave Macy an enthralled look. "My personal best was twice. And in all honesty? That happened exactly one time. Sex with Sean was usually more about him than me, so unless I lent myself a hand I was lucky to get the first O, never mind a second."

"That still made you one up on me. I thought multiple orgasms were a myth." Sex wasn't something she'd participated in even a fraction as often as people around here seemed to think. Still, she *had* had a couple of lovers she'd always assumed were pretty good.

They hadn't come close to giving her what she'd experienced with Gabriel, though. Not on their best day.

Maybe that was why she'd said that stupid you-make-me-feel-safe stuff to him. She'd been mortified when it sunk in what she'd revealed because it just sounded so damn . . . needy. She was a big girl, dammit, and she didn't *need* anything, thank you very much.

Still, for all her self-directed pep talks aimed at assuring herself she'd exercised at least a modicum of damage control, uneasiness over the whole business — the dancing-on-the-edge-of-the-abyss screaming sex Gabriel had introduced her to, her uncharacteristic you-big-strong-protector/me-helpless-little-woman response — continued to slice through the rationales she'd been using to convince herself it was no big deal.

Al*though,* come to think of it . . .

Now that her emotions weren't so raw it occurred to her that *he* might have thought she meant she felt safe with him because he'd rescued her from a burning building.

Her shoulders, which had been creeping toward her ears, relaxed. *Of course.* It made perfect sense that she'd rely on him under those circumstances.

Not that any of it mattered. The moment Janna was up and self-sufficient again, she was out of here.

So what if she was enjoying Sugarville again or that the thought of leaving gave her an unexpected pang? Hell, that was completely understandable. Because of course it was going to be hard to leave Auntie and Uncle and Janna and Ty. But she could hardly come up with cutting-edge video concepts living in a hick-water town.

Could she?

"Between the fire, your, um, stop at Gabe's house and the fuss we all made when you got back home, you've had a hel-luvan eventful day," Janna said. "I have to tell you, I was surprised by how well you held up beneath everyone's concern. And impressed at how calm you stayed when we were all coming at you at once, wanting either to wrap you up in cotton wool or demanding all the gory details. But now . . ."

"Uh-huh." Leaning back against her dresser, she shot her cousin a lazy smile. "But now you know it's because . . ." She pinned down her pinkie finger with her thumb and held up the remaining three fingers.

Janna laughed, but although Macy liked that her cousin thought she was kidding, it was no joke. The way she'd felt when she and Gabriel left the clinic, she would have cracked under the bombardment of ques-tions, felt smothered by the concern that had radiated from her relatives in waves — never *mind* dealing with the boarders' vora-cious curiosity — if Gabe had brought her straight home. Yet his transforming love-making and his *need,* which had seemed to have matched her own — except he appar-ently didn't think it took anything away from him the way she feared hers might — had given her back her equilibrium, not to mention stripping her of all tension.

A private smile curved her lips.

"Wow," Janna said, studying her. "I guess you *really* let down your guard with Gabe."

"What?" Macy snapped erect. *"No."* She forced a laugh. Because she hadn't, had she? She shook her head. No, ma'am. That momentary "feel safe" insanity aside, she was too savvy to get too comfortable — or involved — with any man. That never led to anything but trouble. "It was just . . . all the moons aligning, y'know?" Her shoulder hitched. "Right situation, right time, right guy."

"Sure," Janna agreed, shooting her a knowing smile. "You being such a player and all when it comes to sex." She made a get-real noise. "Admit it, you like him."

"Well, yeah. Of course I do, or I couldn't've —" she waved a hand "— you know, gotten naked with him. But it's not like I'm in *love* with the guy or anything."

"Uh-huh." Janna gave her a look so understanding it made Macy squirm. "You just keep telling yourself that."

"You are so full of it," Macy muttered, knowing full well her cousin couldn't hear as she stomped down the hallway minutes later. Determined to find an opinion she liked better, she made a beeline for Jack's trailer. Hell, he knew her better than Janna did these days, anyhow.

Probably.

Maybe.

Jack hadn't been around when Gabriel had brought her home earlier, however, and now, glancing out the library/rec room window as she passed its doorway, she feared he was still AWOL, since his truck appeared to be gone from the lot behind the house.

Now what? Her postcoital relaxation was fading fast beneath her irritation at her cousin's refusal to accept that she wasn't falling in love. For cri'sake. The idea was preposterous. Even so, Janna's all-but-laugh-in-her-face adherence to the notion made her feel restless and frankly itchy.

Gabe had gone out to the Kilimner place again to investigate the fire, so he wasn't around. And in all honesty, now that she was no longer in the grip of his burn-down-the-town brand of lovemaking, she wasn't all that certain she could even look at him without feeling ten kinds of self-conscious, never mind carry on a coherent conversation. Because, Lord. She had never felt *anything* like that with any man, let alone responded in a way even approaching the brazenness she'd displayed with him.

She wouldn't mind the distraction of

chauffeuring Ty to whatever was on today's schedule — the pool again, if she remembered correctly, followed by tryouts for soccer — but her aunt seemed to think she should be resting. And Auntie so rarely dug in her heels that when she did there was no arguing with her. As a result, Uncle Bud had taken over Macy's usual chores.

She considered throwing herself into a dress-up session to end all dress-up sessions. But in all honesty, even if she could dredge up the least desire to return to her and Janna's room where she'd open herself up to even more comments she didn't want to hear, she was in no mood to muck about with costumes and cosmetics.

Sometimes real life just sucked the joy right out of make-believe.

She went out onto the front porch, but there wasn't so much as a breath of fresh air or shade to be found. So she went back inside to poke her head into the kitchen, secretly relieved when her aunt wasn't there. She wandered into the rec room and shot a desultory, solitary game of pool. Then she decided, heat or no heat, a walk would help clear her mind and settle her down, so she went back to the kitchen, grabbed an apple and let herself out the back door.

She was heading back from the relative

coolness of the orchard a bit later when she heard the throaty sound of Jack's diesel-fueled truck coming up the drive and promptly corrected her course toward his trailer. She was there to meet him when he pulled up next to his trailer and shut down the engine.

Before she could say more than a God-I'm-glad-to-see-you inspired "Hey," Jack had leaped out of the cab and grasped her upper arms. "You all right?" he demanded. "I heard in town that you were trapped in a burning building."

"I'm fine — Gabriel got me out before things got completely hairy. But how on earth did you hear about it?"

"I stopped by the bank to use the ATM and that cute little bird manning the window told me."

"Good God. The Internet has nothing on Sugarville when it comes to instant communication."

"I know." Grinning, he slung a wiry arm around her shoulders and ushered her into his trailer. "I love this town."

Macy felt a strange twinge. Because a huge part of her loved it, too. But it seemed to be constantly engaged in a war with another part that thought matters would be best served all 'round if she hit the road back to southern Cal the instant Janna was up to resuming her responsibilities.

"Clearly they love you, too," she said a bit sourly, "because not a soul has sold your story to the rags and brought the paparazzi down on your head. Me, they want to burn in effigy. Well, when they're not actively trying to drown me, that is."

Jack's countenance promptly darkened. "You'll get no argument from me there's some shitehawk wankers in this town. But a lot of folks have been nice, too — and to you as well as me, luv, even knowing what they think they know about you. I love that I can walk down Commerce Street without being mobbed. And that I can actually hold a conversation that doesn't begin and end with my ability to rock a guitar." He smacked his forehead. "But what a gob I am to keep you standing." Sweeping the Sunday papers off the dinette's bench seats, he waved her in. "Here. Sit yerself down. Can I get you a G?"

"I can't drink a whole Guinness, but I'd love a snort."

He pulled a bottle from the cupboard, opened it and poured a shot into a teacup. The rest he upended into a beer mug and brought them both over. Handing her the dainty flowered cup, he slid into the dinette seat opposite her. "Tell me about the fire. How the bloody bollocks did you get trapped?"

She recounted her adventure, conscious that she didn't have the same discomfort sharing the details with him that she'd had with her family. Jack didn't exclaim or baby a person to death, and she tried to verbalize her appreciation. "One of the things I love about you is your laid-back approach. I gotta tell you I dreaded coming home this afternoon because I knew Auntie and Uncle's first inclination would be to wrap me in cotton wool. Instead I talked Gabriel into taking me out to see the house he's building."

"Sounds like he was an all-around big help today, yeah?"

"Mmm-hmm," she agreed, seeing too late the trap in having introduced the topic. Heat crawled up her throat and onto her cheeks.

Good grief. She'd blushed more since coming back to Sugarville than she had in the entire ten years she'd been gone.

His mug of ale suspended midway to his mouth, Jack stared at her. Then he slowly lowered it back to the table. "Feckin' hell. You did the deed with Donovan."

Her face burned hotter yet.

"What do they bleedin' do, put Spanish fly in the town reservoir?"

"Okay, *that's* an odd little segue," she said, puzzled, as she searched his face. Then a lightbulb went off over her head and she slowly set her own cup on the table. "Oh. My. Gawd. Jack Savage, have you been getting busy with my nephew's schoolteacher?"

His eyes went soft. "She's amazing, Mace. I like her . . . *damn.*" He shook his head. "More than I have words to say."

She didn't know why it bothered her. It wasn't the fact that he had a thing for Grace. She liked the teacher a lot and could actually visualize her with Jack, as Grace was just the nice-girl type he had always gone for. But his easy acceptance of his feelings — *that* made her uncomfortable. "Janna thinks I'm in love with Gabriel," she blurted. Picking up her teacup, she tossed back the last sip, then blotted her lips with the back of her hand. "Isn't that the dumbest thing you've ever heard?"

"Hell, no. Dumbest thing *I've* heard is any word out of that cod Mayfield's mouth. You and Gabe, on the other hand — Jayzus, you've been strikin' sparks off each other for as long as I've been here."

"Okay, sure. But that's just — you know — sex. Janna suddenly claiming I'm in love with the man is something entirely different. Jeez, Jack, I've known him for all of five minutes. I'm not about to fall head over heels for a guy I'm barely even acquainted with —"

He snorted. "I'd say you made a good piece of progress down that road today."

Heat flared, deep and unbidden, as Jack's words triggered a memory of Gabe's hot mouth against her skin and the look that had been in his eyes as he slid deeply —

She slammed a door shut on the memory. "*As* I was saying —" Essaying a coolness she didn't feel, she lifted her chin. "The idea that I'm in love with a guy who I know well only in the Biblical sense . . . well, that's about as logical as you deciding *you're* in love with Grace."

"Ah, well, now, here's the thing, luv," he said with a befuddled smile. "I think I may be."

"*No.*" Macy scratched her arms in an attempt to alleviate the sudden persistent itch just under her skin. "That doesn't make sense. If I've known Gabriel five minutes, you've known Gracie three. That's simply not long enough to fall in love."

He shrugged. "Who's to say what constitutes long enough?" Reaching across the table, he ruffled her hair. "Sometimes, Macy girl, the heart just decides on its own time-table."

CHAPTER NINETEEN

Gabe stared blankly at the slim stack of file folders in his lap. A hot, dry breeze plucked at his hair, rolling in through the open window of his SUV, which was parked beneath the stand of Douglas firs and alders out near the county line. It was the same spot where he and Johnny had gotten together the day Macy first rolled into town.

Maybe that was why every time he let his mind drift, hoping his subconscious would miraculously solve his arsonist case, he found himself thinking of her instead — and about the best-damn-sex-ever morning they'd shared two days ago.

He wanted more. He'd taken a stab at convincing himself that one session with Macy was enough, that the smart money was on backing off. But he didn't buy it. She was sweet and fun and so giving with the people she cared about that it just knocked him on his butt.

The sudden funny pang in the region of his heart — almost as if he desired to be counted among that select group — caught him unprepared for a moment. Then he shook it off. Because that wasn't what their relationship was about.

Still, that kind of sex didn't just roll around every day of the week. So what if it wasn't the greatest love match of their generation? Hell, with the increasing progress Janna was showing in her recovery, Macy probably wouldn't even be around much longer.

They might as well explore the possibilities as long as she was.

It was a damn good idea — maybe even brilliant. The only drawback was that she clearly wasn't on the same page of his game plan. Here they were, two people living in the same house, and his few glimpses of her since bringing her home the day before yesterday had been her shapely butt going out the door of whatever room he walked into.

He shifted in his seat. Then straightened in determination. Well, he'd just have to do something about that. Because damned if watching her run away was an option. Not now that he'd made up his mind to pursue this relationship — at least for the amount of time she was still here or until they tired of each other, whichever came first.

He looked up, his thoughts mercifully interrupted as a car pulled off the highway. Bumping over the uneven terrain, Johnny pulled the sheriff department's Ford Ranger alongside Gabe's SUV until their cabs were aligned, one facing in and the other out, and threw his vehicle into Park. His window rolled down with a quiet hum Gabe barely heard over the birds chattering up in the trees.

"Hey," the deputy greeted him. "What are you doing clear out here?"

He shoved Macy out of his mind and brought his focus back where it should be. "Trying to figure out who the hell's been setting all these fires." He slid the folders onto the passenger seat. "How 'bout you?"

"I had a call over on Palouse Road that turned out to be a nonevent."

"Given our businesses, nonevents are generally a good thing."

"Yeah, it beats being faced with fighting spouses or a loaded gun. And of the two? I gotta tell ya, it's a toss-up which I'd prefer." He gave Gabe a closer look. "So, why are you out here when you've got a perfectly good station house to work in?"

Gabe blew out a breath as he realized he

was about to admit what he'd been trying to deny ever since the unwelcome thought had first crept into his head. But it had burrowed in to take up residence and refused to leave. "Because I've got a bad feeling it may be someone on my crew."

"What?" Johnny stared at him. "Get out."

"Wish I could. But whoever's setting these fires seems to know what he's doing. He's careful, he always uses a long timing device and the places are never all that far from town. They're usually noticed and called in, at any rate, in time for us to reach them before they're fully engaged."

"Gabe. We're talking about your crew, dude. They're *firemen.*"

"Who unfortunately are responsible for setting more fires than you might imagine. Try searching Google for *firemen arson* sometime and you'll get a shitload of hits, most of which are taken directly from the news. And every article seems to agree on one thing — that the majority of firefighters arrested for arson are volunteers." A rough laugh escaped his throat. "Big frigging surprise, considering seventy-five percent of us *are* volunteers. Still, it's a lot rarer for a professional to go renegade."

He speared his fingers into his hair and ground the heels of his hands into his eyes.

Then he dropped them to the steering wheel, staring at them as if they belonged to someone else. "Jesus," he said wearily to the tan fingers flexing against the wheel. "I can't tell you how much I hope I'm wrong. But I can't ignore the possibility any longer that I'm not. Too many things fit."

"*Why* would they do it?"

"Beats the hell outta me." He looked at his friend. "The popular theory leans toward either money — as in volunteers only get paid if the truck goes out — and/or a thirst for excitement and public adulation. Shit, Johnny, the vast majority of firefighters would never dream of starting a fire. But of the small percentage that do for whatever reason, they're often responsible for a large number of them. Once they set the first they tend to become serial fire starters."

"So where do you start?"

"That's what I've been sitting here trying to figure out." Johnny didn't need to know that he'd been distracted by thoughts of Macy.

Then he gave himself a mental shake. Because neither did *he* need to think about that right now. "I tracked down the phone number for my predecessor in Florida —"

"Chief Stoller?"

"Yeah. And between what he told me and

talking to Colin Atkins and Jake Kaufman again about the fires they set, I think we've probably had a problem longer than we thought."

"That doesn't sound good. Hang on." Johnny climbed out of his rig and walked around to get in Gabe's. He settled in the seat Gabe cleared for him. "Tell me."

"Stoller said they had a couple of abandoned-car fires last fall and a tall grass fire that he was never sure if it had been deliberately set or was the result of someone throwing their cigarette out a car window. Both are classic fireman-set fires. So are the abandoned- or secluded-building fires that we've been dealing with."

"Shit. And what was that about the teens?"

"I realized that since they'd copped to the non-building fires, we'd never gone over all the events one by one. So I sat them down and had them walk me through each one." He gave Johnny a level look. "Turns out that while they set the four garbage-can fires, they didn't start the first Dumpster fire we were called out on. They only set the second one and the McFadden Dumpster where we caught them."

"How can that be?" Johnny straightened. "I was there when you specifically stated you had them for X number of can and X number of Dumpster fires."

"Right on top of which I told them I was an arson-forensics wizard. So, between knowing their prints were all over the first Dumpster, since they'd checked it out after the fire, and watching too much TV, they decided to spare themselves our skepticism and just let us lump it in with the ones they were responsible for." He blew out a breath. "But the truth is, they got the idea to upgrade from their can fires after they saw the first Dumpster that someone else had set." He shrugged. "Bigger flames, more fun, I guess."

"Where do you go from here?"

"I wish I knew," Gabe admitted, jerking a thumb at the folders he'd moved to the backseat. "I've gone through my crew's employment records as far back as they're available to me and came up with a big, fat zero. Not one frigging thing popped. So maybe I can pick your brain while I have you here. Can you tell me if any of my crew's ever been arrested?"

"Not as far as I know, but I'll run a check to see if anything crops up."

"Any of them have a habit of disappearing occasionally, even if only for a day or a weekend? No one has since I've taken over, but maybe someone's got a gambling habit or —" Frustration tightening his fingers on the wheel, he gave it a sudden, violent jerk. "Fuck me if I know. Jesus, I'm reaching here. And yet —" He met the other man's eyes. "Whoever set that fire the other day came too damn close to injuring Macy. I hope to God he didn't know she was in there, but I can't be sure of that. And that's my problem in a nutshell. I'm just not sure of anything in this goddamn case. But I know this — I want to stop whoever it is before someone's seriously injured or killed."

He rubbed his eyes again, then looked back at the deputy. "Christ, this sucks. I'm not what you'd call particularly close to any of my crew, but lately I have been getting to know them better. Damn, Johnny, every single one of them has helped me with my house at one time or the other, and I don't like the idea of *any* of them being responsible for this shit. So do me a favor, will you?"

"Name it," Johnny promptly agreed.

"Help me prove my suspicions wrong."

Macy hightailed it out of the dining room after dinner that evening, but not fast enough. Gabriel was hard on her heels, and banging through the screen door onto the porch in her wake, he whipped out a hand to grasp her upper arm. The next thing she knew, she was being whirled around.

Her body slapped up against his, and before she could say a word he was kissing her, all hot lips, strong tongue and an ineffable need that she might not be able to put a name to but to which she sure as hell responded.

Clutching his shoulders, she kissed him back.

When he raised his head an instant — or maybe an aeon — later, he gave her a level gaze. "You've been avoiding me."

She longed to tell him he was full of it, but of course he wasn't. "Maybe."

He stroked his thumb the length of her lower lip. "Come with me to my house."

She shouldn't. He'd made love to her the other day and her world had started moving at warp speed. She felt as if she was *still* running two days later, just trying to catch up — suffused with a twitchiness she'd be happy to go for the rest of her life without experiencing again. She was accustomed to being one jump ahead of the game, but that sure hadn't been the case once they'd quit making love and returned to real life. The sex had been fantastic. The aftermath, however, with her inability to focus for more than a few minutes at a pop and her raft of self-protective coping mechanisms screaming warnings to stay away, to not do that again . . . ? Not so much.

So, no: she really shouldn't.

And yet the lovemaking *had* been . . . *Lord.* Amazing. Stupendous. Out of this world. And *that* she did want to experience again. Boy, did she want to!

But Macy O'James was nobody's pushover. She raised her chin. "I'm not here for your entertainment, Donovan. I'm here to help Janna and Auntie. And I'm probably needed inside right this minute."

"Well, let's find out." He stepped back, opened the screen door and stuck his head in the house. "Lenore! Janna! You need Macy for anything tonight?"

"Nope," Lenore called from the kitchen, and Janna said from her room, "Not me."

"Then I'll have her back in an hour or two." He turned back to her. Moved close. Leaned down and growled in her ear, "Maybe I'm here for *your* entertainment — you ever consider that?"

Hell, no. But she had to admit she liked the idea. She particularly liked that he was making the first move for a change. "Oh. That's okay, then."

Gabe laughed and hustled her around the

boardinghouse to his SUV.

She wondered on the short ride to his place if he'd heard the news about Jack and Grace. She almost opened her mouth to ask but kept the question to herself. Because now that she'd committed to this, she found herself unwilling to destroy the mood. And, face it, when it came to Grace, Gabriel had demonstrated jealousy of Jack in the past. Discovering his ex-girl was definitely having a fling with the rock star might put him off making love to *her* again.

Which after days of telling herself she'd be better off without, she was suddenly wild to experience. And clearly, and most satisfyingly, so was Gabriel. The instant they reached his house he hauled her inside and led her straight to the bedroom in the basement, where he immediately peeled his T-shirt off over his head and reached for her.

Just like the first time they'd made love, contact proved explosive. One second she was on her feet, clinging to Gabe as he strung hot, wet, drugging kisses from her lips to her jaw and down her throat to her collarbone, all the while telling her things he intended to do to her that made her knees buckle. Then they were naked, on the bed. He was over her, inside of her, and, oh, God, she was arching from her heels to the back of her head as fiery sensations detonated one after another around that hard, talented source of pleasure thrusting in and out of her — until finally she melted bonelessly back onto the mattress, Gabriel's weight collapsing atop her seconds later.

She probably should have felt smothered. Instead, she felt safe again, dammit. And although she knew it was just an illusion — and one that wouldn't last, at that — for now she intended to enjoy herself, for she couldn't deny the sheer pleasure of it.

"That," she breathed, "was amazing." She wiggled beneath him. "Let's do it again." Okay, the idea sounded good in theory. She was so relaxed, however, that she doubted she was physically up to the challenge. Still, it was fun to dare him.

And she could probably get with the program if *he* was up for it.

His soft snort fluttered her hair against her temple. "Whataya think I am, sixteen?"

"Hey, I'm only talking about a measly round two here." Grabbing a handful of his hair, she pulled his head back so he could see her sly smile. "When I know you're good for three." She let go, and his face promptly slumped back into the curve where her neck met her shoulder. She snapped her fingers next to his nonburied ear. "Chop, chop, Donovan! Grab another condom."

"Jeez, you're bossy. Think you can give me a minute to catch my breath first?" Pushing up onto his forearms, he looked down at her, then freed a hand to brush a strand of hair away from the corner of her lips. "Tell me how you got started in the music business. I would've thought, after the hard time this town gave you over your reputation, that sexy videos would be the last career you'd have chosen."

"I hit L.A. with nothing more than a high school education and the ability to role-play." She gave him a little smile. "I decided that qualified me to be an actor and decided to give Hollywood the benefit of my brilliance. Mostly that meant waiting tables and catching a bit part here or there. When I auditioned for a character that was barely more than a walk-on in the Aussie Kiss video and Jack picked me for a larger role, I had no idea it was going to be the beginning of a new career. I don't think anyone knew how big that video would become."

Feeling faintly exposed to be discussing a subject with him that no one except her family had ever bothered to ask her about — at least in this town — she decided it was time to change the conversational direction. She gave him a sultry smile and trailed a fingernail from his shoulder to his collarbone, then over a hard pectoral muscle to the flat disk of his nipple. She pouted and heaved a sigh. "*Now* will you get another condom?"

"Wait. This is good stuff. Tell me more."

She flashed him a knowing smile. "You just wanna talk so you don't have to disclose you're not up to another performance, don'tcha? It's okay. You can admit it."

"Funny girl. Me big man." Leaning on one elbow, Gabe thumped his chest and felt like laughing. He'd never met a woman who made him feel so . . . playful. That wasn't generally something he carried in his social bag of tricks. Instead, he gave her an arrogant look down the bridge of his nose. "I'll have you know I can perform anywhere, any way."

"Uh-huh. Just how old *are* you, anyhow?"

"Thirty-four."

"Ah, well, then. Take all the time you need. I didn't realize you were a senior citizen. Holy crap, you're halfway to seventy — I'm amazed you made it through *one* session."

"Why, you little —" Pushing up onto his palms, he looked down at her and almost laughed at the self-satisfied smirk she gave him. Instead, he gave her a faux scowl and, climbing to his feet, snatched his jeans from the floor where he'd kicked them off. He extracted his wallet, which was closer than the chest, fished out a condom and tossed it to her.

She snatched it out of the air. "We'd best get this on you, hadn't we? Before — you know." Holding up an erect finger, she caught his eye as she allowed the digit to droop.

"Okay, that tears it, sister." Falling forward onto his hands and knees on the end of the mattress, he prowled up the bed to her. "You are *so* gonna eat your words. But first —" He dropped onto his stomach between her legs, which he grasped by the ankles to arrange over his shoulders, then splayed his fingers against her stomach to hold her in place. "We need to get you back up to speed."

"That's okay," she protested unexpectedly. "I'm good."

Touched by her sudden look of uncertainty — so much for Macy the sex kitten — he pressed a kiss into her firm inner thigh. Used the tip of his tongue to trace the crease where it joined her groin. Breathed a heated exhalation across the plump lips of her sex as he raised his head to bestow identical attention on her other thigh. Not until he felt her hips commence a gentle bump and grind, lifting toward his mouth, then contracting into the mattress when she failed to make contact, did he glide the thumb and index fingers of his free hand along the slippery cleft on either side of her clitoris. "There you are," he whispered as the tiny organ peeked out of its hood. Giving it a soft pinch, he glanced up to see Macy's head drop back. He lowered his own head. And licked.

She wilted onto her back, reaching out to grip his hair. But not to push him away.

He got so into the flavors, the textures of her that he nearly let it get away from him. When he realized she was getting close — much closer than he'd intended — he pushed back.

"Where's that rubber?" he demanded, looking around the rumpled sheets. Spotting it on his own, he snatched it up. But when he looked up from ripping its wrapper open a moment later, it was to see her hand slipping between her legs.

"Uh-uh-uh." Grabbing her wrist, he pulled it away. "None of that — when you come, I plan to be right there with you. Here." He handed her the opened packet. "Put this on me, okay?"

She did, and then he was sliding inside of her and feeling his eyes all but roll back in his head at the slick, muscular heat pulling, stroking, damn near milking him. He had to grit his teeth and recite the multiplication tables to keep from ejaculating before he had the chance to get her off.

Luckily, he didn't have long to wait. For while Macy wasn't a screamer, she had her own escalating little moan that he loved to hear, as it was a sure precursor to her satisfaction. She started in now, low and sweet, growing gradually less quiet and infinitely grittier in tone the closer he brought her to the edge. Until finally, digging her nails into his back, she shot right over it, that hot sheath clamping down on his dick like a silk-encased, hot-cream-filled iron fist. And he followed only seconds behind, free-falling into an infinity of knee-howling pleasure.

This time when the last shudder of satisfaction faded and gravity kicked in to poleax him, he was careful not to flatten her. Yet even as he held himself above her, she wrapped her arms around his neck and tugged him down. His weight pressed the air from her lungs in an audible whoosh, but she merely smiled against his neck.

"There," she said with sleepy satisfaction.

"That's better."

And he knew then that he was in big trouble. Because this was starting to feel less and less casual by the minute. He couldn't say exactly what it was he felt for Macy. But he knew this much.

It wasn't the least bit casual.

CHAPTER TWENTY

Everything will be Dandy, if I just keep this . . . whatever it is with Gabriel . . . casual. But as Macy headed for the boardinghouse kitchen, she was less than thrilled with her plan. The main problem was that she and Gabe had gotten together an additional four times since last week's encounter — and making love with him hadn't felt casual. Intense, amazing, connective, yes. Casual, not so much.

Still, there was no rule saying she couldn't be more guylike and just take it one red-hot session at a time, was there? That was undoubtedly what Gabe was doing. It remained to be seen whether she could pull it off, but hey, if *he* could, she should be able to, as well.

Spotting her aunt at the worktable as she entered the kitchen, she shoved everything else aside and joined the older woman. "I got Ty off with the Brand X grandparents," she said, pulling out a chair across the table and taking a seat. "And George delivered the mail so I brought it in." She slid the stack over to Lenore. "Need some help snapping those beans?"

"You bet — I never turn down help." Lenore moved the large pottery bowl of string beans to the middle of the table and picked up the mail to quickly sort through it. She stopped at a letter midway through the pile. "Oh, dear." With a sympathetic grimace, she handed it back to Macy.

She looked at the letter she'd written her mother before leaving Redondo Beach. Given the thickness of the long, skinny labels along the envelope's bottom edge, it had been forwarded two or three times before some postal employee had finally stamped it with a telltale purple hand pointing its Return to Sender finger. "Well, this is par for the course. My personal best getting a letter through before Mom moves again is one in three — and since the last one, or maybe it was the one before, reached her . . ."

"I'm sorry, baby girl."

"Nah, don't be." She hitched a shoulder. "You'll notice I put your return address on it instead of my own — and I mailed the thing before I left to come up here. I sometimes feel like I'm wasting my time writing, but having my mail miss or chase Mom sure beats those years I spent living with her when we pulled up stakes once or twice a month. And she calls every few months."

Lenore looked less than convinced, so Macy flashed her an extra-sunny smile. "It really is okay, Auntie." Reaching into the pottery bowl, she pulled out a fistful of green beans and began systematically snapping off the ends. If there was maybe the tiniest niggling in her stomach, well, she knew from experience it would pass — and probably sooner rather than later, as that seemed to be truer the farther away from childhood she moved.

She and the woman who in her heart of hearts she considered her real mother drank iced tea and exchanged comfortable conversation as they snapped their way through the big bowl of beans. Drawing a deep breath, she said, "I think maybe I'll go to our ten-year reunion after all, if Janna feels up to attending."

"Good for you," Lenore approved. "I'm tickled to hear it."

Macy swallowed her immediate desire to take it back and dedicated herself to the beans for a minute or two to avoid telegraphing her doubts. When she looked up again, it was to catch her aunt studying her braided hair and makeup-free face. Oh, she had on lip balm and mascara, but as far as she was concerned that was the same thing.

Lenore gave her a fond smile. "You look about sixteen years old."

"I *feel* kind of naked. But I told Gabriel I'd help him paint his basement." She snorted. "That's prettying it up — painting was the price he demanded, the bastard, for letting me select a nice neutral color instead of the boring white he was leaning toward." She waved the digression away with impatient fingers. "Anyway, it seemed sorta pointless to get all gussied up when I'll probably just end up splattered with paint."

She glanced at the old schoolhouse clock on the wall. "He had some work to do this morning but said he'd be back to pick me up around noon."

"So." Lenore smiled. "You and Gabe, huh?"

"Oh, no, it's not like — we're not a *couple* or anything!"

Her aunt merely looked at her and Macy squirmed. "That is —" She blew out a frustrated breath. "Oh, hell. I don't know what we are." She took an inordinate amount of time getting the next bean snapped just right. "When I'm with him," she admitted in a low voice. "It feels kinda — right. No. More than kind of. *Right* right, y'know? But the minute I'm on my own again, I start picking it to pieces."

She looked up. "I've never had a relationship with a guy that's lasted more than a couple of months. And in truth, Auntie? I don't think I have what it takes to stick with anyone for the long haul. I'm not even sure I know how to love."

"What hogwash," Lenore said. "You have the biggest heart of anyone I know." She reached across to wrap her work-worn fingers around Macy's and squeeze. "You think someone lacking the ability to love would just drop everything to come running the minute we asked for help?"

Macy waved the bean in her free hand. "That's family love. It's the romantic kind I'm afraid I don't have the chops to sustain."

"Trust me, you've got love to spare for that, as well. Honey, Bud isn't your blood relative, but have you ever considered him anything other than your family?"

"Of course not! But he's *been* part of my life for as long as I can remember."

"All right, then take Jack. I've watched the two of you, and you couldn't treat him more like a brother if he was one. The point is, baby girl, most people create their families as they go along. Love in any guise boils down to trust. And communication. So you take some time today to get to know Gabe in ways other than just the sexual. *Talk* to the boy." Releasing Macy's hand, she sat back and gave her a lopsided smile. "You might be surprised what you discover."

Lenore's words played through Macy's head as she and Gabriel rolled out of his air bed an hour or so later and got serious about arranging their painting gear. Because her aunt was right: they'd been using great sex to avoid actually talking to each other for the past week.

Okay, *she* had been more so than Gabriel. He'd tried several times to start a conversation that had more depth than their usual banter, but except for that once when she'd told him a little of how she got into music videos, she'd changed the subject or used sex to divert his attention. Much as she hated to admit it, she'd let insecurity over her ability to sustain a relationship and fear of failure should she turn out to be every bit as lousy at it as she suspected she'd be keep her from even trying.

She opened her mouth now to initiate a conversation but allowed the busywork of laying tarps and getting out rollers, paint trays and brushes to sidetrack her. Finally she said, "It must have taken forever to tape all this woodwork."

That wasn't so stinkin' hard. And while it was a long poke from deep, it was a start.

"No shit, it took up all my free time last night." He squatted in front of the hearth where he'd spread out newspapers and opened a can of paint. "Hey," he said. "This is *nice.*"

She gave him a droll look. "Should I be insulted that you sound so surprised?"

"No, it's just . . ." Glancing up at her, he shrugged. "You kept saying the place needed a nice earth tone, but I didn't have a clue what that meant, since it could be anything from grass green to sunset orange. I like this. It's a color, but not a set-the-wall-to-screaming one." His brows furrowed as he read the lid. "Huh. This says Bennington Gray, but it looks more like one of those fancy steamed-milk and whipped-cream drinks at Starbucks."

They discussed color names and who came up with them as Gabe used a brush to cut in paint from the ceiling molding. The topic ran its course about the time he finished across the top and squatted to begin the same process in from the floorboards. Macy picked up her roller, climbed the ladder he'd set up for her and started filling the gap between the two. But after they'd been silent for a while, she took a deep breath, quietly blew it out — and finally brought up the subject she'd been avoiding all week. Closely watching her color blend into the paint he'd cut in, she said casually, "So, have you heard the news about Jack and Grace?"

She felt rather than saw him look up at her. "What about them?"

"They're having a fling. Well, it might actually be more than a fling — at least on Jack's part. He seems to think he could be in love with her."

"Yeah? Are you okay with that?"

"Me?" Roller halting midapplication, she stared down at him. "Why wouldn't I be? *I'm* not the one who's been acting —" *Uh, probably not a good idea to go there, Mace.*

"How have I been acting? That is your implication, I take it. That I've been acting out in some way?"

She declined to answer and he rose to his feet. Came up to where she perched on the stepladder, his hands on his lean hips as he gave her a slow once-over. *"How* have I been acting, Macy?" It was a low-voiced demand, but a demand all the same.

"Jealous," she snapped. "Okay? Every time you've seen Jack and Grace together, you've acted crazy jealous."

He stared at her with his mouth ajar for a moment . . . then burst out laughing.

Her eyebrows snapped together. "What's so damn funny?"

"I wasn't jealous of *Grace* with Jack, you twit. I wanted to rip his head from his shoulders over you."

"What?"

"You heard me. If I've been acting jealous around him — and I object to the *crazy* portion of that claim — it's because I thought he and you had a thing going."

"Are you crazy? Jack's like the brother I never had."

"I'm happy to hear it — not to mention totally get the concept. Because no matter how much I tried to convince myself otherwise when we were dating, Grace always felt too much like a sister to me. So as long as Jack's not using her simply to amuse himself while he's in town, I'm good with whatever Grace chooses to do."

"He's not like that, Gabe. But that's fair enough." She leaned down, pressed a kiss on his lips, then straightened to give him a quirky smile. "So you were jealous over me, huh?"

"Maybe a little." He smacked her on the butt and went back to his painting. "But I wouldn't plan on thinking that means you're gonna get your way from here on out if I were you."

Macy turned her attention back to the job, but she was aware of a happy sort of warmth infusing her.

A while later she said, "I never hear you talk about your family."

He stilled for a moment, then rolled his wide shoulders. "That's because there's not much to say. I'm an only child of an only child, so I don't have much in the way of relatives."

"Are your parents gone, then?"

"Damned if I know. I never met my old man, so I have no idea if he's dead or alive. As for my mother, well, given her lifestyle she may well be six feet under. She was still kicking when I turned eighteen and left foster care, but I haven't actually seen or heard from her in the twenty years since she decided I was cramping her style and dumped me in the system."

If he was thirty-five, that would have made him — "Your mother abandoned you when you were *fourteen?*" Macy didn't know why she received the news like a body blow, but she wanted to hug him, to cover him in kisses. And she wanted to track down his mother if the woman was still alive and bitch-slap her into next Tuesday. Instinctively knowing he wouldn't welcome anything he'd construe as pity, however, she forced herself to say in a matter-of-fact tone, "Well, that sucks big-time."

His big shoulders rolled. "It did at the time. I don't really care anymore. But what's your story?"

"Mine?"

"I know you're close to Bud and Lenore, but what about your parents?"

This was supposed to be her getting to know him — she didn't want to talk about *her.*

But even as the thought struck, she could see how one-sided it was. She blew out a soft breath. "I didn't know my dad, either. My folks were married, but he died when I was too young to remember. My mother, though? Well, Mom isn't Mother of the Year material, either. She dragged me from town to town until my biggest dream was a stable place to call home."

"Why'd she move so often?"

"You got me." She shrugged as if it didn't matter, but felt a twinge of her old unhappy frustration over the fact that her mom would never discuss it. She'd simply packed them up with an aggravating cheerfulness and hit the road again despite knowing how much Macy hated it. "I guess she was looking for something. She never found it, apparently, because she still is." Her shoulder hitched. "I don't know, I hardly ever hear from her." She shook off the touch of unease this topic gave her and told Gabriel the definitive thing that made it all okay. "But I had Auntie Lenore and Uncle Bud."

"You were lucky there."

"No foolin'. Having them for role models is like holding the winning ticket in the Mega Millions lottery. They made all the difference in how I turned out. Well, the good parts of me, anyhow. I take full blame for the rest."

Once again she turned her attention to her paint job, but now that the lines of communication had been breached, she found herself wild to learn more. "So," she demanded as she climbed down to move her ladder along the wall a couple of feet, "what first got you interested in firefighting?"

Great day. Gabe knotted a towel around his hips, whistling off-key as he leaned into the big mirror of the boardinghouse's upstairs bathroom and used his inner forearm to wipe a clear space in the steamy surface before reaching for the shave gel. Squirting a blob into his palm, he used his fingers to spank it into foam, then spread it on his face. Picking up his razor, he cut a smooth swath through the shaving cream and turned on the faucet to rinse the blade clean.

Even though Macy had spent a decent amount of time with him this past week, he'd had the feeling she was, if not actively avoiding him any longer, still holding back. But today — well, today she'd really opened up for the first time. She'd *talked.* Asked questions and answered his. And he'd liked it. He'd liked it big-time.

On top of which they'd painted the entire rec room. It was pretty much a red-letter day.

Tonight they were going out on a date. Well, not just the two of them, but still their first official date. It was to be a double date, apparently, something he could honestly say he'd never been on. But Macy wanted them to go out with Grace and Jack — and what the hell, since the only option for a night out in this town was pretty much the Red Dog unless there was a special event at the grange hall, they would've been surrounded by a crowd anyhow.

Still, it should prove interesting. *His* ex dating *her* ex while he and Macy bore witness. Weird, but interesting.

Jack's like the brother I never had.

He grinned, and seeing as it tightened his face, tipped his chin up and shaved up his neck and beneath his chin. Jack wasn't her ex, as it turned out. And if that made Gabe a tad smug, too effin' bad. He'd earned it in the sweat equity he'd put into thinking the rocker had been her lover.

Someone banged on the door. "Get a move on, sonny," Mr. Grandview groused from the other side. "I'm an old man. My bowels don't work as good as they useta."

Gabe vacated the bathroom moments later. "It's all yours," he said to the elderly man, who hustled in with his newspaper in hand.

He strode down the hallway to his room. His good mood persisted as he selected a navy T-shirt, his newest pair of jeans and a rust-colored, short-sleeved, loose-weave shirt that he'd leave open over the T-shirt to dress things up. He pulled a brush through his hair, recited, "Testicles, spectacles, wallet and watch," in the age-old checklist a counselor at the Creighton Boy's Home had taught him for making sure a guy had all the essentials before leaving home and exited the room. He was whistling again as he loped down the stairs.

That came to a ragged halt a few minutes later when Macy strolled down the hallway in yet another of her getups.

For Christ sake. Couldn't she just once go out in public without the frigging camouflage?

Then guilt stabbed him as an image of her the last time she had worn regular clothes in Sugarville — at the clinic after the fire — flashed through his mind. And, hell, it wasn't as if tonight's outfit was all that outrageous — she had a kind of film-noir femme fatale look going with that little formfitting, pin-tucked, white satin blouse tucked into a skintight black skirt and those retro blue peep-toed, Cuban-heeled shoes she'd worn the first time he'd seen her. She had parted her hair on the left and must have pinned her bangs to the side, because a glossy wave fell over her right eye. Her left was made up with dramatic eye stuff, including lashes so long they had to be fake, and her lips were a moist red. She looked sexy and a little dangerous, but he couldn't help it: he much preferred the fresh-faced approachable Macy of this afternoon to Theatrical Macy. Hell, she was a video queen, and everybody and his brother knew it. She didn't need a damn costume to cement the fact.

But it wasn't up to him to tell her how to dress. And if watching her hide behind clothing that — no matter how striking — was nothing more than protective covering set his teeth on edge, he'd just have to suck it up. Tonight's agenda was to have a good time.

A big smile spread across her face when she spotted him, erasing his lingering dissatisfaction. She sashayed up the hallway as fast as her pencil-slim skirt permitted.

"Don't you look handsome," she said, then lowered her voice as she came up to him. "I hope you don't mind, but I invited Janna along. I know it sorta takes the date out of the date, but Ty's spending the night with his other grandparents and she's had precious little fun since she was hit by that car." Her hand on his arm, she rose onto her toes, pressed a soft kiss on his mouth, then settled back onto her heels. "I'll make it up to you, though. I'll take you out for dinner and a movie in Wenatchee any evening that works for you. Heck, I'll even let you pick out one of those blow-'em-up flicks."

Warmth spiraled through him. Crazy theme outfits or the simpler clothing he favored, *this* was the real Macy: the woman who came back to a town that had been less than kind to her in order to help her family. "Deal."

Janna came out of her and Macy's room and started down the hall. Her cast was gone and she no longer needed the crutches, but she was still far from running any races.

"You look pretty tonight," he said, recognizing Macy's handiwork in the brunette's makeup and hair — although in a more toned-down style.

She gave her dark hair a self-conscious pat and shot him a look that held a hint of uncertainty. "I hope it's okay that I'm tagging along."

"Hell, yeah. We're just going to the Red Dog. I'll pull the car around front if you two want to wait on the porch."

Macy gave him a big smile, slid soft fingertips down his cheek and went to link her arm through her cousin's.

Later at the Red Dog, as the beer flowed and the noise level ratcheted up, he admitted to himself that there had been a part of him that had harbored a trace of uneasiness about coming face-to-face with Grace, knowing that she was sleeping with Savage. Not because she was having sex with another man, but because he had simply never been able to visualize her as a sexual being — and apparently had a blind spot when it

349

came to putting her in that context.

That had changed the first five minutes they spent together. For he could see her sexuality with Jack. It was in her posture when she spoke to the rocker, in her touches, the look in her eyes and the way her tongue dabbed her upper lip when Jack looked at her — which he did a lot. So how arrogant had *he* been to think that just because she didn't generate sparks with him that she had no sparks *to* generate? He grinned at her now across the table.

"What?" she demanded, catching his look.

"Nothing. I'm just happy to see you with a man who puts that gleam in your eyes."

The flush on her cheeks was discernible even in the dim lighting, but she grinned back at him. "Me, too."

If he thought that was the height of the night's surprises, though, he was wrong. For late in the evening, when everyone was beginning to make noises about going home, Macy turned to him.

"Janna and I decided to go to our ten-year reunion Saturday after next and I was wondering . . . would you like to be our escort? I know other people's reunions can be a drag —"

"I'm in," he interrupted. Hell, yes, he was. He understood it had probably taken a lot for her to make the decision to go. He'd seen the less than great reception she'd received from Mayfield and a few others. So he didn't merely think it was a good idea to be there as a buffer.

He insisted on it. Besides, she clearly saw him as part of her future — even if it was her two-weeks-from-now future. And for reasons he chose not to examine too much, that made him happy.

For now it was enough.

CHAPTER
TWENTY-ONE

For the past two days Gabe had studied call sheets that went back almost a year, trying to determine which of his crew had been on scene most often at not only the arsons since he'd taken over the job but at the fires Chief Stoller suspected had been deliberately set during the older man's tenure. He'd narrowed it down to two firefighters who had most consistently shown up whenever the truck was called out: Johnson and Solberg.

Not that his fire starter was guaranteed to be either of them. If the arsonist was smart — and so far he seemed to be, given he'd gone undetected for more than a year — he'd only show up at every third or fourth fire to deflect suspicion. Still, it was Gabe's best — hell, his *only* — bet and, if nothing else, it gave him a place to start.

The problem, of course, was that he was one man and there were too many hours in the day when he couldn't keep an eye on even one of his men, let alone both. Neither did it help that he genuinely hated the fact that he suspected anyone on his crew.

He said as much to Johnny when they met for their usual discussion on improving workplace efficiency. "This just blows, big-time. Johnson strikes me as a solid guy, and as far as I can tell his farm is doing okay. Solberg keeps to himself more, but if that was an indication of criminal activity I'd be under suspicion myself, since no one's ever accused me of being the most sociable guy in the world. But all I really know about him is that he has good instincts at a fire and liked Macy best in the video she did for *Ain't No Talkin'*."

"Hell, I'd pick him as your guy just for that last thing," Johnny said with a wry smile. "Sure, Macy rocked *Talkin'*. But we all know she was best in *Burn, Baby, Burn.*"

Then his expression turned serious. "Listen," he said. "I can kick in a few hours here and there. My social life's in a slump right now, anyhow — I might as well do something constructive. So why don't I take Johnson tonight? I'll set up a speed trap outside his road. It wouldn't look suspicious, since I've actually used it before — it's a good setup for catching the occasional lead foot. Not to mention that writing a ticket or two'll have the added bonus of making me Sheriff Baxter's Golden Boy, and you know what a hard sell that usually is. Two birds, one stone, dude. Help you and gain me kudos from the boss. It's a win-win."

"That would be great. I'd really appreciate it."

"Not a problem. And tomorrow I can move my trap to town. It just so happens that there's that empty lot next to Albright Welding, where —"

"Solberg has his day job," Gabe said. "Jesus, Johnny. I don't know how to thank you."

The deputy smiled crookedly. "Beer always works. But I wouldn't spring for the good stuff just yet, because there's sure as hell no guarantee I'll be at the right place at the right time. But at least we can keep both of them covered part of the time."

"And I doubt it will be for long," Gabe said grimly. "Because regardless of which of them is setting the fires, he seems to be escalating."

"Yeah." His friend's nod was equally grim. "It's your classic good-news, bad-news sitch, isn't it?"

■ ■ ■ ■

"Come on tour with me."

With a jerk of surprise, Grace stared at Jack standing in the archway dividing her kitchen from the living room, his tattooed and pierced masculinity — that lean, mean, rock-and-roll look — so out of place in her girly nest. Her heart tap-danced a ragged fandango in her breast. They'd spent nearly every free moment together for the past few weeks and she'd been amazed at how compatible they were outside the bedroom — which Lord knew astonished her all on its own. They talked endlessly on a wide range of subjects and laughed at all the same things and had generally just gotten along like a house afire together.

Still . . . he couldn't possibly have said what she thought he'd just said. Could he? "Excuse me?"

He came into the living room, a pilsner of lukewarm Guinness in one hand, a chilled mug of Dr Pepper with ice in the other, and handed her the soda. Clearing a space in the stuff she'd scattered around her for inspiration while she put together her first week's lesson plans, he sat down beside her on the couch. He knocked back a sip of his ale, set the glass on the coffee table and turned to give her a look at once heated and grave. "I have to leave soon to get ready for the tour, Gracie. I don't want to leave you behind. So come with me."

Oh, God, that's what she thought he'd said. For one wild, wonderful moment she pictured it, the two of them, traveling the country, seeing the sights, sharing the nights. Longing washed through her, only to fade as reality set in.

"I can't." Reaching out a hand, she stroked it down his inked forearm, knowing she was probably throwing away the opportunity of a lifetime. "I so wish that I could, Jack, but I signed a contract with the school district. I can't simply renege on it a week and a half before the first day of school." And damn her sense of responsibility! It was probably going to cost her the best thing that had ever happened to her.

"Are you sure?"

"Yes." Regret made her voice tremble.

"Shite." He blew out a breath and tugged her onto his lap, scattering papers from her own. "Forget not wanting to leave you behind, I don't want to leave, period — and that's something new for me. I'm *always* keen to start a tour." He rested his chin atop her head and smoothed a hand up and down her arm. "But this one — bloody hell, this one is going to be the longest four months of my life."

They were silent for a moment, before he slowly said in a considering tone, "Still . . . I've got a few three-day gaps between gigs, so I could likely get back here occasionally."

Her heart lifted. Who would have believed that rock legend Jack Savage would talk about adapting his schedule in order to see *her?* "I could come see you, as well," she agreed, enthusiasm firing. "We don't have any official three-day weekends before the holidays, but I could take a personal day to make one, and I think the day between semesters falls on a Friday this year, so that will make one more. Plus, I'll get a four-day weekend for Thanksgiving and two weeks for winter break in December." She tipped her head back to look up at him and didn't care that her heart was in her eyes as her gaze met his. At the same time, she couldn't prevent the uncertainty that colored her voice when she asked, "Do you really think we can make this work?"

"Too bloody right, we can. You're the smartest, sweetest, most fla—" He shook his head as if he simply didn't have the words, but when her brow wrinkled over the word he'd cut himself off on, he said obligingly, "Most attractive, that last one means. Lord love me, lass, I've never felt like this with another bird. And as much as I wish you were going to be with me, you're right to stay. You've got more character in your wee finger than most people do in their entire bodies. I know it's sudden and we're moving ninety to the dozen, but this feels real to me — more real than anything I've ever known."

He rubbed a guitar-string-toughened thumb over her bottom lip. "So, to answer your question, luv, no. I don't have a doubt in the world that you and I can make this work."

By the day of Macy and Janna's class reunion Gabe was wrung dry, stressed out and pissed off. Because it turned out he'd been wrong. He wasn't a single step closer to discovering who was setting the fires around town than he'd been nearly two weeks ago.

When he spotted Johnny camped out again in the empty lot near Solberg's workplace, he pulled alongside the deputy's rig and filled his friend in on the surveillance he'd put in that day. Johnny gave his account in return. Unfortunately, the conversation was a short one, since neither had much to report.

"Shit," he said in disgust. "I thought we'd have him wrapped up by now."

Over the course of the past dozen days or so, both of them had been in position to catch Johnson leaving his farm once or twice and Solberg leaving both Albright Welding next door to where they now sat and the little house he rented out past Gabe's place. But neither man had done anything more than go into town for groceries or to grab a beer at the Red Dog.

The fact that he deemed that a bad thing was what truly had Gabe on edge. Because he shouldn't be hoping for a fucking fire to be set. Shouldn't be anxious to catch one of his own men in an act that wasn't only criminal but downright traitorous to their profession.

Christ, what a mess.

"Look," he said dispiritedly, "I'm gonna knock off — which probably means this will be the night he hits. But it's Macy and Janna's ten-year reunion, and Macy asked me to escort them —" He cut himself off. Because, oh, hell. "Shit. It's yours, too, isn't it?"

"Yeah, but ask my boss if he gives a rip. I asked for the night off three months ago, but Baxter scheduled me to work until nine anyhow. Still, the reunion doesn't start until seven. I should have time to go home when my shift ends, take a quick shower and throw on something sharper than this. Depending on how long the farmers among us can hold out, I'll get there in time to catch at least part of it." He grinned. "And, hell, even if it's just the tail end, that's not a bad deal. The desperate chicks will have had plenty of time to get drunk, so I'll probably be lookin' pretty good to them by then. Maybe I'll get lucky and end my dry spell."

"You're such a hound, Angelini. Still, I appreciate the fact that Solberg will be covered tonight."

"And you do know that Johnson was in our class, right? He'll probably be at the reunion."

"No. I didn't know that." And for some reason discovering it produced a hollow sensation in his gut. "Macy never mentioned knowing him."

Johnny shrugged. "He was one of the 4H kids — always more interested in the farming stuff than school politics. No doubt he knew what was going on — he just didn't give a shit."

"Huh. Well, I'm outta here. I'll see you at the grange hall then?"

"You bet. I'll be the guy with no date

while you have two pretty women on your arm." Johnny shook his head. "I think I went into the wrong field. I shoulda been a fireman."

"Babes find us hot," he agreed modestly.

Unfortunately, the momentary mood lift he got from slinging the bull with his friend faded by the time he reached his house a short while later. Letting himself in, he headed downstairs for the temporary bedroom he and Macy had painted last week in yet another cool color she'd picked out. Throwing himself on the real mattress on the real king-size bed he no longer had to squat to access — both of which he'd just installed the other day — he ground the heels of his hands into his burning eyes.

As lowering as it was to admit, another reason he was feeling so out of sorts was that all the time he'd spent chasing leads that led nowhere had been time he hadn't spent with Macy. God, he had it bad for her — he felt as if he was going through freaking withdrawal. Because, except for their date in Wenatchee Wednesday before last and the past Saturday spent painting this room, setting up the bed and making it up with the incredibly soft housewarming sheets she'd bought him, the only time he ever saw her these days was at the boarding-house.

Where people were always around. Lots and lots of people.

But she'd be here pretty soon, so he should probably go take a shower in the newly finished half bath next door. Well, the almost finished half bath; the shower stall was done but the rest of the floor still needed to be tiled. Still, the plumbing had finally been installed and was fully func-tional in all three bathrooms, which brought his house yet another step closer to comple-tion.

Which was freaking great.

Following his shower, he'd pulled his jeans back on and was sniffing his shirt to see if it would hold up for another couple hours' wear before he had to change into his reunion duds when Macy arrived.

"Hey!" she called from the top of the stairs. "You down there?"

"Yeah. C'mon down!"

She blew into the room a moment later, amber-ale hair swinging and several layers of clothing on hangers draped over her arm.

"Put those down and come over here," he commanded and grinned inwardly when she promptly dropped them over a straight-backed chair he'd dragged in when she'd complained of having no place to put her clothes but on the floor. Outwardly, however, he didn't crack a smile as she strolled up to him. Instead, he slid one hand into her sleek hair, hooked the other around the back of her neck, pulled her to him and took his time kissing her. When he finally lifted his mouth from hers, he ordered, "On the bed. Now."

"Ooh. I love it when you go all masterful on me." She plopped onto the mattress. "And I really love this bed." She stroked the Egyptian-cotton sheets next to her hip. "I swear it's bigger than the entire bedroom in my condo." She lounged back on her elbows and gave him a cool once-over. "Lose the pants, Donovan. I like my men naked."

This time he did grin. "If you love me being masterful so much, why are you always trying to take over the job?"

She hitched a pretty shoulder. "Control issues." Then she laughed. "Tell you what. We can take turns."

"Deal." And it was — a great deal, the *best* deal, as they wrestled across the sheets, first Macy in the superior position, then he. During her stint on top, she straddled his stomach and pinned his hands to the sheet while she rubbed her breasts against his chest and kissed him. When his control started to fray, he rolled them over and easily held her in place with his weight, his hand spanning both her wrists and holding them to the mattress above her head as their bodies slipped and stroked and slithered against the other's. Then he was pushing inside of her, deep, deeper, deepest, and, God, she felt so frigging good, encasing him in a slick, hot, muscular sheath that gripped him, consumed him, *owned* him.

And not only his dick, he acknowledged just before he plunged off the cliff into a ball-tightening, free-falling, teeth-clenching climax. She'd somehow come to own his heart, as well.

Apparently his skeletal system came with the package, too, because he collapsed on her as if the structure had dissolved at the same instant as the last pulsation faded. His two-hundred-plus pounds all but flattened her, driving the breath from her lungs in an emphatic *whoosh.*

"Sorry," he breathed against her hair. "Didn't mean to crush you. Somebody stole my bones."

"Tell me about it." Her hands slid from his shoulders and flopped to the mattress on either side of her head. "Bastards took mine, too. Least I think they did." She drew in a long, slow breath, then let it unhurriedly escape. "Are my pinkies working?"

With great effort, he raised his head far enough to see her lift both gently curled little fingers a centimeter off the bed. They immediately fell back into line with their sister digits, whereupon his neck lost the little strength he'd managed to dredge up, his face dropping back into the warm, scented hair pooling in the curve where her neck met her shoulder.

"Okay, that was pathetic," she murmured, and he felt her turn her head and press a soft-lipped kiss against his ear. "I guess it's official. I'm jellyfish girl."

Love, in a wave so strong it threatened to swamp him, swelled in his chest. Why something so silly should be the thing to tip him over into a full-fledged case of want-you-in-my-life-forever, he couldn't say. But it had, and because he was a straightforward kind of guy he opened his mouth to tell her how he felt. Before he could say a word, however, a gusty sigh escaped her.

"When we get our strength back," she said, "I'm gonna need your help. This reunion thing tonight's got me spinning my wheels. I want to go, I don't want to go. I think attending is a good plan, I think it's the worst idea I've ever had. So it's crucial that I wear the right thing."

"Seriously?" he mumbled into her neck. "You want my input? I'm a guy, honey. What do I know from fashion?"

"You know what you like, don'tcha? And I brought visual aids."

He had a feeling this was a bad idea but also suspected if he said so, she'd blow it all out of proportion the way women could sometimes do. So he did the next best thing and kept his mouth shut.

She pinched him.

"Ouch! All right, okay. I'll take a look. But you really should've asked Janna's or Grace's opinion, because you know I'm just gonna pick the one that shows the most cleavage or showcases your butt, which in case I haven't told you, is definitely four-star."

"Aw, you sweet-talker." Her boneless moment clearly over, she shoved at his shoulder. "Get up. Time's a'wasting."

"We've got three hours before we pick up Janna!"

"I know. I don't know how on earth I'm going to get everything done."

"Jesus," he grumbled, rolling off of her and sitting up on the side of the bed to dispose of the condom. "You sure as hell know how to take the shine off the postcoital glow."

"We're coming back here after the reunion, aren't we?" she demanded, climbing from the bed and crossing to the chair where she'd left her armful of clothing. "I thought the plan was to sleep over for once."

"Yeah, it is."

"Then we have the entire night to glow." Scooping up the apparel, she headed for the door. "I'll go try on the first one. Keep in mind that I didn't bring shoes or accessories, and that my hair and makeup will have to be done."

"Yeah, I was real worried about that," he muttered as she sashayed from the room. He could feel his mellow mood deteriorating back into the stressed-out, low-grade anger that had defined his frame of mind before Macy arrived, and he tried to rein it in. Because it wasn't her fault the past two weeks had been a fricking washout when it came to moving this case forward.

Deep breath here, bud. He had to remember that while clothes meant dick-all to him, chicks seemed to find the subject endlessly fascinating. So, big deal. He'd help her select her outfit for the reunion, then maybe they could go back to bed for a while.

That idea cheered him right up. But when Macy strolled back into the room a few minutes later, his cheer took a header. He stared at the little blue satin tap pants she'd had on the first day they'd met. They left a yard of bare skin exposed from her thighs to her toes. Instead of the sailor shirt she'd worn then, it was paired with a formfitting little white lace blouse whose collar points were clusters of pearls.

"I know it looks kind of plain right now," she said. "But you have to visualize the right shoes and a forties-style do, or maybe a wig."

The frustration that had been building over his inability to figure out this damn arson business erupted into the mother of all bad tempers. "Oh, for cri'sake!" he snapped in disgust.

Okay, probably the wrong thing to say. But in for a penny, in for a fricking five spot. And if he'd already gone and shot himself in the foot anyway . . .

"When the *hell* are you going to quit with the costumes, already?"

CHAPTER
TWENTY-TWO

Macy took Gabe's reaction on the chin. But inwardly she reeled. How could he switch so fast from making her feel desirable, safe, *special,* to that slap-in-the-face disapproving tone?

She forced a careless smile, however, and murmured, "O-kay. I'll take that as a big fat negative for this outfit." But her feisty inner fighter, which had been her only advocate in too many new-kid-on-the-block situations to count, still lurked beneath her skin.

She turned her back to him before it could burst out of her like some special-effects alien and go straight for his throat. She'd really rather not do something she'd regret.

Not that she was sure she *would* regret it right this minute. Still, she mostly wanted to step back and grab a sec to get her emotions in check before she let the situation escalate to a place where one of them might end up saying something they couldn't take back.

As it turned out, that train had apparently already left the station. Because, in sync with her swiveling away from him, he demanded, "What the hell *is* it with you and playing dress-up, anyway? You wore regular clothes when we went into Wenatchee last week. You're freaking beautiful! So why do you keep going back to the blue wigs, fake tattoos and theme clothing and shit?"

The *freaking beautiful* thing warmed her for all of two seconds before his disdain lashed her like a verbal whip, making her shoulders hunch up around her ears. She quickly corrected the giveaway posture, since self-preservation was a lesson she'd learned young and learned well.

Never let them see they have the power to bug you, hurt you or piss you off.

"Because I look so good in them, sugar," she said, maintaining her back-to-his-face pose. For, while she could keep her voice insouciant, she couldn't seem to stem the fast rise of tears in her eyes — and she was damned if she'd let him see that his judgment had reduced her to a great big crybaby. She blinked rapidly in an attempt to hold back the flood.

"Don't do that!" he snapped, his voice

coming closer. "Don't call me sugar like I'm the enemy. You think I haven't noticed the way you use that to hold people at bay? I thought you and I had gotten past that." His hand, large and warm, started to wrap around the cap of her shoulder.

She whirled, knocking it loose before his fingers could curl into a grip, her tears evaporating beneath the heat of a temper that she'd taught herself years ago never to lose. "And *I* thought that maybe — *maybe!* — you might actually understand a thing or two about me by now. You want to know why I wore *regular* clothes when we had our date? I didn't think I had to play that game with you — that it was safe to just be regular ol' small-town Macy. Because, guess what, honey, I don't feel like that with everyone — especially in this town. So I wear my wigs, my tattoos and my costumes because they say I don't give a shit if you, or you or *you* —" she jabbed her index finger as if pointing out her various detractors "— don't like that I'm different."

"Yeah? Well, guess what, yourself?" Spearing his fingers through his hair, he gave her a narrow-eyed, intent stare. "The things you accomplished after you blew this town say that loud and clear for you already! You left here with — what? — a high school education and maybe a couple hundred bucks in your pocket? Honey, you came back a celebrity. You don't need crazy clothes to —"

She gave him a straight shot to the chest. It didn't budge him an inch, and that made the temper she couldn't seem to get a grasp on flare hotter. "The hell I don't! I need *exactly* that to let the small minds of this small town know that I won't allow them to treat me like I've got no worth, to act like they object to the fact that I *breathe*."

To her horror her voice cracked on the last word, but she thrust her chin up, daring him to even *think* about considering her weak because of it. "I thought you liked me just as I am, though. I thought maybe I meant something more to you than the occasional roll in the hay. I didn't realize that my clothing choices — and by extension me — were something you held in such contempt." She felt those damn tears starting to rise again and whirled away again before he could see them.

"You don't like my wardrobe choices?" She strode for the door. "Problem solved. You don't have to look at them or be embarrassed by association or whatever the hell it is that bothers you so much. I'll just remove myself from the picture." She dashed away another trickle of tears and, with no further attempt at lightness, added, "Oh, and PS, Donovan. You're off the hook. Janna and I will go to the reunion on our own." *Unless, of course, you try to talk me out of it.*

"You're just gonna pack up your marbles and go home? Oh, that's great. I sure as hell didn't have you pegged as a quitter."

Wrong response. Gaze straight ahead, back stiff, she reached for the doorknob.

"Macy!" Exasperation colored his voice. "Will you just wait a damn minute?"

But she wasn't waiting. Not waiting for excuses, for explanations, for further criticism. She wasn't waiting for her damn heart to be broken. He'd made her feel good about herself for a while, but apparently she wasn't quite good enough — and wasn't *that* the damn story of her life in this town?

To the sound track of his curses, she slammed out of the room.

"Dammit, Mace," she heard him roar from the other side of the door. "Give me a chance to get my pants on! Let's talk about this."

"Let's not," she shot back, the damn tears turning from a trickle to a torrent. Pausing only long enough to grab the rest of her clothing from the back of the bathroom door, she sprinted up the stairs and across the great room to the front door, where she slowed down only long enough to let herself out.

She was backing her Corvette in a tight, fast U when Gabe burst out onto the porch, looking somehow more naked in a pair of unzipped jeans that rode dangerously low on his hips than if he'd been wearing just his own skin. His hair stuck up from where first she, then he, had run their hands through it, giving him a sleepy, rumpled look. But his dark brows were gathered over his nose and his mouth clamped at a slant that looked grim and determined.

In no mood to deal with *his* mood, she slammed the stick shift into First gear before he could clear the steps. Popping the clutch, she hit the gas. The car fishtailed before its tires found purchase on the dusty ground that would eventually be his lawn. Find purchase, however, they finally did.

And pointing the hood ornament down his drive, she roared out of his yard.

*"God*damn. *Son* of a. *Bitch!"* Stopping short at the base of his stairs, Gabe punched his fist in the air. Then he locked his fingers together behind the rigid muscles cording the back of his neck and, elbows jutting skyward, scowled at the attenuated dust

374

contrail that hovered above his someday yard. What the fuck had just happened here?

Yes, Macy's costumes bugged the crap out of him. They were a freaking wall she put up between Real Macy and the world. And even though he'd convinced himself he was okay with that, clearly he wasn't. But it was just that . . .

The real Macy was sweet and loyal and caring. She loved big when it came to her family, laughed from her belly, talked in a voice that was free of cynicism.

Threw herself with stop-your-heart enthusiasm into making love with him.

God. The real Macy *shined* with a sort of passion for life, as if she had her own personal Energizer Bunny thumping its drum and running its perpetual battery in order to light her up from the inside out.

And it bugged the crap out of him to watch her hide that light behind a phony facade.

He sure as hell hadn't meant to make her cry, though. His gut clenched tight. Because she hadn't been fast enough to turn away, and the sight of those tears had damn near brought him to his knees. They'd slowed him down for the crucial moment that meant the difference between catching up with her and letting her get away.

Damn. Macy didn't cry. At least he'd never seen her do so, and face it, he'd been in place to witness all kinds of shit raining down on her head since she'd first rolled into town.

So congratulations, Sparky, he thought bitterly. *Many have tried, but only you have made it come to pass.* "Give the man a cigar," he muttered.

Then he snapped erect. Dropped his hands to his sides and squared his shoulders. Because *damned* if he intended to give up. He'd allow her a little time to cool down, then he'd call her. Or maybe it would be better to just show up at the prearranged time to pick her and Janna up for the reunion. Act as if nothing had happened.

Uh-huh. How do you imagine that's *gonna work out for you, Einstein?* He wracked his brain to remember the last time he'd seen Macy ignore or shy away from a confrontation, the last time he'd watched her turn the other cheek. And that would be . . . oh —

Goddamn never.

All right, then. New plan. He'd show up at the arranged time and — *deep breath here, Chief* — apologize.

He winced. Saying the *S* word wasn't something he had a helluva lot of experience with and he expected it would probably sting like a bitch. Still, that seemed like a fair exchange, considering it was pretty obvious he had hurt her.

He also had a hunch that in addition to the apology, the event probably called for a fistful of flowers. Or maybe one of those wrist-corsage things for her and Janna. Knowing Macy, if anything would turn the tide in his favor, it would be including her cousin in the grovel. Couldn't hurt, anyhow.

He loped toward his SUV.

It wasn't until the soles of his feet hit gravel that he remembered not only was he keyless, but he had on neither shoes nor shirt. He looked down at himself and grimaced.

Christ. He used to be so self-contained. A rock. An effin' *island* — or at least a guy who'd taught himself to make damn few wrong moves once he'd left his teens behind. Then he'd had to go collide with a mouthy blonde — hell, not even a blonde, really, but sort of a beer blonde —

Okay, not the point. *That* came in the form of a single question, which was: how could one not-quite-blonde take a guy who'd worked as hard as he had to get his shit together and reduce him to a pathetic specimen dancing barefoot in the gravel?

Jesus. His goddamn fly wasn't even zipped up.

"Macy, why are you lying down? I thought for sure you'd be in the middle of elaborate preps for the reunion." Janna strode across the room they shared to the window, where she snapped up the shade Macy had drawn. Her voice suddenly lost its cheer. "Hey," she said softly. "Are you okay?"

Knowing there was no way she'd be able to hide the less-than-pretty results of her half-hour-long pity party, Macy rolled over onto her back on the bed. She looked up at her cousin through swollen eyes. "Noooo."

Tears started to trickle again and she pinched the bridge of her nose between her eyes to stanch the flow. "God! I'm such an idiot."

The mattress depressed as Janna sat next to her hip. "You're gonna have to tell me why you think so. Because *I* think you're probably the least idiotic person I know."

"Maybe once upon a time. Before I went and fell in love with Gabriel Rat Bastard Donovan." It had T-boned her on the drive home. God. *This* was the reason she felt so horrid. Ordinarily, she could give a rip what men thought of her. And she sure as hell wasn't the type to fall apart over a little criticism. But somehow he had snuck under her guard during the past weeks, had made her feel smart and pretty and exceptional. And in the process he'd sunk his ownership deep.

She moaned and dug the heels of her hands into her burning eyes. "I am so screwed."

"Why? It's clear he's crazy about you, too."

A bitter laugh escaped her. "I wish. Unfortunately, he just thinks I'm crazy." An old schoolyard taunt popped into her head. "Apparently I'm ugly and my mama dresses me funny."

"You're — ?" Janna's slender eyebrows furrowed. "What on earth happened between you two today?"

Macy told her.

Her cousin jolted upright, bristling with indignation. "That bastard! That no-good, two-faced, *sanct*imonious — *God,* I hate men sometimes! What the hell's the matter with them that they're never happy until they've either changed you or cheated on you?"

Macy expected to feel vindicated by Janna's unfaltering defense, to wallow in her cousin's steadfast attack on Gabe's moral fiber. Yet for some reason it irritated her instead. *She* got to assassinate Gabriel's character, but damned if anyone else did.

Sitting up, she grabbed a handful of tissues from the box on the nightstand, then scooted to brace her back against the headboard. She wiped her face and blew her nose.

Leaning to toss the used tissues into the wastebasket, she said reluctantly, because she had no desire to defend Gabe, but with confidence, since she knew this much was true, "He's nothing like Sean, Janny."

"You think not?" Her cousin snorted. "Let me see. He plays fashion police — hmm, that sounds like my ex to me. He stomps on your self-confidence in a town that's already all over your case."

"Actually," she said slowly, thinking back on the conversation with an impartiality she'd been incapable of while the argument had been ongoing, "he said that I didn't need crazy clothes to prove myself. That what I'd accomplished since leaving Sugarville had proved it already."

"Oh." Janna's scowl faded and her shoulders lost some of their rigidity. "That's different. That's actually kinda . . . cool."

"It actually kind of is. At the time I just felt under attack, so I failed to appreciate exactly how cool. But maybe he *wasn't* attacking everything that makes me me.

"Oh, God, am I crazy?" she demanded of

her cousin. "Am I just making excuses for Gabriel because of these stupid feelings I have for him? Because I still think the *way* he said it bites. And yet . . . I can't deny he has a point. Sometimes it's simply fun to play dress-up, but mostly I do it because it's like donning a suit of armor to keep people at arm's length. I've found it pretty effective over the years. But you know what?"

Her posture went proudly erect against the headboard. "I *have* made something of myself since leaving Sugarville. And I did it through my own hard work. Well, okay," she amended. "That plus the killer break I got when I met Jack."

"*After* waiting tables for four years while you kept putting yourself out there even when doors were being slammed in your face."

"Yes!" She nodded fervently. "And I'm making the transition to my behind-the-scenes concept work primarily through contacts that I made on my own. If there is one thing I know, it's that I'm good at visualizing how a song should translate to video."

"Once again, a skill developed through your own hard work."

"So maybe I should scrap-heap the costumes tonight." Her stomach clenched at the thought and she promptly reversed herself. "Or not. This is Sugarville we're talking about. Mayfield and I'm-married-to-the-Mayor Liz are probably just waiting to bar me from the door."

The words echoed in her head and got her off the bed faster than anything else could have. She exhaled an *as if* huff of air. "Like I'm going to let those idiots dictate my choices. I'm tired of reacting to that group as if I'm still in high school. I've actually made a few friends outside the family since I've been back and I've noticed more than once that more folks have let the past go than not. Yet as fast as I become aware of it, I seem to promptly forget and go back to my old knee-jerk ways. *I'm* the one who keeps hanging on to what used to be — it's like this bad habit I can't seem to break. But it's time to put an end to it once and for all."

Peering into the mirror over the dresser, she made a face. "That is not a pretty sight. I'd better go get some ice from Auntie to see if I can bring down the swelling on these puffy eyes. Then you and I have our work cut out for us. Because we've got to come up with something for me to wear that's both attractive and seminormal. And we only have the two suitcases worth of stuff I brought with me to pull it from."

CHAPTER
TWENTY-THREE

Gabe cursed under his breath when he saw the plume of smoke rising near Spindale Gulch.

He had the pedal to the metal as he raced back from Wenatchee, where he'd gone to get wrist corsages — only to wind up having to do a verbal tap dance to get a florist to make them for him. Who the hell knew you were supposed to order the things ahead of time?

It had taken more than an hour and an additional discussion about keeping the arrangements simple, which had grown heated on the florist's part, since he'd taken a big-ass exception to Gabe's insistence that less was more. But he was not about to slide one of those huge, fussy numbers on Macy's wrist, so it had been worth a minor dustup with the guy. Because he now had a clamshell on his passenger seat in which two elegantly minimal rosebud-and-orchid wrist corsages nestled.

He was less than ten minutes from the boardinghouse, and if none of the AAE guys were using the upstairs bathroom, he'd have more than enough time to shower, shave and dress before zero hour. The part he wasn't so confident about was his ability to convince Macy that he should escort her and Janna to their reunion as they'd originally planned.

The woman was stubborn as an ox, and if she was still pissed, there might not be enough hours in the day to change her mind.

He was calculating the odds of making her see things his way when he spotted the slender column of smoke rising against the still-brilliant blue sky. For the first time since joining the fire department, he had fuck-all desire to stop and investigate.

Dammit, he was already running late. And for all he knew the smoke might be from a controlled burn. The only thing down that way was the dream house a couple of retirees from the other side of the Cascades were having built. Maybe their contractor was getting rid of some of the scraps that were part and parcel of new construction.

But maybe he wasn't. "Shit." Hitting the brakes, he waited for his rig to rock to a stop, then put it in Reverse and backed up to the cutoff road he had just passed that would take him down the gulch.

His cell phone rang moments later. Pulling it out of the cup holder on the console as he turned onto the side road he glanced at the readout and saw it was Johnny. "Hey."

"Hey, yourself. Solberg shot by me a while ago, headed out of S-ville. Given that it's almost Saturday night, I thought he was probably on his way to the Red Dog. But he blew right past not only that, but his own place, as well. He's heading west on Two. Look, I know you've got the reunion, and for all I know, your guy could have a hot date in Wenatchee or Leavenworth — or, hell, anywhere between here and Seattle if it comes to that. But I had to hang back to keep him from making me and now I've lost him. Plus, it's a change in his pattern and . . . I don't know, man. I've got an itch at the back of my neck about this."

"I think I know where he is." Mentally stringing together a few of his favorite obscenities, he filled the deputy in on the smoke he was on his way to investigate.

Johnny swore. "That's the place George Fulton's building for those Coasties, isn't it?

"Yeah, so I'm on my way to check it out

and — Christ! Flames just shot up. This is no controlled burn. Where are you now?"

"I just passed Bremer's farm. The Spindale Road is coming up."

"Good. Take that. I'm on the gulch cutoff from this end, so we should have him sandwiched. It stands to reason he's still somewhere on the siding road if you haven't passed him coming back and I haven't run into him headed in my direction. And dammit, he is *not* getting away this time." He gave his head an impatient shake. "I need to get off the line, dawg, and call it in."

"Meetcha in the middle."

Gabe hung up, then called up his truck. After terse instructions to Bundy, who was the first to respond, he tossed his phone back in the cup holder.

With a regretful look at the corsages, he stomped on the gas and sent his rig rocketing down the road toward the gully.

"Hi, do you remember me? Mike Bodendorf?"

Turning away from a spirited conversation taking place with Janna, seated next to her, and the group on her cousin's other side, Macy looked up at the former classmate addressing her. The men, she had noted over the past couple of hours, were the hardest to identify — likely because the last time she'd seen them, most had been ridiculously young-looking. Much more so back in high school than the girls, who had matured more quickly and possessed strong hints of what they'd look like as twenty-eight-year-olds.

This man, however, with his young-bull build, white-blond hair and Germanic looks, struck a cord of familiarity, and she had a vague recollection from . . . "Mr. Rickel's science class, junior year?"

Even as the words left her mouth it felt right. The class in question had been during the halcyon days, before everything had gone to hell, and she tended to remember the guys who'd been decent to her, since they'd soon become almost as extinct as the buffalo hunter. Or at least it had seemed that way at the time.

"Damn." Bodendorf grinned. "You're good. I didn't think you'd have a clue who I was."

"Hey, weren't we lab partners for a couple of weeks?"

"Yeah."

"And if I remember right, I got a whole lot more out of our association than you did, considering you were way better at the lab stuff than I was." She cocked her head to study him. "You were one of the Future Farmer kids, right?"

"Yep." He flashed a crooked smile. "I still am, more or less. I left the wheat fields to my folks, but I've got pear and apple orchards up near Carlton." He looked around the room for a moment, then slid his hands into his slacks pockets and jingled his change as he returned his attention to her. "I'm betting this isn't exactly what *you're* accustomed to," he said dryly.

"Why do you say that?"

"C'mon. Parties at the grange hall?"

She laughed. "I was actually just thinking what a great job the decorations committee did dolling up the joint."

She wasn't being facetious; if this was the work of Mrs. I'm-Married-to-the-Mayor and posse, she had to give them credit. Not only did they possess good taste, but they'd managed some serious changes to the appearance of the hall without breaking the bank. The overhead lights had been dimmed about the same time dinner had ended and the sun had gone down, and LED-lighted paper lanterns in Sugarville High's familiar blue-and-gold had been strung in rows across the ceiling. Candles in matching votives flickered on white linen tablecloths, picking up jewel-toned sparks of color from the metallic confetti scattered around them. Placed about the room was an occasional basket of manzanita branches that had been wrapped in white lights, and on the walls hung four beautiful oversize Turkish rugs. You had to look closely to see the cards giving the corresponding item's price and discreetly advertising the shop that had undoubtedly lent them for the evening mounted next to them.

She refocused her concentration on the man standing in front of her. "So, what have you been doing for the past ten years when you aren't apple wrangling, Mike? Are you married? Have any little Bodendorfs?"

"No kids. I was married, but I've been single again for about two years now." He looked for a moment as if he might go into detail, but merely hitched a brawny shoulder. "What can I say? It just didn't work out."

"Marriages often don't," she agreed.

"How about you?"

"Never been married or had a kid."

Next to her at the table, Janna laughed at something someone said and Macy turned to look. When her cousin twisted around in response to her movement, Macy touched her arm. "Janna, do you remember Mike Bodendorf?"

"Sure. Mike and I used to run into each other in town occasionally before he moved up north." She turned a brilliant smile on the blond man. "How's life in the Okanagon treating you?"

"Can't complain. My folks told me you were the victim of a serious accident last spring, though. How you doing?"

"Much better, thanks. I just recently finished my physical therapy and am definitely on the mend."

"Glad to hear it. You sure look good."

"Thanks." She beamed up at him. "So do you."

Mike edged around Macy to stand closer to her cousin's chair and she thought, *Go, Janny.* A corner of her mouth tipping up in a wry smile, she scooted her chair away from the table. "If you two will excuse me for a minute, I'm going to go visit the —" She waved vaguely in the direction of the hallway hosting the restrooms and wandered off. Glancing back over her shoulder, she saw Mike take her seat and lean in to talk to Janna.

She was waylaid on her way to the Ladies' by a guy who'd once taken her out and promptly become part of the ongoing Macy-is-easy propaganda machine when he'd lied about how lucky he'd gotten with her. Not that it had made him different from all but a few of the high school Romeos who'd dated her after Mayfield started the rumors. But he apparently wanted to regale her now with how much he'd loved her videos. At least the other authors of her bad rep had the brains to give her a wide berth.

She played nice, however, and politely extricated herself. No sooner had she left him when a woman who had been blessedly neutral back in the day asked her if she'd join her and her husband in the memory photo they were about to have taken in front of the backdrop set up out in the foyer. Macy agreed she'd be delighted.

It was the fourth time this evening she'd posed with classmates, so you'd think by now she would be blasé about it. Yet it still managed to catch her by surprise that people wanted her to be in their photographs.

Surprised and, if she were to be honest, tickled. Tonight was turning out much better than she'd anticipated, and after she finished up in the restroom stall she chatted with two women named Jenny and Lisa while washing up and freshening her lipstick.

"I love your dress," Jenny said, and Macy grinned down at her little silver-blue slip dress, which she'd paired with her blue Cuban-heeled, peep-toed forties-look shoes. She was attired more or less like all the other women here tonight. She'd gone a little heavy in the eye-makeup department, perhaps, but as it turned out so had most of the other females. It must be one of those universal evening-wear things.

"*I'm* impressed with your makeup," Lisa chimed in. "How do you get such a flawless look? Just have great skin?"

"It's a little bit inheriting my mother's complexion and a whole lot Diorskin Nude mineral powder," she promptly replied. "It's made with mineralized water so it doesn't settle in to show every imperfection. My favorite makeup artist turned me onto it — she always used it for my shoots."

Lisa sighed in disappointment. "That's what I was afraid of, that it's one of those specialized products you can only get in Hollywood."

Macy laughed. "Sugar, you can get it at most department stores. Check it out the next time you go into Wenatchee." She studied Lisa's makeup for a moment. "You need a lipstick with a warmer undertone," she informed the other woman, digging through her cosmetic bag. Since an evening purse wasn't an accessory she'd thought to pack when she'd left California, she was toting around her regular purse with all its usual paraphernalia.

Locating the lipstick she'd been seeking, she pulled it out. "Here. This one's a shade called All Heart." Plucking a tissue from the box on the counter, she used it to wipe a rosy layer off the tip and extended the tube to the other woman. "If you don't mind that it's not new, you're welcome to try this."

Lisa didn't even hesitate; she grabbed a tissue and removed her own lipstick, then reached for the tube Macy offered. Leaning into the mirror, she applied it, then stood back to inspect the results.

And flashed a huge smile. "Omigawd. This is *way* more flattering."

"It is," Jenny agreed. "It's just like that episode of *The Closer* where Chief Brenda Leigh got talked into giving up her red lipstick for a color kinda like that and ended up looking soooo much prettier."

"Man," Lisa breathed, gazing in awe at Macy as if she were Angelina Jolie and Cameron Diaz rolled into one. "How do you know all this stuff? You must live such a glamorous life."

Macy laughed. "Nah. I've just spent a lot of time sitting in makeup chairs. You either nap or you pay attention." She shrugged.

"I've done both." She indicated the tube in the other woman's hand. "You're welcome to keep that if you want."

"Thank you. I'd like that very much, since I already hate the idea of reapplying my old color when this one wears off." She hesitated, then said in a serious voice, "You know, I owe you a long-overdue apology. I knew, for all your flirting back in school, that there was something a little too contemptuous in the way you looked at all those boys for you to be doing what they said you were doing. But I was afraid that if I talked to you that crowd would make my life miserable, too. It was so cowardly, and I'm really sorry."

"Don't worry about it," Macy said lightly, even as she felt the other woman's words soothe a tiny ache she hadn't even realized she still carried inside her. "High school's a killer for everyone."

"Except a few," Jenny said. "And have you noticed that a lot of them never seem to get beyond it? It's like that was the highlight of their life — and that's kinda pitiful, too."

Macy was feeling mighty fine as she sashayed down the hallway a few minutes later. For the first time in more than ten years she had a clear, adult-driven view of the people in this town, rather than the one she'd been filtering through her high school experiences.

A handful of them were always going to have a problem with her, no matter what. Most of the men and women she'd chatted with tonight, however, had treated her either as easily as Mike Bodendorf or as if she were some big-deal star, a *much* bigger celebrity than she'd ever been anywhere except in her wildest dreams back in the days before she'd gotten a foot in the industry door.

The first was relaxing, the second seriously flattering, considering what a small cog she actually was in the huge wheel that was the entertainment industry.

"What, you couldn't afford a dress, so you just wore your slip instead?" drawled a voice to her right. "Business must not be nearly as good as you'd have everyone believe."

Macy looked over to see — oh, goody — Liz Pickett-Smith and her coterie of yes-chicks bearing down on her. *That'll teach me to get cocky.*

Giving her shoulders an infinitesimal roll, she refused to let the other woman get under her skin. She'd mingled with far too many truly decent people tonight to let Mrs. Mayor spoil her mood. In fact, with sudden clarity she realized that most of Queen Bitch's nastiness likely stemmed from jealousy. Because Gabriel was right about one thing: Macy had made something of herself in the larger world, strictly on her own merit, through perseverance and hard work. In sharp contrast, Liz had climbed to the top of Sugarville's social elite, which was a small pinnacle by anyone's measure, on the back of her husband's accomplishments.

And Macy wasn't above rubbing it in. Facing the group squarely, she gave the other woman a kind smile. "I know it can be terribly difficult for someone who buys all her clothing off the rack to recognize couture when she sees it. But this 'slip,' Lizzy? It's Vera Wang." From two years ago, and she'd bought it at a huge discount from a sample sale. Damned, however, if she owed Liz and the Pucker Ups that information.

Temper mottled the other woman's complexion. "Why did you come tonight?" she demanded through stiff lips. "Nobody wants you here."

"Macy O'James!" called a jovial voice from behind her, and she looked over her shoulder.

Liz's husband strode up to their group. Reaching them, the older man grabbed her hand and enthusiastically pumped it. "I'm so glad to see you!"

She bit back her grin. Who said there wasn't a God? "Hello, Mayor Smith. It's good to see you, too."

"Has my beautiful bride been telling you how happy we are to have you back in Sugarville?"

A choked laugh escaped her. "Not exactly."

"She probably hasn't had time, what with all the effort she's been putting into this reunion."

"Yes, I was just mentioning to Mike Bodendorf what a lovely job she and her committees did decorating the grange."

"She does enjoy her little projects," he agreed with no apparent realization of how condescending he sounded. "But you! I've been meaning to thank you both personally and on behalf of the city and our volunteer fire department for your help at the fair. I apologize for being so remiss — it's as if everything hit my office at once these past few weeks. But I can't tell you what a boon it was to Sugarville's budget — particularly the fire department's — to have you and Mr. Savage volunteer at Chief Donovan's dunk tank. Liz and these fine ladies here have done a *stellar,* an absolutely stellar, job of raising money for our various civic projects over the years. But you and Savage? You two raised more money in one afternoon than they have in the past four years."

Macy nearly winced on Liz's behalf. Any other woman and she would have, because did this guy ever listen to himself? He'd all but given his wife a pat on the head and called her the little woman.

But this was Liz. And Mrs. Mayor's refusal to just let the nastiness *go,* for God's sake, left Macy without an ounce of sympathy to spare her. "I'm glad I could help."

"Me, too," Mayor Smith said jovially. "We could use your clout. I've raved, absolutely *raved,* about you at home, haven't I, darling?" Barely awaiting Liz's terse nod, he added wistfully, "I sure wish you lived here full-time."

"Ah. Hmm." She was blindsided by the strong pang of longing the idea brought. Not that she could make her home here.

Could she?

No, of course not. She had a *career* and friends and a place she'd carved out for herself in California.

Right. And here all you have is a family who loves you unconditionally.

She cleared her throat. "I was happy to help. This is my town, too." She directed that at Liz with a level look. Then she slapped on a breezy smile.

"Well, listen, it's been great chatting with you all, but I should get back to my table and make sure my cousin doesn't need anything." She nodded to Smith. "Mayor." To Liz and the yes-chicks, "Ladies." Then she made her escape.

By rights, she should feel vindicated. Or at least triumphant. Yet even as she rejoined Janna, as she laughed and chatted and fielded compliments (and the occasional snarky remark), she somehow . . . didn't.

Partly, she supposed, it was due to the fact that she truly had moved once and for all beyond the need for approval. But mostly?

Gabriel's image exploded full-blown on her mental screens. *He* wasn't here to see how she'd rocked this event tonight. Gabe wasn't here to see her in her regular-girl party duds, being the goddamn bell of the ball. And without him by her side? None of it seemed that important.

Which was too stupid for words. It wasn't as if she needed any *man* to complete her.

And yet —

She'd half expected him to show up this evening to escort her and Janna to the reunion despite the hot words that had raged between them that afternoon. Gabe was so not the type to let her edicts stand unchallenged; he was much more likely to greet them with a don't-screw-with-me attitude while nailing her with a cool-eyed look that just *dared* her to make a fuss.

She didn't know what to make of the way he'd simply disappeared into the mist instead. She did know, however, that after this was over, she was going to hunt him down and find out once and for all just what this thing was between them. Well, she knew what it was on her part. She loved him.

She might want to smack him at the moment, but she still loved him.

It had crept up on her the past few weeks, inch by inch, but once the emotion had her in its grip — or once she'd acknowledged that it did, at least — she'd known she was a goner. There was no retreating from this feeling. It was well and truly embedded in her bones now; it thrummed through her blood. Because Gabe wasn't just a big, buff guy who could make her body sing.

Not that she discounted those things. Just thinking about what he could do with his hands, his lips, his body, practically made her eyes cross, he did them so well. But he was so much more than just a fabulous lover. Despite practically raising himself, which could have left him bitter and hard, he was steady and humorous and capable.

He was rock solid, a *good* man. And she was crazy about him.

What *his* feelings were, however, were a mystery. One it was time to solve.

So Chief Donovan had better watch his back. Because she was bringing out the big guns and —

A sudden electric prickle touched her spine, and jerking around she glanced across the large room and found herself staring straight into Gabriel's smoky eyes. *Oh, my God. He's here.* Feeling suddenly, uncharacteristically vulnerable, she whipped back and stared at the confetti on the tabletop as she drew deep breaths to get her heart rate under control.

But not before she saw that he was headed straight toward her with a look on his face that suggested he might be packing some heavy artillery of his own.

CHAPTER
TWENTY-FOUR

Gabe winced when Macy turned her back on him. *Damn.* She was still pissed. He'd hoped she'd have cooled down by now, but hadn't truly expected that would be the case.

Well, he'd just have to see what he could do to change the situation. Squaring his shoulders, he started across the room. He'd had a rough night and he needed her. Considering how many years he'd been kicking around on his own, that wasn't an easy thing to admit.

Yet it was true. Coming up behind her, he bent until his lips touched her ear. "Hey, there. Miss me?"

She gave one of those *dream on* sniffs females were so good at, then slowly turned in her seat. "Is that brimstone I smell, or have you been to a fire?"

"A fire." He blew out a tired breath as just the memory of the past couple of hours weighed on him. "It was a mess, Macy."

She studied him closely for a moment, then patted the chair next to her. "Have a seat," she instructed, and swiveled until their knees touched as soon as he dropped into it, focusing her attention on him. "Tell me."

"I will. But I've got something to get off my chest first." He looked her in the eye. "I'm sorry about this afternoon. I was out of line. What you wear is none of my business."

"Too right, it's not, bub. So don't expect me to say it's okay. Or that you were correct." She gave him a narrow-eyed look, but then shifted in her seat. "Still, I'll concede you may have had a tiny point." Leaning back, she posed, her hands spread wide of her body. "So whataya think? Like my regular-girl duds?"

That's when he realized he'd been so focused on her face, her expression, *her,* that he'd completely spaced on the fact she wasn't decked out in one of her crazy-ass costumes. "You look — wow. Amazing. *Gorgeous.*" He spoke the truth. She looked so damn pretty, a woman dressed to kill for a night on the town. She hadn't chosen a fade-into-the-background style, but it wouldn't be her if she had. Yet neither had she donned the usual Macy-centric smoke screen.

He scooted his chair closer still, his right knee sliding along her inner thigh. He had an intense desire to ask if she'd done this for him. But where he ordinarily wouldn't hesitate to press her, this evening had been eventful and he was too wrung out to push his luck. So he said what he should have said during their fight instead. "I think you're amazing no matter what you wear and I swear to God I never meant to hurt your feelings. It was more about —"

"I know," she interrupted. "And what you said about letting my accomplishments talk for me — well, it made me think a little about my motives."

Remembering the corsages that he'd tossed on the table and promptly forgot, he picked up the container and offered it to her. "I got this as a peace offering and was gonna give it to you before the reunion, but got called out on the fire."

"What is — ? Oh, how pretty!" Her face glowed with open delight. But as if to counteract it, she shot him a sardonic look. "A corsage, Gabriel?"

"Yeah, but not one of those old lady pin-on kinds. See the little band?" He leaned forward to point out the feature. "It's kind of like a flower bracelet."

"What are we, at the prom?" But she got that sweet little-girl smile again and wrestled open the plastic clamshell. "Oh! It's two small ones. Those are even prettier — look how dainty they are." She shot him a grin. "Did you get me one for each wrist?"

"What?" He'd been blindsided by her smile but hauled his concentration back on the conversation. "No. The other one's for Janna."

"Ohmigawd, I love you!" Leaning forward she looped her arms over his shoulders, palmed the back of his head and pressed a quick kiss to his lips while he sat there getting a firsthand demonstration of what Savage's expression gob-smacked meant.

But as she sat back and picked one of the corsages out of the box to examine with thorough, flattering absorption, he got his shit together. *It's an expression, Ace.* She didn't mean the hey-let's-run-off-to-the-justice-of-the-peace kind of love. She was just pleased with him for including her cousin.

Whom she was currently poking in the back. "Janna, look at this! Gabriel got us corsages."

When Janna turned, he was surprised at the coolness in her expression when she

406

looked at him. Or maybe he was seeing mirages, because as Macy explained that he'd been out on a fire and after examining him like a bug on a pin for a moment, she suddenly shot him a warm smile.

"Cool." She slid the dainty arrangement Macy passed her onto her wrist and held out her arm to admire it. When she tore her gaze away to look at him again, her dark eyes held their usual softness. "It's really pretty, Gabe. Thanks not only for including me but for not falling prey to those McMansion-size numbers."

"Yeah, I fought the good fight in defense of a simpler style."

She shot him another smile before the man seated on her other side reclaimed her attention and she turned away.

Macy handed him the clamshell with its remaining corsage and thrust her arm out. "Here, let's play prom. I never got to go to mine, so we gotta follow high school rules. Put it on me."

As he slid the flowers over her fingers and settled them around her slender wrist, he realized he wanted to hear her say she loved him as if she meant it. Because, God, he loved the hell out of her.

With a shock he realized this realization hadn't come out of the blue; he'd known on some level precisely what his feelings were for some time now. Not that he'd gone looking to fall in love. But she'd slipped under his defenses when he wasn't looking and now she was burrowed so deep in his heart he didn't think he could get her out again even if he wanted to. Which he didn't.

Fat lot of good it did him, either way. She'd be leaving town as abruptly as she'd arrived any day now.

The thought sent a sharp ache piercing through him, but he ignored it. Damned if he'd ruin the moment. After finessing the placement of the corsage, he raised her hand to his lips. Maintaining eye contact, massaging his thumbs into her palm, he pressed a kiss to her fingertips. "There," he said softly when he raised his head again. "It's official. We're going steady."

"Yet another first for me." She peered at him intently. "What about you? You ever give your class ring or whatever they did in Detroit to a girl?"

"Hardly. Teenage chicks are high maintenance, and until my junior year I was too busy screwing up my future to take one on. The rest of my high school career I spent scrambling to get my shit together. It didn't leave a lot of time to work on relationships." Remembering that part of his life made him recall how ambivalent Macy had been about this reunion. "How has it been going for *you* tonight, revisiting the trials and tribulations of high school?"

"Scarily well." She waved an impatient hand. "But I'll fill you in on that later. C'mon, man. I've been patient."

He snorted, because patient and Macy weren't exactly two words he'd string together.

She shot a knuckle jab to his nearest biceps. "I *have.* Now tell me about the fire."

"Johnny Angelini and I caught the arsonist."

She snapped upright. "You did? Gabe, that's great!" She studied his face. "Except there's a downside here somewhere, because you're clearly not thrilled about it. Was somebody hurt?" Her hazel eyes widened. "Oh, God. *Killed?*"

Her reaction reminded him that, crappy as he felt about tonight's situation, things could have been a helluva lot worse. "No."

"So what is it, then?"

Meeting her eyes, he admitted what he'd secretly hoped he'd never have to. "The arsonist was one of mine."

"He was — what?" She shook her head. "I'm sorry, I heard you, but . . . yours how?"

He blew out a quiet breath. "He was a

409

firefighter, Macy. One of my volunteers. Ryan Solberg."

"Oh, Gabe." She reached for his hand. "I'm sorry."

And he could see that she was, that she truly cared about how it had knocked him back on his heels. It helped. "I've been pretty sure for a while now that it must be one of my crew members, so I don't know why having my suspicion confirmed hit me so frickin' hard. But I guess part of me kept hoping I was wrong. This evening, though, we caught him."

"Setting a fire?"

"No. Close, but not in the act." A bitter laugh escaped him. "And don't think he didn't try to work *that* for all he was worth."

"Okay, you've lost me, so start from the beginning." She glanced around her. "Wait. Maybe we should take this outside."

"Good idea." He escorted her from the building and felt some of his tension lessening as the door closed behind them to mute the cacophony of voices raised in overlapping conversations. Breathing in the verdant aroma of the farmland rolling off into the distance until it touched the midnight-blue sky meeting the horizon, he looked up at the quarter moon in its nightly sail across the sky and the accompanying stars that appeared close enough to catch in his fist.

Threading his fingers through Macy's, he led her over to the grange hall's side yard with its several picnic tables that were mercifully, if temporarily, free of smokers.

The minute they settled on the one farthest from the hall, sitting atop the table and propping their feet on its connected bench, she turned to him. "Spill."

He told her about the call from Johnny. "The pumper truck was on its way and Johnny and I were heading for the new construction that's going up in Spindale Gulch from either end of the siding road. Aside from a possible brush fire sparking dry trees in that area — which, since there's been no lightning for the past few days, didn't seem likely — the Coasties' place was the only thing down that way capable of producing the flames I'd seen."

"But when you got there your guy was gone?"

"No, he rabbited before I got there. Too bad for him he came straight my way." He bared his teeth. "I ran into him driving up the road I was going down. And in that instant when he saw me, Macy?" His smile faded as he experienced again the sick feeling of his idiot optimism, his futile hope that somehow there'd be an explanation, dying a quiet death. "I knew by the look on his face he'd done it."

"So what did he say? How did he explain himself?" She studied him in the dim outdoor lighting, which barely filtered back to where they were seated. And swore softly. "He didn't man up, did he?"

"Hell, no." He expelled a disgusted breath. "He tried to BS his way out of it. Told me how relieved he was to see me, that he'd discovered the fire but hadn't been able to get cell reception to call the truck in and was on his way to get help. But when I asked to see his phone, he knew that I knew. And he bolted."

"But you caught him."

It wasn't a question but he nodded anyway. "Yes. I took him down with a flying tackle just as Johnny got there."

"And did the bastard know I was in the Kilimner place when he tried to burn it down?"

"He swears he didn't," Gabe said. "And I tend to believe it, Macy, given how agitated he got when the subject came up. He kept saying he never would have set it if he'd known anyone was in there."

"How on earth did he get so off track?" she demanded. "It doesn't make sense. Why would someone who's been dedicated to putting out fires begin starting them instead?"

"We spent most of the night down at the jailhouse asking him exactly that. And in the end, Mace? It comes down to the usual when a crime's been committed. Money."

He scrubbed his hands over his face before lowering them to grip his knees. Staring into the distance, he blew out a sigh, then turned to look at her. "A while back Johnny ran my crew through the system to see if anyone had a record. We might've nabbed Solberg sooner if I'd run a credit check instead. Because he's pretty deep in debt. Not because of the things we were looking for that eat up money, though. He didn't have a gambling problem or a drug addiction. He's just a lousy money manager."

"So instead of going to a financial planner to help him consolidate his debts and learn how to handle them, he torched other people's property?" Macy demanded incredulously.

"Pretty much. He'd set the fires, then put himself in place to be called in on the lion's share of them so he could put 'em out again."

"Hey, why stop with just most? Why not all?"

"Volunteers get paid by the fire and it would've been too suspicious if he'd been there every time. As it was, he and another guy on my crew were the two Johnny and I were keeping our eyes on because they had higher percentages of call-outs than the rest. Shit." Planting his elbows on his knees, he dropped his head into his hands and ground the heels into his eyes. "It's so fucked up."

"I'm sorry, Gabe. I know it must be hard when it's someone you trusted."

"He was a good firefighter," he murmured to the bench between his feet. "That's the part I don't get. How can you be so instinctual about putting them out, then turn around and deliberately set them?"

She rubbed soothing circles between his shoulder blades. "Look, you don't have to stay here if you don't want. The reunion's not exactly what you'd call restful."

He lowered his hands and turned his head to look at her, realizing that he felt better, that sharing with her had somehow lessened the weight he'd been carrying. "I'm not sure I could take restful right now. That'd just give me too much time to brood." He glanced at the hall where music had begun drifting out. "Sounds like the band's started up," he said, climbing off the table. He held out his hand to her, something tugging deep

414

and low when she promptly took it. "Let's go get a drink and wait for a slow dance. I need to hold you in my arms."

Looping her arms loosely around Gabriel's neck a short while later, Macy rested her head against the hard swell of his chest and imagined she could hear his heart beat beneath her ear as they swayed to the music. She liked the selections the band had been playing since she and Gabe had come inside. Unlike the usual mix played at dances, this group interspersed a decent number of slow tunes between the faster numbers.

It didn't hurt, either, that she could feel Gabe relaxing more with each dance.

He continued holding her against him for an instant after the song ended. Then his arms slowly slid away until all that touched her was one large hand riding the small of her back. He used it to usher her back to their table, which was rapidly clearing as the band launched into a fast song.

"You never really told me how your night went before I got here," he said, leaning close to speak under the music after they took their seats.

"Yes, I did. I said it was going well."

"Scarily well, I think were your exact

words. But what does that mean?"

"That for the most part I've been having fun." She made a face. "I know that doesn't sound like me —"

"Are you kidding? It sounds just like you."

She grinned at him. "The You-me, maybe, but not Sugarville Outcast–me. But that's the thing, Gabe — I've had a big ol' revelation. I've finally figured out once and for all that high school sucked for most of us and only a select few ever held true enmity toward me." She hitched a shoulder. "They still do, but I think the majority of the kids I went to school with were just too busy protecting their own shaky social statuses at the time to risk getting involved with mine. Tonight I've connected with a lot of people from an adult perspective, though. It's been pretty sweet."

He reached out and brushed a strand of hair away from her lip. "I'm glad."

Over her head a masculine voice drawled, "Long time, no see, Donovan. Hey, Macy."

She tipped her head back to see Johnny standing behind her. "Hey, you made it." Rolling her eyes, she stretched out a foot to push back a chair for him across the table. "Which I guess is sort of evident by the fact that you're standing there."

He laughed and went around to take the

seat she offered.

When people flooded back to their table a few songs later, the three of them were pulled into the conversations that sprung up around them. Janna related a funny story she'd heard. Mike Bodendorf told one that poked fun at himself and pretty soon everyone in their immediate vicinity was laughing their heads off.

In the midst of someone's anecdote, the music abruptly ended. Macy glanced over to see Liz on the stage.

"If I can have everyone's attention," the other woman said, "we've got a few awards to hand out."

Turning to Janna, Macy smiled crookedly. "I'm guessing you and I won't be getting one."

"The first one goes to the person who's traveled the farthest to attend," Liz said. "Ordinarily that would be Jason Patterson, who went away to college in Providence, Rhode Island, and never came back, or to Heather Scopes in Denver. But neither of them could make it. So the award this year goes to Macy O'James."

A surprising amount of applause broke out, but Macy's blood chilled. "This can't be good," she murmured. "Liz looks too pleased with herself."

"Come up on stage, Macy," the mayor's wife called out.

She looked at her cousin as she rose to her feet. "If they pour a bucket of blood on my head and my telekinetic powers fail me, I'm counting on you to take Liz down."

"I'll make it my mission. And not just her, either. I'll take down her whole freaking clique."

"If you start slamming doors and starting fires with your mind I'll call in my truck," Gabe added. "If not —" he shrugged "— I'll join Janna's mission."

"And I'll turn a blind eye." Johnny looked at her defenders. "Long as you don't do it in front of my boss."

Head held high, Macy strode up to the stage. No matter what, she was holding on to her newfound optimism regarding her classmates. And, God willing, to her sense of humor.

But her heart beat a ragged rhythm and her stomach felt as if it were tied in a bow as she climbed the stairs at the end of the stage and crossed to Liz.

Who flashed a big smile and said under her breath, "You were warned to stay away," then gave her a hug.

Macy hugged her back. "Bite me."

The other woman pulled away and handed

her a certificate, raising her voice to say, "Congratulations, Macy. Thank you for traveling the farthest to be at our reunion." She cut a glance to the audience as if expecting something.

"Well, actually, I didn't." Macy had a lot more experience projecting her own voice and damned if she planned to play the chump waiting to take a pie in the face. "I traveled to see my family." She grinned out at her former schoolmates. "The reunion is just a bonus. So the thanks go to all of you who told me I had to attend."

"Who was that?" demanded a female voice in the crowd. "All the guys you slept with?"

"Seriously?" she demanded. For God's sake, was she going to be laid out in her freaking *grave* with this damn rep still chained around her neck? Searching for the speaker, she saw it was — *oh, here's a shock* — one of Liz's stooges.

To her surprise she heard some protests on her behalf, but it was Gabe shooting to his feet and demanding, "Are you serious?" in an echo of her own sentiments that had Macy's eyes rounding. She stared at him as he faced the woman who'd leveled the accusation, his long hands planted on his hips. But his words were directed at everyone.

"What is it with this town that you won't

let the reputation of a seventeen-year-old girl die the death it should have done years ago?"

"Maybe," said the same Mr. Two-faced who had earlier told her how much he enjoyed her videos, "it's because Macy is so *good* at being bad."

"How would you know, Ledger?" she demanded, breaking her own rule of don't complain, don't explain for the first time. "As I recall, I cut you off at the knees when you tried to get me into the back of your daddy's car."

"You know what I'd like?" Gabe said, quiet anger steaming off his big frame. "I'd like a show of hands. Let's hear it from everyone who's never made a mistake in their life, who has never been misunderstood, found themselves on the outside looking in or wished for a do-over." Crossing his arms over his chest, he scanned the crowd with a let's-hear-it level gaze.

No hands went up, but a few people unconnected with Liz's group promptly grumbled about the incident at Buzzard Canyon. "Forget her sexuality," one woman said clearly, meeting first Gabe's, then Macy's eyes. "I don't give a rat's ass who Macy did or didn't sleep with. She still ruined a lot of good boys' lives."

"That's it!" Janna climbed to her feet to stand next to Gabriel. "No," she said to the woman who'd spoken. "She didn't. *I* did."

"Dammit, Janna," Macy moaned as the entire room went silent. For a second she was frozen in place, thrust back into the confusion of that night: the dark woods, the scent of alcohol on Janna's breath, her cousin's fury with her boyfriend and the heat of the two of them arguing in the idling car over Janna's refusal to relinquish her place in the driver's seat.

Of that car rolling forward as Janna lost control and the sickening thump as it struck three boys they hadn't even known were drunkenly crossing their path.

Of reaching across her cousin to turn on the lights, then the two of them tumbling out of the car to see what the hell had happened.

Then someone snorted and broke the spell. "Yeah, right," Phil McMurphy said. "Sure you did."

Macy headed for the stage stairs as her cousin whirled on the speaker.

"Read my lips, McMurphy." Janna marched with only the slightest of limps right up to her detractor. "I was the one behind the wheel — the one with my foot on the brake when I should have had the car in Park. And I've regretted ever since that I didn't fight harder to accept the blame." She gave his chest a poke. "Not that one damn kid there ever bothered to ask who was driving. They just looked at Macy standing next to me and said, 'What the hell, O'James? What have you done?' "

The man looked momentarily stunned by her unusual in-your-face aggression. "I don't remember you insisting we were wrong," he muttered.

"I do."

To Macy's surprise it was one of Liz's friends who spoke up. The woman joined Janna and McMurphy.

"I remember you saying over and over again that it wasn't Macy's fault," she said slowly. "Even after she copped to it, you kept insisting. I just figured you were trying to save your cousin." She looked at Macy as she strode up. "But why? Why *did* you take the blame for something you hadn't done?"

She shrugged. Part of her wanted to continue insisting she *had* done it, but one look at Janna's determined expression said there was no going back. "Janna was planning a life here. I intended to blow this town the minute the ink on my diploma dried."

"But that wasn't for another eight months. You must've known the time in between was going to be hell."

"And that was gonna differ *how* from the spring and summer preceding it? I'd already ended up with one rep I hadn't earned. So what was a little extra baggage piled on top? 'Cause like you said, no one would've believed me if I'd claimed I wasn't responsible anyhow."

She blew out a breath. "It was an *accident*. There was way too much beer, boys stumbling around half-hammered in the dark and Janny half-hammered behind the wheel, just like most of the kids who got back on the highway that night. It was a recipe for disaster even before her foot slipped off the brake." She met the eyes of several people who had been there. "It could have happened to any of us."

A woman she'd talked to earlier in the evening nodded. "*No* one used their headlights in the Buzzard, and I damn near got run down by Corrie Morris's pickup one night. And Jacob here —" she jerked her thumb at the man next to her "— nearly got me on another." She raised her chin. "You're right. It was an accident and we —" She looked around. "We owe you an apology, Macy."

There was silence, but then heads began to bob in concurrence and other voices chimed in to agree.

Gabe muscled his way through the crowd that had gathered, and stood shoulder to shoulder with Macy. His unspoken support allowed her to relax her rigid backbone.

"Well, it's about time," he said easily. "Now, what do you say we get this reunion back in gear?" When nobody moved, he nodded to the band and they launched into a rendition of Nickleback's "I Wanna Be A Rock Star." Little by little, the crowd broke up to either hit the dance floor or gather in clusters to hash over the night's unexpected entertainment.

Macy grabbed Janna's wrist and headed for the exit. "We'll be back," she shot over her shoulder to Gabriel and Johnny, who stood watching them. A moment later they pushed through the front door.

Avoiding the smokers over in the picnic area, they made their way to the far side of the parking lot. Macy rested her hip against a car hood and studied her cousin. "Are you okay?"

Janna nodded. "I am. This is a load I've been hauling forever and it feels good to finally have it off my shoulders. Man." She exhaled gustily. "I should have insisted we tell the truth years ago."

Macy hitched a shoulder. "You tried. And

I'm sorry if I added to your burden by insisting we let it be."

"Don't you go blaming yourself!" Janna said fiercely. "You went above and beyond for me. So, how *about* you? It must feel pretty good to finally have the truth known."

She thought about it. Then smiled. "It does. I feel . . . lighter, somehow." A laugh bubbled up from her belly. "Who knew?" Still, she sobered slightly as she looked at her cousin. "I think you should prepare yourself for when word of this makes the rounds. Not everyone is going to forgive you, you know."

Janna nodded. "It wouldn't be right if they did. You tried to stop me that night, but I was so damn righteous in my anger — and I can't even recall now what Sean and I were fighting about. Something stupid, no doubt. But because of my stubbornness, I wrecked three boys' lives. I don't deserve a free pass. You know, I've often wondered if me getting hit wasn't payback."

"No!"

"I'm not so sure. I kind of believe in karma, and by hurting three people and failing to own it, maybe I opened up the universe to get run down in return by someone else who would run from the truth of what they'd done like I did."

Macy's energy abruptly deserted her. "I'm played out. You about ready to go home?"

"No. I can't just make an announcement like that and then run away."

"All right." She gathered her strength. "We'll stick around."

Her cousin shook her head. "You can't fight my fights for me anymore, Mace. Besides, didn't you have a big night planned before you and Gabe got derailed? Which appears you got back on track, by the way. So head out. Leave me your car and I'll get myself home." A sly smile crossed her face. "That'll be a real hardship, having to drive your 'Vet."

"Are you sure?"

"Yes. This is something I have to do on my own. But I could use a moment or two by myself first. I have to figure out how I'm going to break the news to Mom and Dad and Ty."

"Okay then." Leaning in, she pecked a kiss on Janna's lips. "Remember what your mama always says. Keep your chins up."

Janna laughed.

Turning away, Macy headed back to the hall to collect her date, her thoughts immediately sliding to the conversation she'd promised herself she would have with Gabe.

It was time to fess up to her feelings for him.

She tried to shake off her nerves. Hell, it wasn't as if he was going to laugh in her face or anything. Even ignoring his wonderfully eloquent defense of her tonight, he was simply too decent to do anything like that.

But maybe he'd have done the same for anyone.

I need to hold you, his voice whispered in her mind.

She hadn't imagined he'd said that. And there were the corsages he must have driven into Wenatchee to purchase and the fact that he'd bought one for Janna, as well.

Maybe, just maybe, he felt the smallest fraction of the love that was burning her up inside.

CHAPTER
TWENTY-FIVE

"Don't go."

Gabe watched Macy whirl to face him in his living room. In her heels, she was almost six feet of hot-wired woman, and for a second he could only stare. At her sunlight-through-whiskey hair swinging with her movement, at her bright eyes flashing green-and-gold fire, at that amazing body in the little underwear dress.

God, she was something. She'd been pumped ever since leaving the grange hall, smiling and laughing and talking a mile a minute. She hadn't admitted it aloud, but he was pretty sure she had some kind of euphoria-buzz going now that the truth about the accident in Buzzard Canyon was out. He was in awe of the way she'd managed to keep that to herself all these years, to accept and accept and *accept* the blame for something she hadn't done, never once alluding to the fact that she was being misjudged. But despite her shrug-it-off don't-give-a-damn attitude, the sudden acceptance after more than a decade of being the town pariah had to feel pretty damn good.

She came at him now like a heat-seeking missile locked on target, her long strides eating up the distance separating them. From a few feet away she leaped, and he barely had time to brace himself before she body-slammed him, her arms encircling his neck at the same time as she wrapped strong legs around his waist. The movement had the hem of her short little dress slithering upward to expose the white satin crotch of her panties.

She leaned back to grin at him. "Don't go where, big boy?"

His hands gripping her butt, he held her in place. Too much was riding on her answer to fool around and he met her gaze with dead seriousness. "Don't go back to California."

Her smile faltered, her thighs going lax on his hips and slipping downward over his. "Seriously?" Her voice emerged from her throat in little more than a breathless whisper.

He pulled his hands from beneath her hem and helped her regain her feet, then smoothed down the rumpled fabric of her dress. Because he simply couldn't make himself set her loose, he slid his hands to the small of her back and held her to him. "Seriously."

Her lips were parted as she stared up at him, and he pressed his mouth to hers in a kiss that attempted to convey everything he felt for her.

The instant he raised his head again, he said, "Stay here in Sugarville with me. Pick out all my paint colors. Share my house." *Share my life.*

When she continued to simply stare at him, he found himself getting nervous. This had to be the longest he'd ever heard her be quiet. Jesus, his heart was beating like a maniac's! He was in decent shape so it was unlikely he was having a heart attack, but he sure as hell was as serious as one. Because her answer was more than important to him; it was crucial to any hope of happiness his future might hold. And every second she didn't respond, his odds of getting what he wanted grew poorer. Dammit, why wasn't she talking?

He drummed his fingertips on the upper swell of her ass. "So. What do you say?"

She blinked, then grabbed a handful of his shirt, twisting it in her fist as she drilled him with the intensity of her gaze. "Let me get this straight. You want me to move in with you?"

"I do."

"Because you need someone to pick out your paint colors."

"Well, among other things."

"Among oth—" She narrowed her eyes. "I need more specificity than that. Like what?"

"Jeez, so many things I can hardly keep them straight. I need to see you smile first thing in the morning. To hear you swear under your breath when you slop paint outside your lines. To watch you with your family. I need your laughter and your take-no-bull attitude. God, Macy." He blew out a breath. "I need you to hold me when I have bad days."

Her free hand had crept up to press against her heart as he'd talked. "And how long do you foresee needing me to do these things? Until you get tired of me?"

"Are you kidding me? Hell, I can't even imagine the day I would get tired of you."

"For a *long* while, then?"

He nodded. Swallowed hard. "Maybe forever."

Her throat worked as she, too, swallowed. "I have a job, you know. In California."

"I know, but does it have to be done from there? Because if the answer to that is a big-ass yes, then maybe I'd better start trying to line up a firefighting job in L.A. for when my contract here runs out the end of December."

"You would do that?" Her eyes were big and hopeful, and his heartbeat calmed a fraction. "You told me you were tired of big-city firefighting. But you'd go back to it, give up your beautiful house, to be with me?"

"Honey, I'd give ten years of my *life* to be with you."

"Oh, God," she whispered. "Oh, *God,* Gabriel!" Gripping his shirt in both hands now, she raised onto her toes and kissed him with desperate passion. After several long moments that felt like a red-hot eternity and a blink of an eye at the same time, she ripped her mouth free and settled back on her needle-thin heels. "I love you, Gabriel. I can't begin to even *express* how much I love you. I'd made up my mind to tell you tonight and to ask what your feelings, if any, were for me." A smile spread across her face, making her shine like a candle beckoning him in out of a cold, dark night. "This is *so* much cooler!"

"I'm glad you think so." He pulled her up

to straddle his waist again and carried her across the room. "So, is that a yes?"

"That's a *hell* yes."

He breathed a sigh of relief. "Thank God. I aged five years waiting for your answer." Collapsing on the leather couch with her sitting astride him, he stroked his hands down her legs. And grinned up at her. "I'm feeling mighty fine now, though."

"You haven't actually said it, you know."

"Huh?" For a second he was confused. Then comprehension struck. "Oh. Oh, shit, I haven't, have I?" Wrapping his fingers around her wrists, he pulled her hands from where she'd braced them on his shoulders and held them between his own. "Macy O' — what's your middle name?"

"Joleen. What's yours?"

"I don't have one."

"What?" She sat straighter on his lap. "For God's sake, your mother couldn't even be bothered to give you a damn middle name? I know it's not nice to bad-mouth another's mama, and Gabriel, I'm sorry, but the more I hear of yours the more I think she's an idiot."

He choked on a laugh. Cleared his throat. "Ah, Macy Joleen O'James, I love you. More than I ever knew it was possible to love someone. I want to laugh with you when you're happy and hold you when you're sad and — hell, I don't even know what all. This is uncharted territory for me, but I know that I Buzz Lightyear love you. You know — to infinity and beyond?"

"Yeah? Well, I — can't think of a darn thing to top that. So I Buzz Lightyear love you right back. And do we sound like a couple of middle school kids or what?"

"Maybe, but it's working for us, don'tcha think?"

She laughed and kissed him, then laughed again. "I do." She looked down at her wilting wrist corsage. "And in that vein, I guess it really is official. We're going steady."

"Damn straight. And we're agreed, right? You're going to live with me, wherever we might end up?"

"Yes. I definitely plan to look into how I can make it work from here, though, before I go uprooting everything you've worked for."

He shrugged. "That'd just be the gravy. Because here or California or frickin' Siberia, as long as I've got you?" He tipped her onto her back on the couch and propped himself over her. "Then, baby, I'm the luckiest guy alive."

"Happy Halloween!"

A bitter wind blew into the house as Macy opened the front door to find Grace and Jack standing on the big covered porch. Reaching out, she hauled them into the great room. "Come in, come in. Man, it's cold out there!"

She slammed the door shut behind them, then gave her longtime friend a big hug. "It's so good to see you! How's the tour going?" Laughing, she bent to hug Grace, as well. "Sorry, I'm not ignoring you, but I've had the pleasure of your company lately. It seems like forever since I've laid eyes on Jack."

"Tell me about it," Grace said, her face aglow, and Macy laughed again.

"Yes, I imagine it seems even longer to you. Let me take your coats. Gabe's down in the rec room manning the bar — when he's not stacking logs on the hearth, that is." She smiled wryly. "Good thing he's a trained professional, because I swear he's got enough wood piled up to torch all of Sugarville." She studied Grace's spiked hair, dark lipstick and dramatic eye makeup. "Whoa. I can hardly wait to see the rest of that costume."

"She rocks," Jack agreed with a wicked smile. "Literally." Giving Macy a comprehensive up and down, his eyebrows furrowed. "Which is more than I can say for you. Bloody hell, Mace, you call that a costume? What happened to the queen of dress-up?"

Grace gave his arm a gentle smack. "Be nice." But she, too, looked perplexed when she looked at Macy's conservative skirt and blouse, at her subdued French twist and neutral makeup. Yet all she said was, "Are you hanging the coats in the closet here?"

"No, I'm throwing them on the bed up in our room."

The doorbell rang again and Grace said, "Go ahead and get that. We'll go dump our stuff."

"Thanks, that'd be great. Then head down to the basement." Whirling away, she pulled the door open. "Happy Halloween!"

A short while later, she followed the last of their guests down the stairs, smiling as she looked around at the costumed crowd chatting and drinking and eating the hors d'oeuvres she and Gabriel had prepared. "Where's Grace and Jack?" she asked Gabe when she noticed their absence.

He looked up from the wine he was pouring for the date of one of his crew. "Beats the hell out of me. I don't think they've arrived yet." He handed the woman her glass, who carried it over to the group of firemen by the pool table.

"Yes, they have. They got here a good ten minutes ag— oh, hell. They were headed for the bedroom to drop off their coats the last time I saw them."

He grinned at her. "Problem solved."

"Except that I've been in and out of the bedroom myself a couple times since with other people's coats." She thought about it a moment. "But I didn't go into the bathroom."

"And you didn't hear anything? Grace must be a lot quieter than you."

"Cute." She smacked his forearm. "Jeez, remind me to wipe down the counter before I set my toothbrush on it."

Moments later, the couple in question sauntered in, and Macy had to grin, for they both looked very relaxed. Then she noticed their costumes and laughed out loud. She seemed to spend a lot of time doing that these days.

"That is just too cool," she said, crossing over to give Jack's argyle sweater vest, cords and bow tie a once-over, then grinned at the black heavy-rimmed glasses on his nose. "You're the schoolteacher, I take it?"

But it was Grace who really tickled her. Because the couple had obviously traded personas for the evening and her quiet, conservative-dressing friend was a rock-and-roll queen in an extremely short black skirt and a leather vest over a mesh body stocking that made her look as if she were tattooed from wrist to shoulder and neck to her midcalf boots.

"That is so smack," she said. "I thought Auntie Lenore and Uncle Bud were unbeatable in their pig outfits, but you win best costume, hands down."

"Isn't she great?" Charlie's mom, Shannon, demanded, slinging a psychedelic-fabric-clad arm around her smaller friend. "I thought Gabe's Buzz Lightyear was the best before I saw her." She studied Macy. "You're kind of a surprise, though. I thought you'd really pull out all the stops, so I didn't quite expect this. What are you supposed to be, a junior leaguer?"

"Um, excuse me?" a male voice said

before Macy could answer, and she turned to see Brian Dawson, one of the AAE boys, standing behind her.

"Sorry to interrupt," the Dr. Spock–costumed young man said, "but can you tell me where you put our coats?"

For the next half hour she was busy with hostess duties, but she and Gabe exchanged secret smiles whenever their eyes met. God, she was happy.

Her work was actually going great from here. While she'd flown to L.A. a couple of times to meet with recording artists and present the concepts she'd envisioned for their songs, the truly time-consuming part of her job was coming up with the initial ideas and designing the storyboards, and that could be done from Sugarville as easily as L.A. or Nashville. And since she was still in the process of building her career she was able to figure out things as she went, working into it slowly — although ever since an early buzz for one of her first videos took off a couple of weeks ago, she'd found herself with twice as many potential clients. Talk of a nomination for Best Concept Video at the VMA awards was already making the rounds, but it was too early to put any stock in that.

All the same, it was very exciting — and

good for business.

"Hey, baby girl."

She looked up to see her aunt and Janna crossing the room toward her, and she grinned as she did every time she saw Auntie's pillow-stuffed sow costume. Lenore had added curly tails to her and Bud's one-piece pink union suits and designed ears and snouts for them to wear. But it was the double row of baby-bottle nipples she'd sewn down the front of hers that made the costume such a kick.

"You need any help?" her aunt asked now.

"I was thinking about setting out the buffet so folks can dish up whenever they're hungry."

"Great. We'll give you a hand."

Up in the kitchen, they gathered everything in preparation to taking it down to the table. "Gabriel misses your cooking a lot, Auntie," she said. "But he sure is full of himself for how well your pork *verde* recipe turned out."

Lenore laughed. "Yes, that's a tough one, throwing both ingredients into one Crock-Pot."

"Ah, but we mustn't forget shredding the meat once it's cooked — not to mention cutting up all the condiments that go on the tortillas with it. He even made the guacamole."

Lenore gave her a tender smile. "It's nice to see how much your love has opened that boy up. He smiles much more often than he used to."

"I like the way he's opened himself to his crew. They were all hit hard by Solberg's betrayal, but they've become closer knit, I think, because of it."

"And that's all very important," Janna cut in with an ironic smile, "but I want to talk about the *truly* critical stuff. Like, what is the *deal* with that costume, Macy? I get dressing against type, but what exactly are you supposed to be?"

"An engaged woman."

"A what? What the hell is an —" Her cousin's eyes rounded when Macy extended her left hand and she saw the solitaire gracing her ring finger.

Janna grabbed Macy's hand and inspected the one-carat emerald-cut diamond — only tearing her gaze away from its simple platinum setting when her mother hipped her out of the way and said, "Move aside and let me get a look at that."

Janna eyed Macy. "You're *engaged?*"

Flush with the excitement and happiness she'd been carrying inside since Gabe had presented her with the ring that morning, she nodded.

Her aunt and cousin look at her. Looked at each other.

And screamed in unison.

Hearing it downstairs, conversations stopped midword and Gabe, looking up at the ceiling, broke into a grin.

Jack and Grace, with whom he'd been conversing, looked at him questioningly. "I've sensed something afoot ever since we got here," Jack said. "What the feck is going on, mate?"

"The cat is out of the bag, is my guess."

"And what, precisely," Grace demanded, "does that *mean?*"

"She's an engaged woman!" Janna whooped as she strode into the rec room one step ahead of Macy and Lenore. "That strange-ass costume that nobody gets? It's a freakin' front to keep everyone's eyes off her ring finger until she and Gabe could announce they're *engaged!*"

"Which I guess you've now done for them," her mother said dryly.

"Huh? Oh. Yeah. I guess I have. Sorry." But she laughed and threw herself at Gabe to give him a big hug. "Congratulations! I'm sooo happy for you both!"

Noise and laughter engulfed them as

everyone gathered around talking at once, the women to inspect the diamond he'd agonized over during two separate visits to the jeweler's and the men to slap him on the back in congratulations. "When are you getting married?" Bud demanded.

"We haven't decided," Macy told her uncle as she wrapped her arm around Gabe's waist and leaned into him. "May sounds like a great month to us, but then so does September. We finally decided we'd pick one or the other by Thanksgiving."

"I'm just happy everyone knows," Gabe said, holding her to him as they moved toward the bar where he'd stored several bottles of champagne. "I've got witnesses now. She can't back out."

Everyone laughed, but he was half-serious. He still couldn't believe that happiness of this magnitude was attached to him.

As if she could divine his thoughts, Macy looked up at him, and her beautiful green-and-gold eyes radiated love. "That is such a nonstarter, I can't even begin to wrap my mind around the thought," she assured him with quiet seriousness. "I love you, Gabriel, like I never knew it was possible to love someone. And in no scenario can I ever picture a day when I won't."

Then she laughed, rolled up her skirt, took

off her shirt to reveal the black satin bustier underneath and pulled the wire comb holding her French twist from her do. Shaking out her hair, she reached behind the bar for a pair of translucent black-veined wings and donned them. Then, slapping a little black beanie topped with two big sliver orbs and black antennae at a rakish angle on her head, she looked up at him.

"So, baby?" she said with that smile that grabbed him by the short hairs every time. "I guess you're stuck with this fly girl for the rest of your life."

AUNTIE LENORE'S
OLD-FASHIONED
BUTTERMILK FRIED CHICKEN

3 (3 to 4 pound) whole chickens, cut into
  pieces, washed and patted dry
2 quarts old-fashioned buttermilk
2 cups shortening
4 cups all-purpose flour
1 1/2 teaspoons kosher salt
1 1/2 teaspoons ground black pepper

Place chicken in a large bowl, coat with buttermilk and cover. Marinate in refrigerator *(overnight, if you've got the time, for four to eight hours if you don't).*

Heat the shortening in a large cast-iron skillet over medium-high heat. In a large Ziploc bag, combine the flour, salt and pepper. Remove chicken from buttermilk a piece at a time and shake in the bag to coat, then carefully place in the skillet. Fry over medium-high heat until pieces are browned on one side, then turn and brown other side until chicken pieces are a deep golden-brown, and the juices run clear.

Reminder: These are boardinghouse portions — you might want to cut recipe to one chicken, 1 cup shortening, 1 quart buttermilk, 2 cups flour and one each teaspoon salt and pepper.

AUNTIE LENORE'S (AND SUE BELL'S) SUGAR COOKIE RECIPE

1 cup sugar
1 cup butter
Cream together

Mix in 3 eggs *and* 1 teaspoon vanilla.

3 cups flour
1 teaspoon each soda and salt
2 teaspoons cream of tartar

Mix well with wet ingredients, cover and refrigerate overnight.

Roll out and cut in shapes.

Bake at 375 degrees for 10–15 minutes until golden brown.

Let cool.

Icing
1 egg white, beaten until stiff but not dry
Mix together:
1 1/2 cups powdered sugar
1/2 teaspoon vanilla
1–2 drops food color
Beat in with egg whites. Frost and set.

(Auntie L did the work for you on this one and cut it down for a smaller crowd. Double or triple if you want lots and lots of cookies)